Love and
Other Rituals

PRAISE FOR MONICA MACANSANTOS

"It's not their 'exotic' locations that make Monica Macansantos's stories feel fresh and new, it's the emotional territory she covers. A teacher's compromised longing for the young married father who's become his lover. Two expat Filipinas in Austin contemplating the varieties of loneliness available to them in America. The sudden vision of a teenage girl who has chosen a rough boy as her protector of the potential emptiness of her future. Described this way, these stories sound bleak. They're not. They're stories suffused with tenderness and a keen attention to the wild aberrations of the heart."

Anthony Giardina
Norumbega Park, *White Guys* and *Recent History*

"I loved these beautiful stories by Monica Macansantos, who writes with such beauty and delicacy about desire, home, longing, loneliness, duty, and hope – that is, what it means to be human. Every story is terrific, different, surprising. I can't wait to see what she does next."

Elizabeth McCracken
The Souvenir Museum, *Bowlaway*, *The Giant's House* and
Thunderstruck & Other Stories; winner of the 2015 Story Prize

"Monica Macansantos's writing is immersive to the point of creating its own virtual reality. Set in the Philippines, the US and New Zealand, these are tender and well-crafted stories of heartache and yearning unmet. Macansantos's *Love and Other Rituals: Selected Stories* deftly moves us beyond what some might consider foreign or exotic and instead brings us closer to understanding our own tiny corners of the world."

Oscar Cásares
Where We Come From

"In Monica Macansantos's exquisitely rendered stories about the Filipino experience, both in the old country and abroad, homeland is not a place, but a pang. Wisely and compassionately observed, her dislocated characters long for home with the same restrained ardor they yearn for connection. Because Macansantos knows too well how an upset heart turns, this longing remains always within sight, yet heartbreakingly elusive. Her splendid writing is stirring."

Antonio Ruiz-Camacho
Barefoot Dogs: Stories

"Monica Macansantos draws you into the worlds of her characters and slowly reveals their secrets. I read with curiosity and quickness, intent upon discovery, but she isn't going to give it all away and you wouldn't want her to. Macansantos is a promising young writer who is wise beyond her years."

Mary Miller
Biloxi: A Novel, *The Last Days of California: A Novel*, *Always Happy Hour: Stories* and *Big World*

ABOUT THE AUTHOR

Monica Macansantos earned her MFA in Writing as a James A. Michener Fellow from the University of Texas at Austin, and her PhD in Creative Writing from the International Institute of Modern Letters, Victoria University of Wellington. Her work has appeared in *Colorado Review, The Masters Review, Day One, failbetter* and *Katherine Mansfield and Children* (Edinburgh University Press), among other places. She has received fellowships from Hedgebrook, the Kimmel Harding Nelson Center for the Arts, the I-Park Foundation, Storyknife Writers Retreat and the Honor Society of Phi Kappa Phi. Born in Baguio, Philippines, she spent her early childhood in Newark, Delaware before returning to the Philippines, where she spent the rest of her childhood and young adulthood. A graduate of the University of the Philippines Diliman, she calls Baguio home.

LOVE AND OTHER RITUALS: SELECTED STORIES

Monica Macansantos

Grattan Street Press

Published by Grattan Street Press 2022

Grattan Street Press is the imprint of the teaching press based in the School of Culture and Communication at the University of Melbourne, Parkville, Australia.

Copyright © Monica Macansantos 2022

The story "Playing with Dolls" was previously published by Amazon Publishing.

This is a work of fiction. Names, characters, and places are products of the author's imagination or are used fictitiously. Any resemblance to actual locations, or to persons living or dead, is coincidental.

The moral right of Monica Macansantos to be identified as the author of this work has been asserted by her in accordance with the Copyright Act 1968.

All rights in this collection are reserved. For permission requests or inquiries, email the publisher with the subject line "Attention: Permissions Coordinator", at editorial@grattanstreetpress.com.

Grattan Street Press
School of Culture and Communication
John Medley Building
Parkville VIC 3010, Australia

www.grattanstreetpress.com

ISBN 978-0-6454813-0-3

Printed in the United States of America.

For my parents:

*Francis C. Macansantos (1949-2017),
poet, friend and guiding light,*

and

*Priscilla Supnet-Macansantos,
writer, mathematician and mapper of better worlds.*

CONTENTS

The Feast of All Souls	1
Love and Other Rituals	12
Playing with Dolls	33
Stopover	60
The Autumn Sun	82
Maricel	101
Inheritances	123
Leaving Auckland	153
Notes on the Text	191
Permissions	196
Acknowledgments	197
GSP Staff Acknowledgments	203
GSP Personnel	205
About Grattan Street Press	208

THE FEAST OF ALL SOULS

I clutched a pair of flesh-colored candles as I followed my mother through the crowd. The Baguio Cemetery was awash with sunlight, and the smell of steamed corn, roasted peanuts, car exhaust and newly washed hair gave the air a thick and confusing aroma. At dawn, we had had a quick, simple breakfast of pandesal and butter before taking a jeepney to the cemetery, where the smell of food made my stomach growl. I wanted to ask my mother for money, but she was too determined to find what she was looking for, and she probably wouldn't hear my voice above the din.

A man in a faded brown cap thrust a stick broom in my mother's face. "Ma'am, you need cleaners? We can clean your tomb for you," he said.

My mother stopped. "How much?" she asked.

"One hundred pesos."

My mother raised an eyebrow in surprise, and I followed her when she skirted past him. "Too expensive," she said, brushing him away.

The man caught up with my mother. "What about eighty pesos?" he asked.

"Sixty."

One could always tell by the sound of her voice that she knew what she wanted.

"Take pity on me, Ma'am, I have children to feed."

A short, sunburned woman with a scar on her cheek approached us. "Ma'am, I can sweep your tomb for sixty pesos."

A man in paint-stained overalls spotted us and hurried to my mother. He held a can of paint in my mother's face and said, "Maybe your tomb needs a paint job too? I can do it for fifty pesos."

"Sige sige," my mother said, squinting in the sunlight as she beckoned the pair to follow her lead.

My mother took my hand, and we entered a narrow concrete passageway at the side of the cemetery's main plaza. Rocks, twigs and crushed flowers littered our path. The passageway opened to reveal a hill sloping downwards. Whitewashed tombs were crammed into every inch of space. They looked like tiny unopened boxes and I could imagine myself fitting my shoes into them. Concrete cherubs sat on them, eyes downcast, hands clasped.

My mother stepped on a tomb that read *Baby Michael Flores, RIP*. "Watch your step," she said, and squeezed my hand.

We stepped on these concrete boxes as we made our way downhill. "When your dad and I came here last year, we were able to find the spot where your cousin is entombed. It's always hard for me to find. The adults are taking over and edging out the children."

I nearly tripped on an overturned tomb with a decapitated cherub. Nearby, two boys and a woman stood on a small, grimy box, praying before a larger, freshly painted box that rose to their waists. Another family sat in a circle atop a marble grave, eating rice and longganisa from paper plates.

Farther down the hill, a group of dark-skinned men in work clothes stood on a white tomb at the foot of a pine tree, hauling away a pile of leaves and branches and dropping them into a wide rectangular hole in the earth.

"If my memory serves me right, it's right in front of that tree," she said, and when her gaze settled on the group of men, her face fell and she dropped my hand. One of the men returned her gaze, and she yelled, "What do you think you're doing?"

She scrambled down the hill. I held my breath, hoping she wouldn't slip and fall. The men looked at her and exchanged glances. The woman with a scar on her cheek clicked her tongue and said, "Naku, Ma'am is angry."

"That's my niece's grave you're turning into a dump!" my mother hollered. My ears burned as people turned to look at her.

A gray-haired, mustached man scratched his head. "Sorry ha, Ma'am. We were hired to clean this tomb."

"Uy," he hissed at his companions, waving a hand at them, "clean up your mess."

One of the younger workers jumped into the hole. "But where do we throw these?"

"Anywhere," the mustached man answered, waving a hand at the sea of white boxes on the hillside.

∼

This was the first time my mother brought me to the cemetery to visit Erika, my cousin. My mother and father had gone the year before to pay their respects, but this year I was taking my father's place.

A week before our visit, my mother announced that the Feast of All Souls was again fast approaching. We were having breakfast, and my father tossed his newspaper aside after my mother spoke.

"Shouldn't you tell Manang Carmen to visit her own daughter? She comes to Baguio all the time," he said.

"You know how Manang Carmen is. She can't be talked into doing something she doesn't want to do," she said, stirring her coffee.

I poured a heart on my pancake with the honey bottle my mother had handed to me. I drew hearts everywhere – on my notebook pages, on the sketchbooks my father bought me for my birthday, in my diary, on my food. I did it especially when I was bored, like when grown-ups talked to each other without talking to me. But when I sensed that my mother was looking at me, I closed the lid of the honey bottle, set it down on the table and swung my legs.

"Seems like your father doesn't want to come with me to visit your cousin's grave. Do you want to keep me company instead?" my mother asked.

"So now Ina's officially part of the family tradition too," my father grumbled, giving me a quick apologetic glance.

"I can come with you, Mom." I knew this was what my mother wanted me to say, and a smile broke on her face. I wondered what I was supposed to do when I came with her and why she needed me to be there. I didn't know how to behave in a cemetery, especially one that had babies buried in it.

∼

"It's Erika Gallardo. Born June 1, 1971, died June 3, 1971," my mother told the painter after he had lowered himself into the pit.

Erika died ten years before I was born, and I only knew her from the photos of her burial tucked into the pages of our family album. In one picture, a group of adults and children surround a tiny wooden coffin. They're in the middle of a grassy field. My tita Carmen stands at the center of the group, her face half-hidden beneath a veil of black lace while my mother, dressed in bell-bottoms and a black buttoned-up sweater, stands beside her. This was before my mother was married, and she was still slim and sexy because she was yet to have me. I am a ghost in this picture, a child who hasn't yet been born. There weren't as many dead babies back then.

I sometimes wonder whether Erika and I would've been friends had she lived. She would've been a grown woman by this time, perhaps as pretty and stylish as her mother. Maybe she would've been fun to be with, or maybe she would've been like her brothers who never spoke to me whenever they came to Baguio with my tita in the summertime. I had always wanted a big sister, but she was just a tiny baby my mother visited every year. I wondered if she even knew us, or whether she was just waiting for her mother to visit her instead.

After Erika's death, Tito Mar was offered a job in Manila, and Tita Carmen and their children followed him. Manila was good to Tita Carmen, my mother said. The women Tita Carmen played mahjong with didn't know she was the daughter of a jeepney driver, nor did they know she had a child named Erika.

Now the painter raised his head. "Wait lang Ma'am. I have to scrub off the dirt." He opened his bag of tools, pulled out a rusty pair of scissors and proceeded to scrape off bits of caked mud and moss from the tomb's surface.

We sat at the edge of a stonewashed tomb that overlooked the pit, facing the group of men who were now whitewashing the cleared tomb. Whenever the painter stood, his head brushed my feet, and it would've been easy for me to give his head a painful bump with my baby-blue sandals. Erika's tomb wasn't originally in a pit – over the years, people had piled soil around it and placed their relatives' tombs on top of these heaps. The tomb we sat on had a corrugated iron roof. The relatives of *Ariel Macaraeg, RIP* had not yet arrived and we sat under his roof for shade.

Smoke rose from a pile of burning garbage at the top of the hill. The wind blew the smoke in our faces, and my mother tied a handkerchief around my nose and mouth. At the bottom of the hill, the ground rose again, and at the edge of the cemetery a patch of sunflowers swayed in the breeze. It was the first day of November and a chill was beginning to set in. I wondered whether Erika ever got scared out here, or lonely, or if she even remembered her mother. When my mother tucked me into bed the night before, she spread a comforter over my thick Ilocano blanket and pulled socks onto my feet, and a sudden loneliness swept over me when she switched off the lights and closed my door.

∽

My tita Carmen would make frequent business trips to Baguio and was a regular guest in our household. I looked forward to her visits because of the gifts she'd present to me: teddy bears, faux gold jewelry, beaded hair scrunchies and, on one occasion, a Barbie doll. My mother chided her for spoiling me, upon which she'd laugh and retort, "Your daughter will only be young once!" Sometimes I imagined Erika staring down at us from heaven, wishing she could be mean to me.

My parents would pick Tita Carmen up at the bus station in the evening, and when a clicking of heels echoed across our pine-wood-paneled house, I'd rush to the living room and there she'd be, smiling brightly, jingling with gold jewelry. She'd bend down, take me in her arms and press a powdery cheek against mine.

"And how is my little pamangkin? What grade are you in na ba?" she would always ask, no matter how many times I had answered these questions before.

My mother would trail behind her, clad in her usual black slacks and denim jacket, while my father would hobble into the living room, carrying my tita's brown Louis Vuitton suitcases.

"You know naman that I was in Hong Kong last week to do some shopping for my business," she said the last time she visited. "I bought early Christmas gifts for you na rin. You have to be ready for 1992 as early as now. As for me, I'm more than ready to get rid of this year of volcanic eruptions and massacres." She unzipped one of her suitcases, rummaged through the odds and ends inside and fished out a pot-bellied buddha. "I noticed that you don't have any of these in your house so I got one for you. Leave it in your living room and it will attract luck."

"Do you have one in your office?" my father asked, amused.

"Of course! It's good for business," Tita Carmen said. She sauntered across the floorboards and placed the buddha on top of our upright piano. Its fat arms were raised in glee, and I wondered whether the sad-faced Mama Mary standing beside it took offense.

Over dinner, Tita Carmen talked about her Chinese herbal medicine business, Tito Mar's law practice, and my cousins Nico and Raul whom my parents called rich, spoiled brats behind my tita's back. "They're both on the San Agustin High basketball team right now, can you imagine that? I never imagined them growing up so fast! One of their teammates is the son of Congressman Webb and there's another boy on their team who's the son of a senator," she said, slicing her steak.

"That's good. They can make the right connections in case they want to enter politics," my father said, cupping his glass of wine.

"Hay naku, politics is so messy. It's good enough to know some people up there in case one gets into trouble."

"Patronage politics. That's how corruption begins," my mother said.

Tita Carmen rolled her eyes. "Our parents never required you to become an aktibista, Vicky. God knows where you got your rebellious streak."

Tita Carmen brought out her gifts later that night. There was a set of three wooden monkeys that were supposed to attract luck, incense sticks for the living room, a silk tie and a bottle of Tiger Balm for my father, a blood-red cheongsam for my mother and Chinese silk pajamas for me. "Good heavens, where on earth will I wear this?" my mother cried as she lifted the cheongsam from its box.

"In the office, while teaching. Why not?" Tita Carmen said.

"Manang, do you want me to look like Mother Lily? My students would laugh at me if I wore this."

"Why, can't you be a donya in the classroom? It's better for them to know who's the boss," Tita Carmen said, raising a pencilled eyebrow. "Besides, red is a lucky color. The Chinese wear it to attract good fortune and ward off evil spirits."

"I guess we need all the luck we can get," my mother said, folding the cheongsam and putting it back in its box.

∽

A fog descended on the valley as I dug into the cup of hot taho my mother bought from a wandering vendor. We were waiting for the paint on Erika's tomb to dry. Meanwhile, the painter had disappeared, perhaps to look for another customer, another tomb. "When are we going home?" I asked, spooning out a mixture of dark syrup and soft white bean curd.

My mother gazed into the fog. "After the man returns and finishes the lettering. Naku, will the paint ever dry in this weather?"

"Ma, why didn't Tita Carmen come with us to visit Erika?"

"Your tita Carmen is a busy lady. She has to attend to her business in Manila and can't stay long whenever she's here," my mother said. "Besides, can you imagine her walking down this hill in her high-heeled shoes?"

The image of Tita Carmen tripping on a tomb and rolling downhill made me burst into laughter. My mother smiled, relieved perhaps that she could still make me laugh.

"Be careful, child. You might fall." My mother's smile faded, and she put her arm around my waist.

Fog was shrouding everything now: the grove of pine trees in the distance, the tombs that surrounded us, the iron poles that supported our roof, the families who combed the hill clutching flowers and candles as they searched for the tombs of their departed. Even my mother's wispy hair seemed to be fading into the mist, and for a split second I pictured her vanishing into the whiteness.

∼

Tita Carmen would always bring a certain lightheartedness into our home, and whenever it was time for her to leave it seemed as though her good humor would leave our home as well. Maybe this was because my parents had no one else to laugh at when she was gone, or maybe we had more things to talk about whenever she was around. Over dinner, she'd share stories of her clients and the people she called her "marketers" whom she'd meet whenever she was in town. There was the student who sold skin-whitening cream to her classmates to finance her college education; the housewife whose husband went to Saudi Arabia, then became a Muslim and took a second wife; the old tomboy who lived alone and couldn't bend her joints unless she smeared Tiger Balm on them; and the elderly priest who drank seven-herbs tea and could now lift weights and jog around Burnham Lake. Every story she told had a happy ending, and it seemed as though every problem could be solved with the help of her merchandise.

Tita Carmen dined with us the night before she returned to Manila and as my mother served dessert, she said, "Vicky, you could be one of my marketers too. Just start small and who knows, maybe you could make enough to buy a new car for Eddie."

My mother set a bowl of sweet rice cakes before my tita. "You know that I'm not good at selling things," my mother said.

"All you have to do is smile more often."

My mother giggled. "Oh Manang, you know how hard it is for me to smile without a reason."

"Just think of your future prosperity whenever you make a sale. That's a good enough reason." Tita Carmen beamed.

My mother's smile faded as she returned to her seat. "Not everyone's like you, Manang."

∾

"Shit," my mother muttered under her breath as she relit the candles on the edge of Erika's tomb. The fog had lifted, the whitewash had dried and the lettering was finished, but a smart November wind was blowing, descending into the pit where my mother stood. She'd cup her hand around a freshly lit flame and the wind would sneak through her fingers, extinguishing whatever she managed to ignite.

I sat at the edge of Ariel Macaraeg's tomb and tapped my empty plastic taho cup with my spoon. "Ma, I'm hungry," I called down to her.

"But you just had taho!"

"I want corn now."

"Ina, don't be a brat."

She finally managed to get two candles burning and kept her hands spread over the flames as she stood up. When the wind still hadn't blown them out, she made the sign of the cross, clasped her hands and bowed her head. I stopped swinging my legs and fixed my eyes on the cherub sitting on Erika's tomb, wondering if it had been preparing all along to mirror my mother's gesture.

Men in work clothes combed the hill as my mother prayed, eyeing the unpainted tombs and the families who kept searching. A frail gray-haired man descended the hill, leaning on a wooden cane for support, nodding at what he saw. When he passed the pit where my mother stood, he stopped and looked down. He raised an eyebrow when he spotted my mother, as though he never expected to find any living thing where she stood. My mother opened her eyes and made the sign of the cross, and when she looked up, she saw him.

"I wasn't expecting anyone to be visiting a tomb this old and hidden," he said.

My mother narrowed her eyes. "Who are you?"

"I'm the caretaker of this cemetery. I've been working here for years, and I've seen some of these babies abandoned for good. But this one always has a fresh coat of paint after the Feast of All Souls."

"We come here every year."

He looked at me, smiled and asked, "Are you visiting your brother or sister?"

"She's my cousin."

"And where are the parents?"

"They're in Manila. I'm the one who visits now," my mother said.

The old man leaned on his cane as he gazed down the hill. "I always think that people will build a tomb over your niece, but thankfully only weeds cover her."

"That's why I come here every year. When they see a clean tomb with a fresh coat of paint, they'll think twice." My mother sighed and looked at me. "I can't just leave her here."

I sat still, out of respect, the way my mother wanted me to.

The man looked at me, winked and walked away. As my mother struggled out of the pit, I took her raised hand, even though I was afraid I would fall in.

We held hands as we made our way up the hill. I wondered whether the babies inside the tombs got mad when we stepped on them. But where else would we steady our feet? We didn't do it on purpose. They were just in our way.

"God, I hope I can find that tomb next year," my mother said, scowling.

"I'll help you find it, Ma," I said.

She stopped in her tracks and turned to look at me. Her shock seemed to wash away the scowl on her face, and her eyes softened. "Would you do that for me?" she asked.

"Yeah."

Children in rags tripped down the hill, their slippers slapping against concrete. Some had already made it to the bottom of the valley and were picking melted candles from abandoned tombs, pressing these together to form balls of wax they would later sell.

"I'll get you ice cream before we go home." She squeezed my hand. I let her lead the way.

LOVE AND OTHER RITUALS

The sun was setting when Kardo slid from Rene's arms and lifted a pair of threadbare jeans from the hook on the door. "I have to go home," Kardo said as he pulled on his pants. As it always was whenever he was about to leave, his back was turned to Rene.

"Don't you want dinner? There's beef caldereta on the stove," Rene said. He let out a sigh as the sweat of their lovemaking sank into his skin.

"It's getting dark. I have to go home," Kardo said, buckling his belt.

"Stay for a while. You've only been here for thirty minutes. I'll heat the caldereta. It's my mother's recipe." Rene got up and plucked a T-shirt and a crumpled pair of boxer shorts from his metal bedpost. Kardo drew the curtains and looked out the window, his gaze far away.

"Elena shouldn't already be back, should she?" Rene put a hand on Kardo's shoulder.

Kardo placed his hand on Rene's and fixed his eyes on the corrugated iron roofs of the neighbors' houses. "It depends. She could be delivering laundry at this hour. The kids are at home by now, though."

"Oh, they know how to take care of themselves. Don't worry." Rene wanted to stroke Kardo's hair, to plant a kiss on his warm, moist nape, but Kardo's mind was elsewhere.

Kardo set the table as Rene switched on the stove and stirred the caldereta in its aluminum pot. When it was time to eat, Kardo sat facing the TV screen. He laughed with his mouth full when a girl in a fuchsia-colored bikini slipped into a tub of bubbling water and a gangly game show host did an awkward jig. Rene had moved his television set to the dining room, noticing that Kardo hovered around it like a moth whenever he paid Rene a visit.

"Dance, Nene, dance," Kardo sang as he clapped.

"Have more ulam. You must be hungry," Rene said.

Kardo nodded, got up and piled another mountain of rice and caldereta onto his plate. He sat down, mixing the orange-red sauce into his rice and hunching over.

"I have a question," Kardo said.

"What is it?"

Kardo put down his fork and spoon and leaned back in his chair. "One of the boards on our wall was blown off by the last typhoon and we've been using a sack to cover the hole. Elena's working extra to have it patched up, but we don't have enough money to buy plywood to cover it. My children sleep near that hole at night and I'm worried they'll get sick."

"Why didn't you tell me earlier? I would've given you money for repairs."

"Well, you know po, it's so shameful. We ask for money from you all the time."

Rene tossed his head and struck the air with his palm. "Hay naku, stop saying that. You say that all the time and ask for money anyway." He reached for his wallet, opened it, counted his money and handed Kardo a wad of bills. "Here's one thousand pesos. If there's anything left over, buy your family a good meal."

"Thank you." Kardo took the bills, counted them and pushed them into his jeans pocket.

"Kardo, I just gave you money. Why do you look so sad?"

Kardo shrugged and smiled.

"You're cute when you're being shy, but it can get annoying too."

"Ikaw naman, don't be such a drama queen." Kardo's voice melted into a whine and he got up, approached Rene's chair, put his arms around Rene's shoulders and dabbed his lips on Rene's cheek.

"That kiss costs one thousand pesos," Rene said, touching Kardo's arm.

"You know that's not true."

Rene closed his eyes as Kardo's fingers curled against his chest. During moments such as these, Kardo's calloused hands could feel so warm and promising. Then the hands fell away and Kardo returned to his seat.

Rene stared at Kardo's bowed head. *I would've given you the money anyway, even if you didn't ask*, he wished he could say. It was easier on the tongue than, "I love you", and less cloying too. But he was afraid of sounding petulant and, anyway, Kardo was too busy feeding himself to listen.

~

Whenever a boy's beauty caught Rene's attention in the introductory calculus class he taught, he'd recall a conversation that he'd overheard in the office years ago. As the years passed, it would come back to him in snippets.

"I heard Eric invites them to his apartment."

"And these kids allow him to do whatever he wants with them?"

"Don't tell me you didn't know anyone in college who sold themselves for tuition money."

"Or for grades."

"So you can do anything you want when you're tenured."

"Why, you're thinking about it too?"

He would've wanted the other details of that afternoon to slip away from his memory, but they lingered in him like the ghosts of physical pain: the conspiratorial snickers that emerged from the office kitchen, the silence he walked into when he entered the tiled room and saw three of his colleagues gathered near the watercooler. They were young and untenured, just like Rene, and when they saw him, they lowered their eyes. As he smiled at them, pretending he'd heard nothing, he slid his hands in his pockets, clenching and unclenching them. He struggled to squeeze out the mannerisms he knew his colleagues couldn't wait to encircle and dissect: the telltale softness of his wrists as he plucked pieces of chalk from the blackboard tray in front of his wide-eyed students, or the suspiciously delicate touch he used to comfort a distraught colleague.

He felt the months, then years, pass before he could say with some certainty that they weren't waiting for him to provide them with juicy morsels of scandalous behavior. It wasn't that he lacked desire – it was just that he didn't want his yearnings to be laid out on the faculty kitchen table to be examined, trivialized, joked about. Despite their suspicions, he wasn't one to compromise the efficient, sanitized relationship he maintained with his students.

~

He was working in his garden on a cold afternoon in January when he heard a tapping at his gate. Strangers selling fruit, rice cakes and sometimes labor often knocked as he worked in his garden. He bought their fruit and ate their rice cakes, but he rarely hired people to clean his house or trim the hedges of his garden. He was afraid of the questions they'd ask once he allowed them to set foot in his house: why he lived alone, whether he had more money to spare.

"What is it?" he called out.

"Do you want to have your garden fence fixed?" It was a male voice, and a large sunburned hand emerged from behind the gate to point at the wooden fence that separated the garden from the driveway. Rene turned to look at it and noticed the holes that riddled the graying planks, the old nails that bled rust into the wood. A carpenter whose name and face he had long forgotten hammered it together years ago, and it took a stranger to spot these symptoms of neglect.

Rene returned to his work. "I don't see anything wrong with it," he said, gripping the stalk of a stubborn weed with his gloved hands.

"It doesn't match the beauty of your garden, that's what's wrong with it."

Rene sensed a teasing lilt in the man's voice, and he raised his head to look at the face that peered at him from behind the gate.

It was a young man who smiled, revealing a set of crooked teeth. He had the round, dark eyes of a child and the calloused hands of a working man. Rene remembered the hands of his father, a man who never wore gloves when he plowed his field back in the village. Rene sent money to his parents whenever he could, even after his father stopped speaking to him years ago. Rene could never be the son that his father wanted, no matter how persistently he wrote checks. He still hoped that they'd show up at his gate one day, if only to ask for money. They had nothing to be afraid of.

Instead, a stranger stood at his gate, grinning.

Rene walked through the arched gateway of his garden and approached the front gate. He took note of the man's crooked nose, the scar under his left eye, the smile that could easily be mistaken for a sneer.

"Or maybe you need help digging. Or cleaning your house."

"I'm not looking for a houseboy."

"Please, sir. I just lost my job and my wife is pregnant."

Rene took another look at the man's face. *Looks like he's been in a couple of fights*, Rene said to himself. And yet there was a youthful glow in the man's fine, unwrinkled skin and a warm, almost cheerful look in his eyes.

"Why should I trust you?"

"I've never stolen from any of my bosses, ever." The man looked at Rene's bungalow, as though he knew what lay beyond its clapboard cerulean facade.

Rene sighed. "I have to think of what you can do for me."

"We could start with your garden fence."

Rene looked at the broken fence and saw the weeds that had sprouted around it. He was becoming careless in his gardening, and even this young man noticed. Did he also seem to be the kind of person who could easily be swayed by a sob story? He remembered the young man he once was, a man who needed help but who was too ashamed to show it. He pulled off his gloves, lifted the latch of his gate and ushered the young man in.

The man showed up at eight in the morning the next day, and Rene gave him money to buy wooden planks and nails. When he returned from the hardware store, the man handed back Rene's change before he dismantled the old fence. His name was Kardo, he said when he was asked. Rene insisted that Kardo dine with him at noon. When Kardo gave in and sat with Rene at the kitchen table, he ate the food spread before him in silence. Rene could tell he was hungry by the heaps of rice he piled on his plate, but he slowly worked through his food as though he were ashamed of his own hunger.

"Do you also have a garden at home?" Rene asked.

"We don't have enough space for one," Kardo said.

He told Kardo to come for work on Saturday mornings. He couldn't leave the new boy unsupervised, he told himself, and Saturday was the only time of the week Rene could be at home the entire day. One never knew what could happen if one's back was turned.

On Kardo's next visit, Rene sipped his morning coffee as he watched Kardo lower the roots of a tree sapling into a hole in the ground. Rene cooked lunch for two people, coaxed the young man into his house at lunchtime and sat by the living room window when Kardo returned to work. Having a stranger touch the leaves of his plants, water their roots and pull out the weeds that sucked the earth dry, was easier than Rene thought it would be. Once,

Kardo glanced at the window and caught Rene's eye, and when he waved, Rene nodded back.

Later that afternoon, he handed Kardo a five hundred peso bill and watched him walk through the gate, wondering how a day slipped away whenever he wanted it to trickle slowly through his fingers.

When Kardo came to work again, they sat at Rene's kitchen table at noon, finishing a pot of fish sinigang Rene had cooked that morning as Kardo worked. Rene opened the kitchen windows to let in a warm wind, and their hinges rattled as he filled Kardo's bowl with soup.

"How is your wife?" Rene asked, taking his seat.

"She's all right, but she gets tired a lot these days. I guess I have to look for a full-time job so that she won't have to work too much." His wife was a laundry woman and was sometimes hired to clean the homes of the families she worked for.

"You could come here on a weekday, if you need extra work." Rene didn't have much more to give, but Kardo's husky, timid voice coaxed forth his pity.

"What else do you need me to do?"

"I'll have to think about that," Rene said, drowning the rice on his plate with spoonfuls of soup. "You could scrub and wax my floor. Or dust the knickknacks in the living room."

"Come on, I know you want more than that."

When Rene raised his head, he thought he sensed a sneer flicker across Kardo's face. The young man's insensitivity struck him cold – Rene had expected him to respect his quiet admiration, to exercise tact.

He stood, walked around the table – and slapped Kardo's face. Stunned, Kardo cupped his reddening cheek in his hand.

"Sorry, I just thought you were—"

"Get out of my house," Rene said, pointing to the front door.

Kardo stood and brushed past Rene, leaving a faint trail of warmth on Rene's skin. "You'd understand if you were in my place," Kardo said, before closing the door behind him.

Rene threw Kardo's unfinished meal in the trash, cleared the table and ran water over the dirty dishes. In the days that followed, he had nothing else to look forward to after work beyond the solitude he had once treasured. When Saturday came and Kardo didn't show up, he found himself working alone in his garden and eating a meal meant for two people in his empty kitchen. He heard a rapping at the gate and when he rushed to his window to see who it was, a woman with a fruit basket on her head pointed a wrinkled finger at her produce and asked, "Would you want to buy fruit?" There was too much food in his refrigerator for him as it was, and he waved the old woman away.

His nights were filled with a vacuum-like silence. In one dream he shared a bowl of wonton soup with Kardo, licking clean the spot where Kardo's lips left a mark of sour moisture. One night, he dreamed that they lay side by side in bed, a cold wind whipping their bare skin.

The next Saturday afternoon came and he jumped from his kitchen seat when he heard a knocking at his gate. He spotted Kardo standing behind the locked gate. Kardo had never seemed so small to him before: this time Kardo slouched, avoided Rene's eye.

"I'm sorry," Kardo mumbled when Rene came to the gate.

Rene straightened himself and folded his arms. "Is that all you can say for yourself?"

"It was a misunderstanding. I'm sorry."

"Is that what you think of us baklas?" Rene said. "That we're all Miss Moneybags?"

"It's not like that. I just thought that you were about to make an offer. My other bosses have done it before." Kardo scratched his head.

Rene looked into Kardo's eyes. Was his restraint so uncommon, so farcical? He was punishing himself, holding himself back when there seemed to be no reason to do so. He knew this man wouldn't give him what he truly wanted. But what he needed right now, as he stood behind his closed gate, was a temporary balm for an ache that lingered.

Children walked home in groups that afternoon, dribbling basketballs down the road, jostling with each other, soaking themselves in their own petty rivalries. Elderly women tapped the ends of their umbrellas against the pavement as they inched down the street, and Rene ducked as they passed. When the last gray-haired woman disappeared beyond the bend of the road, he unbolted the gate.

"Come in."

Kardo stepped inside and stood before Rene, waiting, as always, to be told what to do.

"What kind of work do you expect me to give you? I've watered and weeded my garden. I've had enough time to clean my house. Don't tell me you're going to cook for me this time."

"I don't know where else to go, Sir Rene."

"Come to my bedroom, then."

"What?" Kardo's face fell, as though he had come unprepared for this.

"Isn't this what you wanted to do?" Rene opened his front door and held it open for Kardo. Kardo hesitated, but then followed Rene inside.

"Second door to your left. Go inside and sit on my bed."

When Kardo disappeared into Rene's room, Rene hurried to his kitchen, opened his cupboard and took down a bottle of virgin olive oil he had received as a gift from a colleague at an office Christmas party. Sweat gathered in his palm as he clutched the neck of the bottle, and in his mind he went over the notes he had picked up from movies, from the magazines he had read in quiet private moments.

Kardo was in his briefs when Rene walked in, sitting on the edge of the bed, eyes averted, rubbing his arms as the cold settled inside the room. Rene placed the bottle of oil on his nightstand and turned his back to Kardo as he pulled off his T-shirt and wriggled out of his boxer shorts. "If I could help you with that by showing you a Tanduay girl calendar, I would," Rene said, shivering as he eased his naked body under his sheets.

Staring at the floorboards, Kardo pulled down his briefs and tossed them to the floor. Rene got up as Kardo turned to face him, and he felt an ache blossoming between his legs when his eyes fell on Kardo's exposed protuberance: an ugly, veined and vulnerable thing.

"Come closer," he whispered, picking up the bottle and unscrewing its cap.

Coated in virgin olive oil, it tasted a little less revolting when his tongue fluttered around its tip, ushering forth a faint moan from Kardo's lips.

Rene patted Kardo's chin when it was over, watching Kardo avert his eyes and turn away in the gathering darkness.

They had dinner in silence afterwards, and before Kardo left, Rene handed him a one thousand peso note. Rene knew Kardo needed much more money than that, but he needed Kardo to come back for more.

When Kardo left, Rene sat down to watch the evening news, more aware of the strange tingling in his body than the images of scam artists, Senate hearings and traffic-clogged Manila streets that formed a colorful, unending blur. Had he known it could happen so fast, he wouldn't have rehearsed the event in his mind as though it were some fearful, life-changing experience. There was shame that accompanied the act, but that only came afterwards. In the thick of it, he'd forgotten everything else and allowed his pleasure to take over. He'd never had a man inside him before and he'd never expected to take joy in his own breaking, his own humiliation.

Kardo visited Rene, unannounced, on weekday afternoons, appearing at the gate after Rene parked his car in the driveway. Rene took Kardo's hand as he led him into his bedroom, and drew the satin curtains before they unbuttoned their clothes and made love on his bed. Rene gulped down his own moans so that the neighbors wouldn't hear, and covered Kardo's mouth if a grunt escaped from his lips. In the privacy of his bedroom, this young man took him back to the earth, to the rankness of his own body, and his heart soared.

∼

When Rene opened his front door, a girl with sun-darkened skin stood wide-eyed next to Kardo's lanky figure. It had taken Kardo a week to visit him since their last meeting, and Rene was about to give Kardo a proper scolding when he spotted the girl.

"I had to pick up my daughter from school today. Elena's still cleaning Mrs Cornejo's house. Can we come in?" Kardo asked.

"I guess," Rene said, pulling the door open. He had never expected Kardo to deliver a part of his life, much less a daughter, to his doorstep. As she entered the house, the girl turned to look at the olive-green curtains, the cabinet of fine china, the high ceiling, the angel figurines displayed on the divider.

"And what would your name be?" Rene asked, looking at the girl.

"Her name's Cecile," Kardo muttered, letting go of his daughter's hand. "Is there food? I'm hungry."

"I was about to make tinola. Can you wait?"

Kardo winced. "Can I have a sandwich first?"

The frayed hem of Cecile's sleeve caught Rene's eye. "Yeah, there's bread in the bread box. There's leftover hotdogs in the fridge, if you're really hungry."

Kardo strode to the kitchen and opened the refrigerator. "Your tito Rene is a rich man. He has a lot of food in his house," Kardo called out from the kitchen.

"You're my tito?" Cecile asked.

"If you can wait, I can cook tinola for you two. You might want something hot," he called out to Kardo.

"You're my tito?" Cecile repeated.

"Ah, yes, I'm your tito Rene. You must be hungry too." Rene took her hand, which fit snugly in his, and led her to the kitchen.

Kardo sat at the head of the table, legs spread, munching on a hotdog wrapped in a slice of white bread. Rene pulled up a chair and Cecile sank into it, staring at the plate of cold, wrinkled hotdogs and the bag of bread set before her.

"What do you want to drink?" Rene asked.

"What I want to drink?" Cecile asked, puzzled.

Kardo pierced another hotdog with his fork and dropped it on his plate. "He means juice, soft drinks."

"Do you have Royal?"

He didn't, and he wished he did. "What about orange juice?"

"Okay."

Cecile watched as he walked to his refrigerator at the corner of the kitchen, opened it and pulled out a box of Fontana. He took a glass from the dish rack, uncapped the box of juice, poured the juice into the glass and set it beside Cecile's plate. Cecile took the glass with her two hands and tilted it until the juice inside touched her lips. After taking a few sips, she lifted the glass from her lips and smiled at Rene. She had a thin mustache of orange that Rene patted away with a napkin.

"I would've licked that off," she said, giggling and kicking her legs.

"You don't use saliva to clean your face, darling," Rene said. It was a long time since he met a child who could be so easily pleased. As long as this little girl was fed and entertained, she wouldn't ask questions. Perhaps she would even come to like him. He wrapped a slice of bread around a wrinkled hotdog and set it on her plate. She took the sandwich and closed her eyes as she bit into it and chewed. Inside, Rene breathed a sigh of relief.

After Rene slipped into an apron, he worked near the kitchen sink, dressing chicken, plucking malunggay leaves from their spindly stalks, peeling the green, watery sayote fruit he had harvested from his backyard. He watched Cecile as she wandered to the parlor and stared at the angel figurines displayed on the divider. She found a plastic stool and placed it at the foot of the divider, then stood on it and took a blushing cherub from a dusty shelf.

Kardo's eyes were glued to the TV set, its sound a curtain he drew around himself.

"Kardo!" Rene hissed.

Kardo gave a start and looked at Rene. "What's wrong?"

Rene eyed Cecile who had sat, cross-legged, on the floor, and was cradling the angel in her palms as though it were a tiny baby. He had wanted to tell Kardo to keep an eye on Cecile, but on second thought, it seemed better to let her be.

"Did you get that hole in your wall fixed?" Rene asked, turning back to Kardo. The alarm on Kardo's face receded, and he smiled.

"Yeah, I patched it up yesterday. Thanks for the money."

"And is your family eating well?"

"Actually, that was what I was about to tell you. We're running out of rice."

"Sige, I still have lots of rice in the dispenser over there. You can get as much as you want," Rene said. He pointed with his mouth to the plastic box at the corner of the kitchen. "There are bags in the cupboard. Whenever you need rice, you just get here ha?"

Kardo grinned. "Sus, you're so kind," he said as he got up from his chair. Rene was afraid that Kardo would make the mistake of kissing him on the cheek in full view of Cecile. But when Kardo walked straight to the cupboard and pulled it open, Rene glanced in her direction, and was relieved to see her playing with the cherub in the next room, too self-absorbed to notice them.

The cherub danced in circles as Cecile balanced it on her hand, and Rene was about to shout "Careful!" when the cherub rolled off her palm, shattering on the floor.

Kardo peered through the doorframe that led to the living room.

"Naku Cecile, look what you've done! How shameful you are!" Kardo yelled, storming into the living room and grabbing Cecile's hand.

Rene dried his hands and ran to the parlor, watching a frightened Cecile as her father tugged her arm. "Don't worry, Sir Rene, I'll take care of this," he said as Rene approached them. He took off his rubber slipper, lifted Cecile's uniform skirt, and gave her buttocks a quick, forceful slap.

"Please, stop!" Rene yelled. Kardo paused, letting the hem of his daughter's skirt fall.

Rene stared at his fallen angel. Its wings had fallen off and its body had split in half, exposing its hollow insides. Cecile's head was bowed, and she used the worn sleeve of her blouse to wipe her eyes. Rene approached her, took a handkerchief from his pants pocket, and patted her cheeks dry. She avoided his eyes.

He rubbed her back. "Don't cry, dear. We can easily replace it."

Kardo scratched his head. "Well, I thought you were angry," he said.

Rene looked up at him and said, "She's just a child."

After a silent, awkward dinner, Rene handed Kardo a wad of bills, "to buy more rice and to have a new school uniform sewn for Cecile." Kardo clutched the bills in one hand and the bag of rice in the other, avoiding Rene's eye as he made his way out the door with Cecile. Whether Rene had given these out of pity or because he wanted Kardo to come back, Rene wasn't so sure.

That weekend at the Chinese bazaar, he bought two angel figurines: a female angel with flowing blonde hair, silvery-blue robes and large gold wings, and a pink-skinned cherub that held a harp in its fat arms. The adult angel took the place of the cherub that had been broken, while the new cherub was to be Cecile's. Her hot tears emerged from Rene's memory as he wrapped the gift. He could not protect her.

It wasn't his right.

∼

When Rene had bought his first car, he'd found a shortcut to work that skirted past an open field dotted with sunflowers and squat banana trees. As the years fled past him and Rene grew older, immigrants from the countryside gradually invaded it, building rust-colored shanty homes that seemed to sprout from the land like mushrooms after a heavy rain. Smoke from their aluminum chimneys mingled with car exhaust from an increasingly busy street. Wet underwear hung like heavy flags from their window grills, reminding Rene that modesty was one of the many luxuries not everyone could enjoy.

This was where Kardo lived. It was a familiar eyesore that grew in size every year, and Rene expected it to be a neighborhood where gossip, like the smell of sweat and fried fish, spread quickly.

These thoughts filled Rene's mind as he sat at his front porch in the afternoon, waiting for Kardo's return. A week, then two, passed. As monsoon rains saturated the soil in his yard, he paced from one end of his now dusty porch to the other, wringing his hands, wondering if he had been too harsh in scolding Kardo. He knew Kardo couldn't possibly love him, but he missed the way Kardo announced his presence at the dinner table by switching on the television, the way Kardo laughed when Rene brushed against him, complimenting him for the way he made his garden – their garden – flourish. Kardo had no reason to be ashamed of his own ardor – he had a daughter, yes, but did that matter? Rene was beginning to grow fond of the girl too.

He began to picture how Kardo went through the motions of life inside this shantytown. Kardo babysitting his children as his wife went to work. Kardo coming home at night in a crisp white uniform, setting down a bag of roast chicken on a plastic kitchen table. Kardo was good-looking enough to be a salesperson in the newly opened mall downtown. Even if the pay wasn't good, at least his wife wouldn't need to worry about sharing her husband with another man. Maybe it was only right for Rene to give Kardo back to her. Like a tenant in a boarding house who had overstayed his lease, it was now time for Rene to return his key to the tiny, cheap room his money had once afforded him.

The sun came out after another week of rain, and as he drove home from work, his eyes fell on the familiar cluster of shanties and he clutched at the steering wheel, unable to drive any further.

Rene parked his car by the curb and stared at the shantytown, wondering if it really had to come to this. He then got out of the car and his own reflection in the car window caught his eye. His hair was slicked back, his white polo shirt was rolled up at the sleeves, his shirttails were tucked beneath the waistband of his slacks and his leather belt hoisted up his growing belly. He took out a handkerchief from his shirt pocket and wiped away the sweat on his forehead and nape. What would Kardo's neighbors think if they saw an older man looking for him? Regaining his composure, he turned and began walking.

Two girls in school uniforms leaned against the walls of an alleyway, sucking popsicles encased in plastic.

"Sir, what are you looking for?" one of the girls asked, revealing her crooked, yellowing teeth.

"Do you live here, hija?" Rene asked, doubting she'd appreciate his politeness.

"No, we live in that mansion at the top of the hill!" the other girl exclaimed. The girls exchanged looks before bursting into a harsh fit of cackling.

"We live here. Why?" the girl with crooked teeth asked, regaining her breath.

Rene hesitated, but since he'd already been ribbed by these girls, he felt he had nothing left to lose. "Does Kardo live here?"

"Kuya Kardo? Yeah. Why, are you his boss?"

She was making it easier for him now, and yet he stuttered. "Yes, I—I am."

"My dad says he's sick. Are you looking for him?"

If she were an older woman, he would have found her tone accusatory. If she were his daughter, he would've scolded her for her impoliteness.

"Yes, I have to talk to him."

She turned her back to him and walked away, and her friend followed her, looking at Rene and shrugging her shoulders. Just when Rene was beginning to think they were pulling his leg, the crooked-toothed girl looked over her shoulder and wiggled a finger at him, as though she were beckoning a small child to follow her lead.

The ground underneath them was muddy and uneven. Rene stepped around the rocks that littered their path, careful not to scratch his nice leather shoes. Wet T-shirts and blankets hung from flimsy plywood windows and flapped in the wind. Women squatted in the alleyways as they scrubbed their soiled clothing in plastic tubs, while shirtless potbellied men sat on wooden benches outside their houses and smoked. The smell of damp and raw sewage was everywhere, and he resisted the urge to cover his nose, for he was afraid of what these people could do to him when slighted. A troop of chickens crossed Rene's path, and they flapped their wings and cackled when a young man in basketball shorts stepped out of his house and chased them away with a stick. He spotted Rene and, stunned, straightened himself.

"Are you looking for anyone, sir?" the young man asked.

"He's looking for Kuya Kardo," the crooked-toothed girl said.

"Are you his boss? He had to be rushed to the hospital two weeks ago."

Rene felt relief wash over him – Kardo hadn't abandoned him, he had just gotten sick. *Who wouldn't fall ill in a dump like this?* he thought. It was as though he were learning, for the first time, that Kardo's body could succumb to illness. "What happened?" he asked.

"Typhoid fever. Everyone's been getting it. But he returned from the hospital yesterday. He's still in bed, I think," he said. "Elena!" he yelled, walking past two houses before pounding on the door of a two-story shack.

"What's that?" A woman's head emerged from a window on the second floor. A pink plastic clamp held together her long straight hair, and she brushed away the stray wisps that fell across her oily cheeks. She had the face of a teenager, and Rene felt sorry that her figure had to be framed by rotting wooden planks.

"Is Kardo in there?" the man yelled. The two girls wandered away, throwing glances at Rene as they sucked their popsicle sticks.

"Where else do you think he is?" Her harsh, high-pitched voice did not match the softness of her features.

"His boss is here." The man pointed at Rene with his thumb, slapped the door and sauntered back to his shack.

Elena stared at Rene as though he were an apparition.

"You're Sir Rene, right?" Elena asked.

"That's me."

Her face twitched in panic. "Kardo's been sick and couldn't go to your house. We're so sorry. Please don't fire him."

"Hija, I won't," he said, hesitating. Seeing the doubt on her face, he smiled, tried to regain his composure and asked, "Is there anything you need?"

"You don't have to worry about us. Have you eaten yet, sir?"

It was an offer he hadn't expected, and he didn't know how to politely decline it.

"Please come inside. You came all the way here to visit us and you won't even have anything to eat? How shameful of us to let you go." She shut the window, clambered downstairs and opened her front door. "Please come in, sir. Our children aren't home yet from school."

She stepped back to make way for him as he entered her house. It was surprisingly clean – the linoleum floor had been mopped and swept, and the plastic table at the center of the room smelled of Lysol and boiled rice. A poster of a bikini-clad woman caressing a bottle of Tanduay Rum hung from one of the plywood walls, next to a plastic reproduction of *The Last Supper*.

Shutting the door, she said in an embarrassed voice, "Our humble home." When he turned to look at her, she gripped the plastic door handle, bit her lip and giggled.

There was a crib in the corner of the room next to a long plastic bench, and as soon as Rene sat down, a cry emerged from the crib's netted walls.

Elena rushed to the crib and took the baby in her arms. She bounced on her heels, patted its back and cooed into its ear. The baby turned to look at Rene and grimaced, as though it had read his thoughts, before letting out another pained cry.

"If you want to see Kardo, he's in our bedroom on the second floor. But I'm sorry, he's still asleep." The baby's cries slowly ebbed and when it fell asleep, she lowered it into the crib.

"Is it a boy or a girl?"

"A girl. Sorry, didn't Kardo tell you?"

Elena walked to the kitchenette at the other side of the room and opened a sideboard. Rene waited for her to speak as she emptied a pack of instant noodles into a pot, filled it with water and set it on the stove.

"You don't have to make anything for me," he said as she turned to face him.

"No, it's fine. You're our guest." She smiled to herself as though amused by what she had just said, and then sank into a chair near the kitchen table. "I'm sorry that we couldn't tell you what happened. You were probably worried sick."

"I wasn't worried sick," he said, the annoyance in his voice becoming too sharp for polite conversation. "I was just worried."

She had to stop apologizing, for it was hard for him to maintain his calm. She seemed so sincere in her generosity, to take anything more from her would be criminal.

"But then you came all the way here to visit us," she said.

"Do you think he's the only reason why I'm here?" He couldn't admit to her that he hadn't been generous with his love, that he had given all of it to her husband, not knowing that she'd expect something from him too.

"What else would bring you here?" she asked, her voice faltering. Then, avoiding his gaze, she got up and glanced at the pot on the stove.

"I'm sorry if I have nothing better to serve," she said, lifting the pot cover and stirring the soup with a small fork. "When Kardo was well enough to work for you, we had fried chicken for dinner almost every day. We were eating three times a day."

Rene got up and pulled out his wallet from his back pocket. He took out four five-hundred-peso bills and placed them on the kitchen table. "You'll probably need more than this. I'll come back tomorrow and give you more." He felt trapped by this woman's unflinching hospitality and prepared to leave.

Elena stared at the money. "We haven't done anything to earn that much. I could clean your house or do your laundry."

"You've done enough for me, Elena. Enough is enough."

"All right. Kardo will be well enough to work next week." She nodded, as though she could read his thoughts and was giving him permission to have them. He stared at her, not knowing if he was supposed to apologize or to mention the unmentionable.

The front door opened and Cecile walked in. Her face lit up when she saw him. "Tito Rene!" she exclaimed, skipping towards him. He found himself laughing in relief as he bent down and caught Cecile in his arms.

"I have a gift for you, but I left it at my house," Rene said, stroking Cecile's hair.

"Sir Rene, you shouldn't have," Elena said.

Rene turned to Elena. "And why not?"

A boy, smaller than Cecile, walked through the front door and took a step back when he spotted the unfamiliar guest.

"Nicolas, this is . . . your Tito Rene . . . a friend of your father's. Ask for his blessing. You too, Cecile."

Rene got up and the two children pressed the back of his hand to their sweaty foreheads. Nicolas ran up the stairs right after letting go of Rene's hand, while Cecile skipped away.

"Don't be noisy! Your father's still asleep!" Elena yelled. She laughed and looked at Rene.

When her children had disappeared upstairs, she said, "There was this rich couple who came by the other day. They were offering me ten thousand pesos for Cecile and the baby. They said they'd raise the children as their own and send them to a good school."

Rene was shocked. "What did you tell them?"

"I told them I couldn't do it. It's not as if I haven't thought about it. I just don't know these people. Who knows what they'd do to my babies?" Elena switched off the stove, took a chipped bowl from the cupboard and poured out the noodle soup. "I didn't want so many babies when I got married, but I keep on getting pregnant. Sometimes you have no other choice but to love what the Lord gives you."

She set the bowl at the center of the table, slipped in a spoon and drew a chair. "Let's eat, Sir Rene," she said, nodding at him.

"I could feed Kardo if he's awake. I have so much food at home. You're making me feel guilty," he said.

Elena shrugged. "All right, if that's what you want. I'll come with you upstairs."

He cupped his hands around the bowl. It wasn't within his powers to do what was right – to walk away from this woman's husband, to stop exploiting this woman's desperation. It seemed that Elena depended on him to not walk away from them. He had offered to feed her husband and now she was waiting for him to do it.

"You're very concerned about him," she said, her head bowed.

The soup's steam warmed his face. It felt heavy in his hands and he put it down on the table. He couldn't look at her. Closing his eyes, he said, "Hija, you don't know what you're talking about."

She said, "But I understand."

He picked up the bowl with both hands and followed Elena upstairs to the bed she shared with her husband, knowing there was no turning back. This was probably what Rene had wanted all along.

PLAYING WITH DOLLS

Before Dad left, it was easy to get away from the parties my mother held at our house. As waves of laughter and conversation swept my mother from us, he and I would get into his Porsche and drive off, leaving her to drown.

I was ten when he eloped with one of our maids. After he left, there weren't any parties to escape from and I became a willing prisoner of our house, like my mother. Sulking and sniffing back her tears, she'd appear in a plush robe that needed laundering. We all waited for the dam of mourning to break, for all the small details of her old self to return. After a couple of weeks, it dawned on me that I didn't know what we were waiting for. I barely knew her, after all.

I can't say I was fond of my mother's thin laughter. It was a special treat that was reserved for guests who came to our house to partake of our caterer's hors d'oeuvres, play tennis on our lawn when the sky didn't bode rain, or share gossip with her and my lola Marie over a game of mahjong. However, its absence jolted me awake, like an unexpected rebuke.

I began to suspect that my father was the secret source of my mother's rare bursts of joy. Before he left us, I was sure this wasn't so. At night, when all my mother's guests were gone and my nanny, Yaya Dayang, pulled my blankets to my chin and switched off the lights in my bedroom, I'd hear my mother taunting my father from a few walls away. My father would fire back at her with insults that were worse than the ones used by my American classmates at school. I stayed awake, wondering why my parents reserved their cruelty for each other. They were both good-looking, and they both had lots of friends – she only had to wait at our house for her amigas to come flocking to her like frantic butterflies, while he only had to pop in at the Baguio Country Club to earn cheers and slaps on the back. Their friends liked them so much that my mother and father forgot how much they liked each other. It seemed that they had built their own individual lives around themselves, and there was no way they'd meld these two together. My mother had taken over our house, while my father had to get away for fresh air.

My father joked about it with me, especially when my mother attended to the well-dressed people who swarmed around her on Saturday afternoons; she was too busy to notice my father's boredom, or mine. He'd lead me by the hand to our garage at the north end of our house, open the front passenger door of his red Porsche convertible, usher me in, buckle my seatbelt and slide into his seat behind the steering wheel. The roof of his car would part from the windshield, folding neatly like an eyelid behind our exposed heads. This was our "great escape", as he often said, even if we hardly did anything to secure our safe passage – there were no prison doors to unlock, no fire-breathing dragons that guarded the exits of our house. Mang Danny, our family driver, would hold the front gate open for us, waving and smiling at me as Dad drove the car beyond the boundaries of our compound.

We'd sail out of our subdivision, down the pine tree-lined avenues of our section of the city. When we'd drive past the entrance of my father's beloved country club, he'd tell me to check my seatbelt, saying, "We're going from thirty to eighty in ten seconds, so buckle up, my honey bun!" I'd scream as we sped up, and laugh when I stopped being frightened. We'd sail up and down the hills of golf courses and fly past the pine trees that dotted the sidewalks.

Once, a golf ball flew across the road as we drove by, grazing my head and my father muttered, "Punyeta, that was close." We got off the road and pulled into the parking lot of a small pastry shop. A wedding cake was on display behind the shop window, the tiny bride and groom marooned on an island of white frost.

He turned to me, took off his Ray-Bans and asked, "Are you okay?"

Before I could reassure him with a response, he leaned toward me and parted my hair with his fingers, searching for a wound or a bump on my head.

"Dad, it's all right. I don't even feel anything," I whined.

He withdrew his hands, leaned back in his leather seat and breathed a sigh of relief. "Gosh, that was close," he said. "If anything happened to you, your grandpa Joaquin would've skinned me alive." I knew that my lolo Joaquin couldn't literally skin my dad alive, but I was sure he was capable of confiscating my dad's car keys. After all, my dad was still his son, and the car was still my grandfather's.

"Oh." I scratched my head, wishing for a second that I could find a wound hidden underneath my hair.

"But did you have fun?" he asked, his eyes lighting up as he clutched the steering wheel with both his hands.

"Mmm-hmmm." I nodded vigorously.

"Do you want to do it again?"

"Maybe we should go home. Mom or Lola Marie must be looking for us by now."

He laughed. "You saw them a while ago. They weren't missing us."

He was speaking the truth, and my limbs grew weak as I turned away from him. I fixed my eyes on the domed awning of the pastry shop before us, remembering how strange our house had felt to me that day, as guests trickled in and out of our front door, taking ownership of every piece of furniture, every potted plant, with their appraising eyes, their hollow laughter.

As though to interrupt my train of thought, my father said, "I'm sure they miss you, but I'm not sure if they miss me." He looked tired as he put on his Ray-Bans, but as soon as he had them on, he looked as cool as he had when we had driven out of our compound earlier that afternoon.

"You look like James Bond, Dad." What I said was true, in many ways – he was a charmer who dressed well and liked fast cars as well as James Bond movies. His occasional gaffes – such as mismatched socks or a dried spot of shaving cream on his chin – were details I chose to endear myself to, rather than scorn.

He turned to look at me and beamed. "Really?"

"You have the clothes and the look. The only thing you don't have is the English accent."

My father was easy to cheer up, easy to please, and this was something my mother failed to understand. If only she hadn't been too anxious to please her guests and mahjong partners, she would've noticed my father. She would have seen him pacing around our living room, waiting for someone to take him away from the chatter of our house, drowning his boredom with alcohol, intoxicating himself with the promise of speed and the company of his only child.

∼

My dad's Porsche waited in the garage, having taken part in the temporary escapes my father had staged with or without me. This time, my father had left without me or his car, and there was a certain finality to this exit, as though he could truly escape this house only by traveling light. A few mornings after my father's departure, I was walking to the garage and saw Mang Danny breathing steam onto the taillights of the Porsche, wiping the beads of moisture away with the diaper my father had instructed him to use when cleaning the car. I began to entertain the hope that my father was coming back soon and that Mang Danny – cued in to his arrival – was getting the car ready for his master's return. But when he turned to look at me, there were tears in his eyes. Whether these tears were for me, my father, or the abandoned car remained a mystery to me.

"Oh, Margot, poor little Margot," Mang Danny said, rushing toward me and taking me in his dark arms. He had been my father's driver from the time my father had been in elementary school until my father married, and with us, he had become an old man with graying hair. I had already bawled like a baby in Yaya Dayang's arms the day after my father had left, and now it was my turn to comfort this old man who had been abandoned by his little master, Senyorito Linus. In the flurry of weeping and shouting that had filled the rooms of our house those past few days, Mang Danny had been left to grieve alone in our garage. I had rubbed his back and shushed him as he'd wept, mimicking the gestures Lola Marie used when she consoled my mother. We had neglected the men who lived in our house, and I knew – even at that age – that my father had left, with a woman we barely knew, to seek solace somewhere else.

Mang Danny wiped his face with the diaper and apologized to me as he tried to rub away his tears from the sleeve of my dress. The taillights of the Porsche were as round and bright as lizard eyes, and the rim of its hood seemed to form a smug smile when we both returned the car's stare.

"Do you want to sit inside?" Mang Danny asked.

I nodded, and he opened the door to the driver's seat, pushing it shut when I had stepped inside and taken my seat. I stared at the deer logo on the steering wheel, wondering if Dad had gone to Europe, where there were lots of deer. Once, he had told me that the roads were better in Europe and that you could race down those roads in a Porsche, or an Alfa Romeo, or a Ferrari, if you wanted to. Maybe he had gotten a newer, faster car wherever he had gone, and was speeding down a highway with his girlfriend – a young, new maid whose presence in our house we had barely noticed. He had left me here, with a mother who couldn't recover from the humiliation of being ditched by her husband for her maid, with a car that I couldn't yet drive. He couldn't expect me to save myself from this castle, but this seemed to be the least of his concerns.

Perhaps children's tales contain an element of truth. I never believed in the aswangs and half-bodied sorceresses that populated the bedtime stories Yaya Dayang told me, no matter how vehemently she insisted that they walked the streets of her childhood village disguised as ordinary women. She had the right to her own superstitions, considering what little education she'd received before coming to our resort town in the mountains to look for work. I was beginning to learn how adults used codes to lock away certain truths that refused to uproot themselves from the world we inhabited, and that some became so enchanted with these codes that they came to accept them as literal truths. The husband stealer becomes a malevolent aswang who eats the hearts of men, while the abortionist operating on the fringes of the village becomes the manananggal whose legs stay rooted to the ground while her upper torso flies away at night, searching for unsuspecting pregnant women who make the mistake of leaving their bedroom windows open as they sleep. Gina – my father's mistress – was an aswang, and Yaya Dayang wasn't quick enough to see the connection between the fabular and the real. The fabular was vividly real, while her everyday reality was too oppressively banal to captivate her.

Three weeks after my father's departure, Lola Marie received a phone call from Lola Consuelo, my father's mother. Before I knew it, Lola Marie was in my bedroom, choosing my dresses and shoes and handing these to Yaya Dayang, who packed them in my Hello Kitty suitcase. My father was in the southern city of Cebú with his mistress, and he had asked his mother to ask Lola Marie if I could pay him a visit. Lola Marie said she didn't want me to be exposed to my father's immoral behavior, but he was my father, after all, and they needed to know what my father was up to. Mang Danny was to drive me to Manila in the family van and from there, I'd take a plane to Cebú.

"If I weren't so angry, I'd come with you all the way to Cebú – but if I ever lay my eyes on him, God knows what I'd do," Lola Marie said, appraising my lavender-colored dress before handing it to Yaya Dayang.

"Margot, when you're in Cebú, act like a lady and show that Gina what she's worth!" Yaya Dayang said.

Lola Marie laughed. "And keep an eye on your dad and his mistress," she said. "Observe their every move, hija, you promise that to me, ha? Tell me everything when you come back, down to the last detail. I know you're a smart girl."

As Mang Danny carried my suitcase downstairs, my mother sat before the TV in our living room, hair uncurled, face sadly unmade. I had gotten used to seeing my mother wearing makeup, and her bare, shiny face disarmed me with its honest vulnerability. It was as if happiness were a mask she had lowered all of a sudden, forgetting that the curtain hadn't fallen yet, that the drama in which she took part hadn't yet reached its conclusion.

Lola Marie, who was descending the stairs behind me, seemed to notice this too. "Clara, we're going to the salon later," she said. "Your friends will see you looking like that and you'll be the talk of the town."

"Let them talk," my mother said, folding her arms. She glanced up at me and said, "And tell your father that I don't care if he won. I still have the house."

"If only your mommy were a big girl like you," Lola Marie said, ushering me outside before my mother could speak another word.

It was easy to spot my father at the Mactan airport because of his attire – Ray-Bans, Lacoste T-shirt and khaki pants – and even though I had dreamt on the plane of slapping him in the face and yelling, "You have no shame", the way women did in the telenovelas Yaya Dayang watched, I ran into his arms and sobbed when he caught me. He paid a porter to carry my luggage, and we walked hand in hand to the cab that would take us to his hotel.

"I'm sorry if it's so hot here in Cebú," he said when we were seated in the cab. "That's what I miss about Baguio – the pine trees and the mountain breeze."

I wasn't used to this tropical heat and sweat collected under my starched summer dress. We whizzed past palm trees and Toyotas as we made our way into the city center.

"So why don't you come back?" I asked. I meant it – why would anyone choose the heat and smog of this city over a life in our secluded mountain paradise?

"I don't know. I've been asking myself that question." He took off his Ray-Bans and turned to look at me, and I noticed the blue circles under his eyes.

"How's your mother?"

As I thought of a way to describe my mother to him, I remembered my mother's words. "She says she doesn't care if you won," I said. I was about to add "She still has the house anyway", but I reined myself in.

"Women. They refuse to give up control." My father sighed. "Gina was in the salon when I called her from the airport. I didn't know she was so high-maintenance. When she was working for us, she was just a simple barrio lass."

I couldn't control myself anymore. "What a pok-pok," I said.

"Margot, don't talk like that," he said. He rubbed his eyes, as though to scrub away the truth from his field of vision, and then said, "All right, I know you're upset. I'll try to make it up to you. I'll get you anything you want when we go to the mall."

I scooted away from him and looked out the window. Small, dirty houses made of tin and rice sacks spilled onto the road and when I looked closer, I saw more of these tiny shacks behind the row that faced the street. Shirtless men with fat, sweaty bellies stood in front of their houses watching cars pass, and as traffic slowed, I spotted a woman giving her baby a bath on the sidewalk. I wondered what Yaya Dayang would've said if she had seen what I saw. The water poured onto the baby looked almost as dirty as the water that trickled down the gutters of the sidewalk.

"Gina's family lives in one of those shacks," my father said, pointing at the scene rolling past my window as though I hadn't seen it already. "Now she expects me to feed and clothe them all. Jesus. I wonder why these people have so many children."

When we stepped into his hotel room, a woman was sitting at the balcony, her back turned to us, her hair draped over the back of her chair. My dad asked her something in halting Visayan and she got up, her shoulders hunched as though burdened by a heavy, invisible load.

As she turned to look at us, strands of frizz popped out from her head of shiny salon-styled hair. The powder she had piled on her face failed to lighten her peasant-girl skin, and her nose wasn't as straight and matangos as mine. She had a pretty dress on too – it was shiny and tight at the waist – and even my mother wouldn't have worn such a dress at home if she weren't expecting guests. Maybe Gina was imitating my mother this time, and I began to realize that I was a guest at this woman's house, a prisoner of her hospitality.

I had once thought that I possessed no memories of the woman who had taken my father away from us but as I stood before her, I remembered a small-boned girl who had this woman's face entering my bedroom after a friend from school and I had spilled glitter on the carpet. She vacuumed it up for us, not looking us in the face, not answering back when Yaya Dayang nudged her head with a finger, scolding her for not giving the lunch dishes a thorough washing.

Once a maid, always a maid, I said to myself, and I backed away as she approached me.

"Ohhh, Margot, how's the bebe gurl?" she asked, arms outstretched. I could tell she wasn't used to speaking English, and the words of a language I had been taught to love by my parents and teachers now drifted toward me like mutant children her mouth had spawned. Before she could reach me, I darted away from her and hid behind my father.

"Now, Margot, don't be like that," my father said. Gina's exuberance faded, and her eyes narrowed as she frowned. She muttered something in Visayan, the words sliding easily from her tongue. I could tell her dress made her feel uncomfortable – she pulled at its cinched waist and scrunched up her powdered face. Stepping from behind my father's back, I folded my arms and said, "I'm fine, and how are you?" in the best American accent I could muster.

"Gina, I'm bringing Margot to the mall in a bit. You don't have to come with us," my father said, and she bit her lip as she nodded.

"I have my own room here, don't I?" I chirped, rubbing in my sense of triumph.

My father averted his eyes from Gina, as though ashamed for having been caught staring at a dirty picture. "Yes, of course. You must be tired," he said. He then turned to Gina. "Have you made her bed yet?" he asked.

This seemed to have put her in her place, and she stared at my father in disbelief. "Ask the maid service, not me," she said, choking on her words. She turned away from us and returned to the balcony, slamming the glass door behind her and gripping the railings with her manicured fingers.

Soon, soon, she'd lose her grip on this world. I wasn't like my mother, who had parted easily with what was rightfully her own.

That night, my dad helped me brush my teeth. After reading me the Edward Lear book he had bought for me at the mall, he pulled the hotel blanket to my chin and kissed my forehead. He was about to switch off the lights when he turned to me and said, "I think that was the first time I ever tucked you into bed."

"Yeah. Yaya Dayang usually does it."

"Did I do okay?"

"You were better than Yaya Dayang. She tells me all these scary stories about aswangs and manananggals." I sat up and leaned against the headboard.

"She shouldn't be telling you scary stories."

"I never get scared, Dad. You know that."

Dad walked to my bed and sat on its edge. Rubbing his eyes, then turning to me, he asked, "Could you do me a favor? After all, I bought you that book and tucked you into bed."

"Okay."

"Well, if you ever get to talk to your Lola Consuelo on the phone, tell her they need to add a little more money to my allowance. Tell her that I have to buy a house here because I can't live in a hotel forever. You can come visit us, of course."

I frowned. "Whatever."

"Your Lola Consuelo is very fond of you. She'll do whatever you say."

I turned away from him before he could kiss me again. "You just want to build a house for that maid," I muttered, pulling my sheets over my head.

My mother and Lola Marie had a good laugh when I returned home and described the maid to them. I began imagining myself sharing gossip with them over a game of mahjong, tossing my head back and giggling about the misfortunes of the other women who came to our parties. I was happy that my mother was cheering up. A few days after I got back, my mother was wearing makeup again, going to the gym and entertaining friends at our house. Even if my loyalties were with my father, my mother's victories were mine too.

Once, while my mother was keeping score at a tennis match being held on our lawn, I slipped into my parents' bedroom and tried on some of my mother's dresses and shoes. Although I was growing taller, the skirts of her dresses trailed behind me even when I walked around in high-heeled shoes that were several sizes too big for me. The king-sized bed that was already made when I came in was now solely my mother's, and I wondered if she felt lonely as she lay in bed at night, now that she had earned sole ownership of this immensity. At a corner of the room was my mother's antique dresser, which had a round mirror framed with flowers and leaves carved into the wood. There were no traces of male vanity left on this dresser – only brushes, powders, perfumes, and a basketful of lipsticks of all sizes, shades and brands. I picked out a blue tube labeled "Fire Engine Red" and rubbed its contents all over my lips, like a crayon. It was true what they said, that I had my mother's Cupid's-bow lips and hazel eyes, but my father's long lashes and puppy-dog look. I imagined him waking up one day from the spell cast on him by his maid and coming back to our house to see me ripening into a lady as beautiful as the woman he'd once loved. Like my mother, I'd outshine Gina, the mud-complexioned aswang.

"Margot, what are you doing in my room?" my mother asked, and when I turned, she was standing in the doorway, hair tied back in a ponytail, glowing with perspiration. When she saw my face, she burst into a fit of laughter and I felt my cheeks burning. "Oh, Margot," she said, walking toward me, and she pulled a tissue from a box on the dresser and scrubbed the lipstick from my lips. "You're supposed to put on enough to catch a boy's eye, but not too much or else you'll end up looking like a payaso," she said, rummaging through the basket of lipsticks and picking out a gold tube with a light-pink sticker at its base. "And don't wear makeup at school, or else those American teachers of yours will scold me for teaching you how to be a little flirt," she said, opening the tube. "Young girls start with pink. It's an easy shade to manage, and it's appropriate for your age. Hay, these are things you won't learn from that old Yaya Dayang of yours."

My childhood was ending, and even my mother approved.

∼

My father's Porsche remained in our driveway, its engine turning into what I imagined to be an unused knot of rust. After school, I sat in the driver's seat, dreaming that I was at the wheel this time and that my father was sitting beside me as we sailed out of our compound, onto the streets of our city, down the two-lane highway that slithered down the Cordilleras, into the sun-drenched rice fields of the central plains. After a while, my father disappeared altogether from the dreams I had. I'd be alone in this car, driving away from my parents' house which was haunted by the presence of my grandparents, into a bright, blurry future.

My mother's father, Lolo Gregorio, had been in London for a few weeks and when he returned, he presented me with a wooden dollhouse. It was fashioned after the English manors I'd seen in *The Secret Garden* and *Pride and Prejudice*, and came with a toy father, mother, brother, sister, dog and chauffeur. Their private lives were conveniently exposed to me whenever I slid a key into a lock at the side of the house and its two sides popped apart. At night, I placed the dolls on their beds, pushed the two sides of the house together and locked it shut. I sometimes imagined them escaping their locked house at night, running into the garden, and returning to their rooms just as the sun began to rise.

I was sitting in the driver's seat of my father's Porsche one afternoon when Lolo Joaquin's black Lexus rolled into our compound and stopped in front of the garage. He got out, slammed his door, and when his eyes fell on the Porsche, it was as though I were invisible to him. Mang Danny raced toward him from the gate, and I could tell by Mang Danny's panicked look that Lolo Joaquin had come to our house unannounced.

Lolo Joaquin traced a line on the hood of the car with his finger, brought his fingertip to his eyes, frowned and said, "Danny, you haven't been polishing Linus's car."

"I polish his car every day, sir. It's just that I had to wash Senyorita Clara's Golf today, and I forgot to wipe down this one."

Lolo Joaquin waved Mang Danny away, as though he were shooing a fly.

"When I bring this back to my driveway this afternoon, you will come with me and wash it down."

Mang Danny hesitated. "But I don't know what Senyorita Clara would say."

Lolo Joaquin scratched his beard, suppressed a laugh and said, "Danny, I bought this car for my son. Technically, it's mine."

"No, it's not!" I cried.

He turned to look at me, as though he were surprised that I could actually speak. He rarely visited us since, after all, our house belonged to my lolo Gregorio, not to Lolo Joaquin's son. Lolo Joaquin maintained an air of aloofness during the rare times he appeared in our compound, as though threatened by the abundance of space that my mother's family possessed. I had never really warmed to him even though I received blushing wide-eyed dolls from him on birthdays and at Christmastime.

"Child, I'm not taking away your daddy's car. I'm just borrowing it." He spoke to me slowly, liltingly, as though I could be easily fooled.

"Why?" I asked.

"Your father says he needs it. You still love him, don't you? You'd do anything for him, and you'd get out of the car right now and lend it to your dear lolo."

Standing beside my tall, muscled lolo Joaquin, Mang Danny was a shrunken old man, and he shook his head in surrender as he put his hand in his pocket and pulled out a key. The deer-logo key chain briefly caught the light on its laminated surface. Lolo Joaquin took it and he dangled it in my face.

"You see, child, I have the key now, and you do not. I can drive, while you cannot. Besides, that car you're sitting in is in my name. So, get out before your mommy sees us, or else she'll get very, very mad."

Gripping the sides of my seat, I yelled, "It's our car, not yours!" Lolo Joaquin unlocked my door, seized my arm and tried to pull me out, but I dug my nails into the edge of my seat. I screamed when he finally dragged me out of the car and pushed me aside onto the pavement. As he climbed into the driver's seat, Lola Marie came running from the back door. "Margot, what's the matter? Where are you?" she called out, searching for me at the mouth of the garage. When she spotted me crouched on the floor, sobbing, she rushed to me and helped me up.

Lolo Joaquin didn't waste time in starting the car, and he tossed another car key to Mang Danny, yelling, "You take my Lexus home or else!"

"Joaquin, I can charge you for trespassing and battery," Lola Marie said, brushing away the gravel that had cut into my knees.

"I'm taking what's mine!" Lolo Joaquin said, slowly easing the car out of the garage.

The back door slammed shut again and my mother rushed toward us, the golden butterflies of her Japanese silk robe flapping against her thighs. When she saw Lolo Joaquin driving out of our compound, she yelled, "Hey, come back with that!"

"You're not having my son's Porsche!" he yelled back.

"I have every right to it! Linus left it with me, and it's conjugal property!"

"Conjugal property, you say? My dear, neither this nor anything you own is in your name!" He smirked at us as he made a roundabout turn toward the main gate, and the car made one last purr before he sped off.

Now I had to look for another hiding place in our house, for my dreams threatened to spill out of my head, into a reality of closed spaces, locked doors.

First, she bewitched my father, then, not being content with that, she took away his car. I sat in my bedroom in the days that followed Lolo Joaquin's visit, playing with my dolls, making them go on picnics far away from their pretty house, in another pine-paneled corner of my room. It didn't take long for us to see the Porsche again. We found it parked at the Baguio Country Club one Sunday morning when Lola Marie brought us to a charity brunch organized by her amigas. My mother told us over breakfast the next day that one of my father's fraternity brothers – a man named Cedric – had bought it from Lolo Joaquin, and that he had asked for her forgiveness, saying, "Don Joaquin told me that Linus needs the money to stay alive in Cebú. You know me – I help friends when they're in need." At the brunch, I saw her laughing beside Cedric, a pale, slit-eyed man, on the veranda overlooking the golf course, and a week later he drove the car into our compound, parked it in our driveway, and leaped out of the driver's seat when he saw my mother rushing to him and offering her hand.

"Don't tampo to me, Margot. I rescued it for you," he said to me when he saw me gazing at the car through the lace curtains of our living room window. He offered to take me out for a ride, but I shook my head and refused. With him behind the wheel, the car seemed to have undergone some kind of chemical change, since it was now incapable of emitting the subtle glow I hadn't seen but felt, when it was still my father's toy.

Maybe I was blind to whatever my mother saw in it, for she slipped into the passenger seat before my father's friend drove out that afternoon.

∽

Her name was Sarah and she had merged into the crowd that flowed in and out of our house on weekends. She had blonde hair and blue eyes, wore native tribal clothing, and her hyena-like laughter was capable of reaching the far corners of our house. She was like a rare and exotic animal that cast a spell on those who laid eyes on her, and though she came to our parties uninvited at first, she soon made herself a welcome guest at our house.

Not everyone was charmed. "It looks like finishing schools are a thing of the past in America," Lolo Gregorio said as we stood in the living room, watching my mother's friends buzz around this tall, turbaned Amerikana. I couldn't understand, at first, why people enjoyed her presence at our parties. Maybe it was her lack of table manners – I once saw her downing a slice of blueberry cheesecake in three gulps – or maybe it was because of the way she dressed. She stood out like my naughty classmate at school whom all the teachers treated better just because he was an American. Once or twice, I caught a glimpse of her long, blonde armpit hair when she placed a hand on her hip while talking loudly with my mother, who nodded at whatever Sarah said, blinking as though hypnotized.

"I heard she came here to Baguio to buy property," one of my mother's amigas said, brooding over her wall of mahjong tiles and taking another drag from her cigarette. Another party had just ended, and the maids were sweeping up the clutter on our lawn as my mother and three of her closest amigas played a round of mahjong on the table of our first-floor balcony. I sat in a garden chair a few paces away from them, my legs dangling from my seat. The small hardbound volume of Edward Lear limericks that my father had bought for me in Cebú lay open in my lap, begging for my attention with its silliness. Sarah deserved a naughty caricature in this book, perhaps even a limerick. But my imagination had to do the work, and this sneaky female conversation intruded into my thoughts, luring me back into a reality that Sarah's voice and flesh occupied.

"And who told her about Baguio?" my mother asked.

"Oh, you know these Caucasians, they're desperate for some cool air."

"Well, this city was built by Americans for that purpose," another friend of my mother chimed in.

"That's why they behave as if they own the place!" the woman with the cigarette said.

"Where did she get her money?" my mother asked.

The woman with the cigarette giggled and nudged my mother's shoulder. "Believe me, she didn't bring her money from America. I wouldn't be surprised if she was born in a trailer park. What I heard is that she was married to a Perez, from Bacolod. Their marriage was annulled and she received a nice separation package from him. I heard he was glad to get rid of her."

"She's living the dream," my mother said. "She has her own money, and she can do whatever she wants."

"It's not her money – it's her husband's. She just got lucky, and she needs us because Bacolod society cast her out."

When I turned to look at the group of women, my mother looked in my direction and smiled. For a moment it seemed as if she weren't smiling at me, but at something in the air that had materialized before her eyes. She was looking through me at some imagined scenario where my presence wasn't necessary.

Even if Lola Marie and Lolo Gregorio weren't particularly fond of Sarah, she continued to be a guest at our house. One afternoon when I got back from school, Sarah's far-reaching voice punctuated the silence of our compound. I walked inside and found my mother and Cedric seated beside each other in the living room, sipping tea and listening to Sarah speak. From her seat, Sarah talked rapidly as though to fend off any possible interruptions, while my mother and Cedric politely nodded in agreement whenever she punctuated a statement with a sigh or an upward, asthmatic lilt. Cedric tried catching my mother's attention with a furtive smile, but my mother was too absorbed in what Sarah was saying to notice this small distraction. However, my mother saw me standing near the piano, and she beckoned me toward her. After ordering a maid to get me a glass of orange juice and a bowl of cookies, she patted the vacant space on the couch beside her and placed an arm around my shoulder when I sat down. When she turned to look at Sarah, her smile wasn't of mild tolerance, but of sincere curiosity.

"What I don't understand about the locals is that they embrace Western culture as if it were part of their historical heritage," Sarah said, crossing one fat leg over the other. She was wearing a wraparound batik dress, and her pasty flesh spilled over her cinched neckline. "Well, I know you were under Spain for three hundred years, and then you were under the United States for fifty years, but three hundred and fifty years shouldn't be enough to wipe away all the traces of your native culture. Wherever I go, I see poverty, inaction, jadedness. Women are prisoners of the houses of their husbands. The ruling class remains a slave of Western consumer culture, spending their energies acquiring useless goods instead of leading the people toward the path of dharma." She paused to take another sip from her cup of tea and then said, "I had to leave America because I was just sick of being another guinea pig of the capitalist system. And then I come here to see that they've placed you on a leash too."

"So you expected us to be living in trees?" Cedric asked.

She seemed unprepared for this interruption, for she pursed her lips as she placed her teacup and saucer on the coffee table. "You had a culture before the Spaniards came to destroy it. It was a culture rich in meaning and wisdom," she said. Her last sentence made Cedric roll his eyes, and my mother shot him an angry look.

Cedric said, "My grandmother was Spanish, if you didn't know that. And Clara's grandparents are Spanish too."

"Oh, but what about that Babaylan blood running through your veins?"

"Babaylan blood, my ass," Cedric said, slamming his teacup and saucer on the coffee table and rising from his seat. He pouted at my mother and said, "It's jazz night at Pilgrim's Café. Wanna come?"

If I had been my mother, I would've said yes right away. A lock of his slicked-back hair fell before his eyes, casting his pale Chinese features in shadow.

"Cedric, Sarah's our guest, and she hasn't finished talking," my mother said.

"Well, you entertain her, while I find some entertainment for myself," Cedric said, making for the front door.

"When you've been kept blind for more than three hundred years, it's hard to accept the truth," Sarah said, fingering the patterns on her batik dress.

"Tell that to your ex-husband," Cedric said, before opening the door and slamming it behind him. My mother's hand fell from my shoulder, and she got up and followed him outside. Left alone with this tall, big-boned woman, I clasped my glass of orange juice and bowed my head. When she stretched, a wave of body odor spread across the living room. I was afraid she'd ask me a question that I wouldn't know the answer to. She was a puzzle whose presence bore down on me, like unfinished homework. I heard my mother pleading with Cedric in the courtyard, and then raising her voice when Cedric called Sarah crazy. I felt more nervous in front of this woman than anyone I had ever met – even Gina, whom I detested, could be easily subdued.

When I raised my head, my eyes met Sarah's. While I knew I had met the standards that my American teachers at the international school measured me against, it seemed that this woman was dissatisfied with what she saw. She looked at me from head to toe and snorted.

"Looks like they turned you into a little brown American too," she said.

I heard Cedric starting the engine of what was now his car, and when my mother returned, she looked at Sarah and put on a smile. "Now, where were we?" she asked, settling back into her seat beside me.

Sarah seemed to be excited by my mother's enthusiasm, and the condescension she directed at me was replaced with matronly approbation. "Your friend doesn't seem to like hearing the truth from a woman," Sarah said, taking her teacup and saucer from the coffee table.

"He's just your typical Filipino man," my mother said.

They both exploded in laughter. It wasn't too difficult for me to sense the undercurrent of a shared secret I was too young to be let in on, and I felt excluded from the sudden warmth that grew between these grown women. When my mother turned to me, a look of calm triumph flickered in her eyes, and she pulled me close. I put my arm around her back, realizing that I had missed her.

With Sarah at the helm of my mother's parties, we began to attract a different crowd. Many of them were Americans or American mestizos dressed in the geometric-patterned wraparound garb of the Igorot tribes that used to inhabit the hills of our city before the Americans came. They ate our hors d'oeuvres and began to complain that they had come halfway across the world just to feed on snacks they could have purchased in some restaurant in America. And so, my mother fired our caterer and hired an American cook who had just set up shop near the city hall, and who was keen on learning how to prepare the dishes that native highlanders once feasted on.

My mother's amigas rolled their eyes and giggled as the American guests tried to imitate the young loinclothed Igorot man who danced around our tennis court and spread his arms as he imitated an eagle. But they chatted with our American guests and listened in silence as a bearded white man, who also wore a loincloth, gave them a lecture about how the white man had forced us to give up the unique relationship we shared with nature. As soon as he turned his back to them, they burst into giggles, but at the next party they showed up wearing wraparound skirts, beaded vests and clay-bead necklaces.

At one party, my mother descended our staircase wearing a low-cut evening gown made of thick, irregularly patterned ikat fabric, eliciting cries of awe from her old-time guests who were now coming to her parties wearing tribal garb. My mother insisted that I wear a red-and-black wraparound dress that Igorotas wore, and when I threw myself on my bed and beat my pillows, she ordered Yaya Dayang to force me into my costume.

"Child, if I could only take you away from this place, I would, but I have nowhere else to go. Please put this on, or else I'll lose my job," Yaya Dayang said to me, and I got up from my bed and raised my arms so that she could undress me. I wasn't doing this for my mother. I was doing this for my dear yaya.

"Oh, children. They're the closest to nature, the closest to God," a blonde in purple beaded pajamas said, as I descended the stairs in my Igorot costume.

"If only the locals returned to the basics, wouldn't this country be a less corrupt place?" a bearded white man with clumpy hair and tattered pajamas said, taking a quick glance at my mother's Filipino friends. They were gathered near the front door, feeling the fabrics of each other's clothes and comparing prices.

"There's this specialty store in Intramuros that sells these heirloom clothes of tribes that have disappeared from the map. I got this dress for fifteen hundred pesos. I feel possessed by the spirit of the head-huntress who once wore it," a woman said, and the beads of her turban glittered as she struck a pose before my mother and her amigas. I had gravitated to their group after having woven through the crowd of Americans who chatted among themselves, too absorbed to notice my presence or to cross over to the other side of the living room to talk to my mother's Filipino friends. They only addressed us whenever they delivered a speech. I wondered why they shied away from us. We could all speak English.

Our front door opened and Cedric walked in, wearing a turban tied at the front of his head, a cloth jacket with diamond shapes embroidered on its sleeves and soft gray trousers with rolled cuffs. This was the first time he had shown up at our house since he had stormed away weeks before. When he saw me, he spread his legs, folded his arms, pretended to gaze into the distance, turned to look at me, opened his mouth and winked. I laughed as I approached him and when he offered his fist, I offered mine. His amused detachment made him stand out at this party and for that reason alone, I felt relieved that he had come.

"Margot, I'm just gatecrashing. You think your mom would like the way I look?" he asked.

"You look funny," I said, before turning to take in the throng of costumed adults who hung about in our living room and wandered around our lawn. This time, Lolo Gregorio had had enough of these parties, and he left in a huff with Lola Marie when a group of costumed Americans showed up at our gate, asking if they had come to the right place. My mother ushered in the Americans and told my grandparents to stop telling her what to do. As more guests showed up, Lolo Gregorio said she could do as she chose, as long as he could stop bankrolling her parties.

"Fine. But let me have my party first before I pack up," my mother said.

"She's depressed, that's all," Lola Marie said, and she waved at my mother and the guests, telling them to have fun before escorting my scowling grandfather out the door. In their hurry, they had forgotten to take me with them. Now I was stuck with these adults, wearing a costume that bit into my armpits and scratched my skin.

"I know, I know, we're surrounded by weirdos," Cedric said, lowering his voice, and when I turned to look at him, he gave me a knowing nod. He seemed to be the only adult at this party who knew my mind wasn't a blank slate that remained blank as they talked about clothes, my mother and me.

"Margot, you know how your mother changes her mind so easily. Soon, she'll be looking for another diversion." He broke into a smile when my mother called out to him.

"My Muslim prince!" my mother cried, and he walked toward her, leaving me standing alone beside the door.

There was no one at this party with whom I could share my misgivings about the changes my mother had undergone and what our lives would look like after this. Sarah held court at our balcony, coconut shell in hand, and my mother disappeared into the crowd that merged to listen to Sarah speak.

Sarah handed her empty coconut shell to one of our maids, who disappeared into our kitchen. A dark-haired woman faced the crowd and yelled, "Quiet. The chief is about to speak." Silence fell over the living room.

Sarah clasped her hands and closed her eyes, and the crowd followed her lead. As though by instinct, my mother's Filipino friends made the sign of the cross. An old American man threw them dirty looks and hissed, "We aren't in a Catholic Church, you sheep."

"I call on you tonight, eternal mother, because the children of this beautiful country have been kept blind and searching for the longest of time by forces of Western patriarchal capitalism and imperialism. They have lost contact with their true selves and have become oblivious to the forests that surround them. Oh, we must become children again, all of us children!"

I felt a tapping on my shoulder, and when I looked up, Cedric was grinning at me. Bending down, he whispered in my ear, "Your mother needs your prayers." I nodded, made the sign of the cross and closed my eyes. I knew I had to pray for my mother, but I didn't know what to ask for. I asked God to make Sarah leave us alone, but then the thought of my father entered my mind. I knew there was no harm in asking God to bring him back. No one else could come to my rescue.

A month later, as Yaya Dayang dressed me for school, she told me she'd overheard my grandparents say that my father had returned to Baguio, unaccompanied, and that he was living with Lolo Joaquin and Lola Consuelo. "They say that Gina left him for a politician. Maybe things will return to normal after this," she said, buttoning up the freshly ironed blouse she had draped over my back.

Sarah had bought a house two streets away from ours and my mother was a frequent guest at her garden parties. Once, Lola Marie scolded her for taking me to one of Sarah's parties, saying, "Don't force all this nonsense into the child's head." It was in my grandparents' power to keep me at home, but they couldn't prevent my mother from rushing out of our house whenever she received an invitation from one of Sarah's maids. She'd come home dazed and taciturn, and even Cedric, who had stopped dressing like a Muslim warrior, couldn't coax a laugh from her. He still came to our house, expecting, perhaps, one of the parties of old. Once, when he put a hand on her shoulder, she pushed him away and called him a "patriarchal, colonial-minded fool." He left our house, never to return.

Indeed, my mother's mind had changed. Even my mother's amigas had kept up with these changes, flocking to Sarah's house, wearing the clothes she had prescribed. I wanted to imagine them playing mahjong at the country club, sharing the gossip they had gathered about Sarah, calling her an aswang behind her back. But I knew they preferred to sit on the grass of Sarah's garden, listening to the woman who called herself the chief.

One Saturday, after my mother had gone out, Yaya Dayang helped me into the same lavender dress I had worn when I had visited my father in Cebú. An old gray sedan pulled into our driveway as I sat in the living room with Lola Marie. We got up and walked outside to meet my father. Lola Marie stood at the doorstep and, sensing my hesitation, put a wrinkled hand on my shoulder and said, "Go on. He came here to see you, not to see me."

I could see my father through the window of the driver's seat, his hand on the steering wheel, his eyelashes fluttering behind the lenses of his aviators as he opened and closed his eyes. Bowing his head, he finally pushed the door open and stepped out.

He looked at me and said, "You've grown taller."

"Uh-huh."

He opened the passenger's seat for me and I stepped in. The interior of the car smelled of dust and the moldy remnants of afternoon rain. Crushed soda cans and water bottles littered the floor. He got behind the steering wheel, pulled the door shut beside me and turned on the ignition.

"I learned how to drive in this car," he said, pulling out of our driveway. "It's an old clunker, but it brings back memories." His lips strained into a smile. "I heard my old friend Cedric has been taking the Porsche to the house," he said.

"He used to. I haven't seen him in weeks."

"So that grocer's son finally learned some delicadeza." We passed Sarah's house, where wind chimes made of glass and clay hung from her striped awning. Smoke rose in dirty, heavy puffs from behind her house. I imagined Sarah spinning around a bonfire and tap-dancing barefoot on the grass, and my mother watching her in silence, waiting for her turn to dance, to let go.

"Has he taken you on a ride?" my father asked.

"He offered once, but I said no."

"Good. I hope it breaks down on him."

We were silent as we drove through the pine forests of South Drive. My father's reticence seemed to provide the answers to my questions. I knew he was ashamed, and I knew his silence was a wall he had erected to hide his own clumsiness. He had used whatever money he had to hide this clumsiness from Gina and when the money ran out, so did her love for him. For in truth, he needed us, or at least he needed me.

We stopped at the gate of the Baguio Country Club. The guard waved us away, and my father pulled out his wallet from his back pocket, flashing his member ID. The guard scratched his head, laughed and said "I didn't recognize you at first", before opening the gate for us.

"My parents say I should go out more often and see friends. I don't know. I need you to back me up when I meet the guys again," my father said, as we pulled into a vacant parking space.

"I could do that," I said, unbuckling my seatbelt.

"Sure you're not ashamed of stepping out of this ratty car?" he asked.

I imagined us acting in a comedy sketch, my father's old Porsche waiting for us offstage to bear us away.

"It doesn't matter," I said.

My father took off his sunglasses, rubbed his eyes and sighed. "I'm sorry, Margot."

"I forgive you."

"Do you think they'll forgive me?"

When I fell silent, he pressed his forehead to the steering wheel and began to sob. I put a hand on his back and leaned my head against his side. His shaking wouldn't subside – his sobs grew heavier, deeper, when I squeezed him. The main club building loomed before us, a silent, stony witness to my father's shame.

"I can't go in there. They'll laugh at me," he said in between sniffles.

"Dad, we can leave if you want to. We could go to the beach," I said.

When he turned to look at me, he looked like a little boy who had just been told that he couldn't get any more candy.

"But we belong here, don't we?" he asked.

"Of course," I said, feeling my anticipation waver, then drown in a pool of disappointment.

"Be strong for me, kid. Be my backup if they start heckling me." Swallowing and closing his eyes, he opened his door.

Maybe he was right. My father needed something to return to if he were to come back to me at all.

STOPOVER

When Cathy's plane began its descent into Austin, Texas, she lifted the shade of her window and peered outside. From where she sat, the city streets trickled from the downtown area to the sparsely populated fringes of the dust bowl below. A vein of water wound its way through the city grid, appearing and disappearing as the base of her window bobbed up and down beside her. As the plane tilted to its left side, a bell tower emerged into view and the trees and brick buildings that surrounded it seemed to reinforce its genteel authority. She imagined Evangeline biking to class under those trees, her wavy hair streaming behind her the way it did in those tin-framed, open-air jeepneys they rode together to class in their sprawling college campus in Manila.

She and Evangeline had both been English majors in college, and when they graduated, Evangeline took a teaching job at a college near the foothills of Mount Makiling, while Cathy left the Philippines with her family to begin a new life in the suburbs of San Francisco. She wasn't even "Cathy" back when Evangeline knew her, and when Evangeline called her by the name "Katrina" on the phone, she felt her old life tightening around her like an ill-fitting dress she had outgrown. She hadn't intentionally cast away her old name or her memories of the old country during her three years in America. Like scales she had shed, she had hardly been aware that some of her old habits had gradually fallen away.

This wasn't her hometown, but as she walked up the tarmac and into the small, glass-paneled airport, she felt as though this were a sort of homecoming, and she pictured Evangeline being awed by her accent as well as the ease with which she dealt with Americans. She hadn't been back to the old country since she had left and this was the next best thing to coming home – meeting a character of her past whom she could overwhelm with her knowledge of America. One of the fringe benefits she enjoyed as a check-in clerk for an American airline was free domestic flights. She took advantage of this to explore her adopted country, and she posted pictures of her trips to New York and the other big cities on Facebook religiously. She followed every "like", every admiring remark about her success in this land that everyone back home called "the land of the free". It came to a point that she needed to get on a plane to hear their comments in her head, for only by doing this could she remind herself of the freedom she now possessed.

When Evangeline messaged her, telling her that she was moving to Austin, Texas for graduate school, Cathy looked forward to having a couch to sleep on in a town she had only read about in in-flight magazines. Evangeline was probably as bewildered as she had been when she first arrived in America, but Cathy was sure she was smart enough to navigate the town or at least to know how to buy a couch from a local thrift store. Cathy could take care of the other parts of this trip, like coaxing Evangeline to a bar, or teaching her how to flirt with American boys.

Plane just landed, Cathy typed into her phone, her boot heels neatly clicking against the grooves of the airport escalator. You can pick me up now.

All right. I texted you my address. You can rent a car or take a shuttle to my place, Evangeline replied.

What? You don't have a car? Cathy texted back, alarmed.

I said so in my email. Car rental companies near the exit. Sorry, was Evangeline's reply.

Sighing, Cathy pushed her phone into her jeans pocket and made her way through the crowd of families, students and returning servicemen in khaki boots and camouflage uniforms who stepped aside as she passed without making eye contact with her. She felt as though she were walking through a forest of towering bodies that were too indifferent to do her harm. She approached the Avis counter and fell in line right behind a family of South Asians and a bespectacled old man in a gray suit who carried a battered leather briefcase. The crowd that had gathered around the baggage carousels thinned out, and she watched on as families in light summer clothes entered the airport, letting out excited screams when they spotted their uniformed sons lumbering towards them. Her friend was too poor to extend the same welcome to her, and when the uniformed teenager behind the Avis counter handed her a bill, she realized she didn't have enough money saved up for this trip to be as mobile as she wanted to be.

At Evangeline's suggestion, she reserved a seat on an airport shuttle and shared a ride with a quiet Asian girl who peered nearsightedly into her iPhone, and two middle-aged women in jeans and T-shirts who chattered about a bridal shower as they clasped their newly bought cowboy hats to their bellies. The houses they passed on their way to the city were just as seedy as the clapboard bungalows that surrounded her apartment building on the outskirts of San Francisco. Outside her shuttle window, mothers pushed strollers across the street as small children grasped the hems of their worn thrift-store skirts, while men in baseball caps and baggy pants walked along the roadside, ignoring vehicles that barreled past them. A twin-sized mattress and box spring peeked from the mouth of a dumpster that faced the road, and she remembered the futon mattress she and her boyfriend had retrieved outside a vacant lot near her apartment building just months before. It creaked beneath them during their make-out sessions and her boyfriend complained that it was giving him back problems whenever he slept over, but the two hundred dollars she had saved was enough to pay for a two-night stay at an airport hotel in one of those sleepy Midwestern towns whose names she didn't bother to remember. Money passed through Cathy's fingers like water, and again she was back to scrimping. The shuttle that bore her to her friend's apartment was like a sealed capsule with its windows rolled up, shielding its passengers from the grayness that spread itself before them like the stale pages of an unread book.

After skirting past the university and entering a quieter neighborhood of oak trees and clapboard houses nestled behind flower bushes and evenly mown lawns, the shuttle pulled into a parking space in front of a gray, benign-looking apartment building, with arched entrances and a pair of curved staircases that wound their way from a raised platform on the first floor, to the right and left sides of the second floor. She dialed Evangeline's number and a door on the second floor opened. Evangeline stepped outside, holding her phone to her ear, and when she spotted Cathy at the foot of the stairs leading to her floor, she flipped her phone shut, smiled and waved.

In America, Cathy had learned the habit of spreading her arms as a friend approached, and Evangeline whispered "I missed you so much!" into her ear as they hugged. The touch of Evangeline's palm against her back awakened memories of long ago, when Evangeline brushed Cathy's arm teasingly whenever Cathy asked her to explain Derrida's definition of différance to her, as though gleefully surprised that anyone she considered her friend could find such easy concepts so difficult to understand. Evangeline never lacked friends despite spending hours in the library, and when she did socialize with the likes of Cathy, she'd guard her secrets of success with a lighthearted friendliness. She was a favorite of the professors, a perpetual guardian and dispenser of answers when no one else in the classroom was bright enough to follow a professor's train of thought. The tidiness with which Evangeline conducted her own life bewildered Cathy. Evangeline had left her hometown in the northern provinces to study in Manila, locked herself up in her dorm room to study and despite her shyness with boys, had defied her classmates' expectations by dating the president of the student government. Her life, it seemed, had been carefully planned out – even two years of teaching in a sleepy farming town south of Manila seemed to have gotten her places.

Evangeline grasped her shoulders, pulled back and inspected her. "You've gained weight!" she said in Tagalog. Cathy was sure she would've felt insulted if Evangeline said the same thing in English, but in their native tongue it was a common greeting. Evangeline knew just how to tell a friend the embarrassing truth.

"At least I'm gaining some weight. You've remained a stick since we graduated," Cathy said.

"You know me. I jog every day," Evangeline said, letting go of her shoulders. "I made adobo for dinner, by the way. My dad's version." She turned and led Cathy upstairs.

"Great. That's one less meal to spend for," Cathy said, pulling at the straps of her backpack.

"This country's crazy," Evangeline added, with an airy, resigned voice. "You have to swipe your card for every move you make. That's what I miss about the Philippines."

"I know. Back home, they just laze around and expect us to send them money from abroad."

Evangeline turned and gave Cathy a hard look of reproach.

"Well, not all of them," Cathy said, forcing a smile.

Evangeline's face softened. Cathy was amused by her friend's sternness, a habit acquired, Cathy joked to herself, from having to deal with minds that weren't as sharp as hers.

"I see what you mean," Evangeline said. "My aunt thinks I'm making enough to save up for a house back home. If ever she knew how expensive it is to live here." They had reached the door of her apartment and Evangeline turned the knob, pushed it open and stood aside to let Cathy pass.

"My futon was delivered a week ago. Just in time for your visit."

Cathy spotted the black futon pushed to the right side of the living room, behind a chocolate-brown coffee table with a growing stack of magazines. The entire living room was bathed in the afternoon sunlight that shone through the room's floor-to-ceiling window. Cathy would've been hesitant to sign a lease for an apartment with such a large window, but if she lived in such gentrified surroundings there wouldn't be the constant threat of break-ins to sharpen her instincts. She felt a pang of envy as she paced around the apartment, spotting a large hardwood desk beside the futon couch and a bookcase pushed against the wall that marked the end of the living room. It would've been the perfect writing space for her: a room with a view, offering enough space for the mind to wander.

She took off her backpack, set it down on the floor and approached Evangeline's desk. "This is a beautiful desk," she said, running her fingers along its varnished surface and closing her eyes.

"Forty dollars, from a poet who was moving to Chicago," Evangeline said, leaning against the wall dividing the living room from the kitchen. "It's cherrywood."

"I wouldn't even have made the distinction," Cathy said.

"Poetry used to be written at that desk. It's a desk meant for you, not for me," Evangeline said, and she laughed as though wanting to ease Cathy back into the past, back into the ill-fitting dress.

"I just have enough space in my apartment for a futon and a coffee table," Cathy said, sinking into the futon and pulling her backpack towards her feet.

"So your coffee table doubles as your writing desk?"

"As a reading desk, it does." Cathy unzipped her backpack and peered into it, feeling Evangeline's eyes following every twitch on her face.

"I miss reading your stories," Evangeline said, retreating behind the kitchen wall.

Cathy pulled out the library books she had brought with her and set them on the coffee table. Both were due in two weeks: H.P.

Lovecraft's *The Dunwich Horror* and Nicole Krauss's *The History of Love*. It was an odd pairing, but there was no need for her to follow any syllabus or thematic grouping now that she was out of school. She was educating herself, not enslaving herself to any institution or order.

The smell of soy sauce and bay leaves wafted into the living room, and a wave of memories washed away the antiseptic calmness of the present, revealing the comforting confusion of her past. She was in her grandmother's house in the old country, sitting on a bamboo bench as her grandmother puttered about in her stone kitchen. Her grandmother's adobo smelled sweeter, more acrid. America, back then, stood for everything her adulthood meant to her: an unrealized vastness into which her parents, after getting their visa petitions approved, would initiate her. She was in college by this time and she was telling her grandmother, who was ladling the pork and chicken stew into a bowl, that she wanted to be a writer, maybe a journalist. "But before you leave, you should learn how to cook our food," her grandmother said, setting down the bowl on a linoleum-covered bamboo table and inviting her to eat. "In America, you'll have food on the table all the time. But unless you learn how to cook our food, you'll never be able to feed that belly."

The first adobo she made when she had moved out of her parents' house was too bland to awaken memories of her grandmother's cooking. She gave up after her first try and now subsisted on a diet of TV dinners and canned chili. As long as she kept her stomach filled, she could keep her longing for the past at bay. A more skilled cook like Evangeline, on the other hand, could afford to be oblivious to the longings she awakened in her friend.

"You must be thirsty. Would you like some tea?" Evangeline asked, emerging from the kitchen with a wooden spoon in her hand.

"Do you have beer in your fridge?" Cathy placed *The History of Love* on her lap and opened it to a random page.

"Oh, I don't keep alcohol in my house."

Evangeline's cheerfulness only served to fan her disappointment.

"For real?"

"I just can't drink alone."

"The only liquids I drink are alcohol. And water."

"I'll get you a glass of water, then." Evangeline disappeared behind the wall, opened her fridge and cupboards, and re-emerged with a glass of cold water. Placing the glass on the coffee table, she looked at the book in Cathy's lap and asked, "What are you reading?"

"*The History of Love*. I was just looking at a random page. Haven't really started yet."

"Oh, that's such a good book," Evangeline said. Then, straightening herself, she said, "I'd like to see one of your stories in print someday."

"That wouldn't happen." Cathy bit her lip.

"Sure it will."

"I don't have time to write these days," Cathy said, snapping her book shut and returning it to the coffee table. "There are just too many good books to read."

"Don't you remember Dr Cruz comparing my failed attempts at writing with your polished prose?" Evangeline was behaving like a mother this time, and it seemed as though she took joy in dispensing kindness to her less fortunate friend.

"Why write if there are so many good books to read?" Cathy asked.

"I don't know. You were just so good at it. I still remember that story you wrote about two blind men."

"I've been doing some living too, you know." For how could she justify her own laziness to Evangeline? Life rolled on, whether Cathy liked it or not, and she had other pressing concerns to deal with like rent, bills, and coworker exes who nagged her with handwritten letters filled with misspellings and grammatical errors. She didn't see any reason to be choosy – it was bad enough that her coworkers had turned her bookishness into a running joke, and she chose to laugh along with them rather than alienate her new friends. After all, it was the ones who had never been to college who treated her as though she were one of them – the college-educated among them behaved as though they were too good to be hauling suitcases onto conveyor belts and working alongside new immigrants like her. Traveling allowed her to forget the less savory details of her life, but the sheets of stationery she left blank on the writing desks in the rooms where she slept reminded her of a larger emptiness she preferred not to face.

Evangeline withdrew again behind the kitchen wall and re-emerged after a few minutes with a bowl of steaming hot adobo which she set on the dining table. Like Cathy's grandmother, Evangeline nodded at her in invitation. "There's no pork in here," Evangeline said. "Just lean, skinless chicken breasts. I also made salad."

On the table she set two embroidered placemats on which she placed two matching floral plates. Cathy sometimes suspected that Evangeline's orderliness was a tic meant to disguise a hidden chaos. But Evangeline executed these gestures with so much ease that Cathy wondered if this wasn't a mask, but the foundation on which her life had been built. It seemed, at this point in their friendship, that Cathy had to give her friend a cleaner justification of her failure to accomplish her goals, since cleanliness seemed to be the only language Evangeline was capable of comprehending.

Cathy suspected that Evangeline saw life as a series of signposts pointing on to a desired goal, and that every wrong turn Cathy made was the result of her own miscalculations. Over dinner, she told Evangeline that she had sent her résumé to fifty newspapers upon arriving in America, and that only one of them asked her for a writing sample, after which she was informed that the position for which she applied had been filled.

"Then you could've applied to fifty more places," Evangeline said, as though her mind were immune to reason.

"Vangie, you don't get it, do you? I needed a job. I couldn't get one at a newspaper. Americans don't like our English." This conversation was exhausting her, and she leaned back in her chair and pushed away her food.

"That's not true. Look at me. I got into an American graduate school with my Filipino English."

She groaned. "But I'm not you."

Evangeline nodded, and in her silence, she seemed to give Cathy her half-hearted assent. But then Evangeline said, "I'll edit you. Send your essays to me." She met Cathy's stunned gaze with a reassuring look.

"You could always write travel articles. If I were you, I'd take advantage of those free trips. And then you could send me your drafts and I could line-edit them." Evangeline placed a salad leaf in her mouth and chewed.

After a few seconds of silence, Evangeline swallowed and said, "Oh come on, don't be offended. Everyone knows you're the better writer. You just said that Americans don't like our English. Sometimes it's just a question of nuance."

"And you're the expert on nuance."

"Well, I got into grad school here. Maybe they thought I could learn something."

"Vangie, you're making me want to get drunk."

Evangeline smiled. "Is that the real reason why you came here?"

"You just read my mind. I have to get drunk. Dead drunk."

"Plastered, you mean?"

Cathy sighed. "Yeah, whatever. And you have to get drunk with me too."

A look of nervousness passed over Evangeline's face, and it amused Cathy to see her facade of calm goodness crumble. Cathy put her hand over Evangeline's and said, "Don't worry, I'll watch out for you. You have to trust me."

"After tonight, you're gonna thank me for not having a car."

"Tama."

As Evangeline ran water over the dirty dishes and pots, Cathy took out the dresses she had brought and draped them on Evangeline's futon. Apparently, it wasn't too difficult for her to gain the upper hand. While there were things that Evangeline was better at doing, there were things she had yet to learn, and to turn her into a willing pupil, Cathy would first have to expose her ignorance.

"I'm glad you came. I've been feeling lonely ever since I arrived here," Evangeline said.

"Don't you have friends here?" Cathy asked, staring at her dresses, wondering which one her friend might be willing to wear.

"I get along well with my classmates, but you know how white people are. They're comfier when dealing with their own kind."

"You mean most of your classmates are white?"

"You could say that."

"Now that would make me very uncomfortable."

"Don't you work with white people?"

"Just white passengers, and they can be so stuck-up sometimes." Cathy picked up the fuchsia-and-black striped tube dress from its sleeves, and carried it to the dining area where she turned to face Evangeline. "Now, what do you think of this?" Cathy asked, draping it on her chest.

Evangeline stared at it and said, "Very daring. Very Latin."

"You're wearing it," Cathy said and threw it at Evangeline. Evangeline was too surprised to let it fall to the floor, and after catching it, she held it before her, her face registering a faint disgust.

"We're probably the same size. I have another dress on the futon if you don't like that one."

Evangeline walked to the living room and raised an eyebrow when she saw the neon-green one-shoulder dress spread on her futon like a mislaid piece of merchandise. "I can't wear that one either," she said.

"Unless you have something better to wear."

Evangeline lowered her eyes and it dawned on Cathy that it wasn't modesty that made Evangeline hesitate. Cathy had bought both dresses at Ross, the only place where it didn't pain her to part with her money, and the brightness of these dresses now flashed at her embarrassingly. They had both been brave choices, but her bravery could have been a result of her carelessness, or her simple lack of taste.

She covered up her embarrassment with a laugh and said, "Oh, come on. This isn't the Philippines. No one's gonna go after you for being slutty." She knew Evangeline was embarrassed to admit to her own lack of experience in these matters, and Evangeline giggled.

"Oh, what the hell. This means I'll really have to get drunk." Evangeline withdrew to her bedroom, draping the fuchsia-and-black tube dress on her arm.

She chose to ignore the hint of disappointment in Evangeline's voice, taking solace in her prediction that she'd outshine Evangeline later that night. "I'll do your makeup too," Cathy yelled with relish. "After all, you said you'd edit me!"

This wasn't Cathy's town, and she stood out in the bar-going crowd of Sixth Street. The faces of the doormen lit up when they saw her, as though hungry for variety after watching blonde after blonde walk past them. When she flashed them her California driver's license, they'd joke about knowing that she wasn't "from around these parts" as they offered her a crooked arm, which she gladly took as they escorted her into their music-filled bars. Evangeline trailed behind her, taking her Texas ID card from her clutch purse and returning the doormen's patronizing smiles.

"Oh my God, I think the drummer just gave me the eye," Cathy said as they carried their drinks to a table near the stage.

"How do you notice all these things?" Evangeline yelled above the music.

"You don't go out a lot, do you?" Cathy yelled back, stirring her chocolate whiskey.

She felt hungry after they had visited four bars, and they found a Mexican restaurant after walking several blocks. After they had settled into their leatherette seats and given the waitress their orders, Cathy observed her friend from across the table. Evangeline radiated a carefree alcoholic energy from her seat and she leaned forward, blinking and laughing before she spoke.

"There's this guy I met. His name's David," Evangeline said.

"And he's making you all giggly," Cathy said, nodding at the waitress as a bowl of chips and salsa was set before them.

"I know. He's not my type, but I'm beginning to like him."

"Sounds promising." She pulled a chip from the pile, dipped it in salsa and popped it in her mouth, giving Cathy a mute, prodding look.

"A classmate introduced us at a party. He's doing his PhD in Anthropology."

"Wow," Cathy said, her mouth full. Swallowing, she said, "At least you get to meet smart guys here. That's what I miss about college, you know? Talking to people about books, meeting smart guys."

"Hello, you could always go back to school here. You'd qualify for federal aid."

Cathy smirked. "I don't know. I'm too lazy to go back to school."

"I don't believe you," Evangeline said, drunkenly slapping the air between them with her palm. "You with your cum laude."

Cathy rolled her eyes. "I didn't work for that. Besides, all the forced writing we did in college made me want to quit school for good."

"Forced or not, you were good at it."

Service at this restaurant was quick. Cathy's plate of quesadillas was placed in front of her, while Evangeline looked on in horror when the brownie à la mode she had ordered was served.

"The newspapers I applied to didn't think so," Cathy said. She picked up her fork and knife and sliced off a neat corner from her quesadilla, putting it in her mouth and munching evasively.

"But you could still write while doing your airport gig. Keep a blog or something."

"Yeah. And then you'd edit me." Cathy stared at the abundance of food on her plate, wondering why no one else in this country seemed to take notice of this habitual overindulgence. Food was so plentiful in this country, it almost seemed like they didn't have to strive for anything else.

"This is a lot of brownie," Evangeline said.

"You're still not used to the portions here?" Cathy asked.

"How can I be? They always serve us too much food."

"You say that because you're used to eating much less."

"But this is too much."

"I said it's too much for you because you're used to eating much less." She liked the pathetic look on Evangeline's face, and how much it seemed like an admission of cluelessness.

"Come on, eat up. You look like a hungry African child. And tell me more about David."

Evangeline laughed and dipped her spoon into the scoop of vanilla ice cream.

"Well, he's a blond, blue-eyed Texan who's writing a dissertation about Indian culture. He has an adorable drawl. He's really smart too."

"So, he's a white guy."

"Yeah." Evangeline paused and gave Cathy a doubtful look. "Do you have some beef with white guys?"

Cathy pursed her lips then said, "Not really. It's just that I've never dated a white guy."

Evangeline was incredulous. "You mean out of all the guys you told me about over the phone and on Facebook—"

"The guys I've dated so far are either coworkers or friends of coworkers, and none of those people are white." She flipped through the laminated beverage list on their table. "But I'm okay with that." She ran her fingers through her hair, giggled and said, "Did I tell you yet about the guy I'm sleeping with right now? His dick's huge. And his endurance, my God! It chafes after a while, you know!"

Evangeline smiled.

"You, girl, have to go on birth control soon. As in *soon*. Because that white boy of yours is gonna ask for it soon."

Evangeline dug into her brownie. "He already did. But I told him I'm not ready."

"That's not the only thing you should be worried about. White guys suck in bed."

Evangeline narrowed her eyes. "How do you know that?"

"You'll know when you sleep with your white boy."

If Cathy could ever convince herself to write a story about that night, she'd probably mention how she took Evangeline home after her friend had nearly passed out on the sidewalk in front of the fifth bar they had gone to. She'd admit she had known that Evangeline wasn't used to marathon drinking, but that Evangeline didn't seem to mind. Maybe she'd describe how Evangeline's laughter buzzed in her ears like flies' wings as she had asked Evangeline for her address, and how she watched the lights of downtown Austin illuminate the interior of their cab with their indulgent, wasteful glow. Evangeline had sobered up when they had gotten home and they helped each other fold out her futon, laughing when they realized that they couldn't figure out how they had done it when the futon finally gave in to their pushing. If words fractured a friendship, alcohol healed it, and she wished it were possible to drown in the amber-colored recklessness of that night forever.

But with sunrise came the unwanted resurfacing of the mind, and she awakened to a bright throbbing in her head and a dismal awareness of her surroundings. As she turned, her sheets rustled – she hadn't remembered Evangeline spreading these sheets – and the detailed attentiveness of her friend annoyed her as her eyes fell on the drawn blinds of the living room window. The sputtering of cooking oil and the smell of brewed coffee and fried eggs reminded her of the calm domesticity that Evangeline was apt to return to after what was probably, for her, a temporary relapse. Cathy wanted to remain in bed the entire day, and felt too conscious of how the rhythm of her body was out of sync with the rhythm of her surroundings. She sat up and glanced at the clock near the kitchen. It was almost nine.

Evangeline peeked at her from behind the kitchen wall. "Did I wake you up?" she asked.

"You did," Cathy grumbled, scratching her head.

Evangeline laughed. "I just got hungry, so I made coffee and fried eggs. I made some for you too, in case you woke up."

Cathy stretched and smiled. "Oh, I don't eat breakfast."

Evangeline politely raised a hand and rushed back to the kitchen. "Sorry, the eggs might burn. My God, Kat. I'd faint if I didn't have breakfast," she said from behind the wall. "Besides, we have a long day ahead of us. You'll need the energy for walking."

"Right. We're going to walk," Cathy moaned, getting up and walking to the bathroom.

Her head continued to throb as they walked around the university. When they passed the bell tower on which the words, "Ye Shall Know The Truth And The Truth Shall Make You Free", were inscribed, Cathy found that her usual urge to take pictures of everything she saw evaded her this time. She hadn't taken pictures ever since she had arrived, and there would be no evidence of her brief visit here, aside from a few lingering memories that would probably disappear under the pile of worries and drunken nights in the strange cities she'd visit after this trip. For what was worth remembering in Austin? All she wanted to take with her was the freedom she felt the night before when music and lights swelled around her, eliminating the need for conversation.

She complained about the heat and the dust, and fanned herself furiously with her baseball cap when Evangeline tried to appease her by pointing at a statue or an empty expanse of grass. These surroundings did not pull her in the way the downtown bars did. In the clear light of day, the stucco buildings impressed her with their aloofness, and Evangeline's familiarity with them spoke of a sense of entitlement that Evangeline could afford to be gleefully oblivious to.

"The travel guide mentions a Zilker Park and Barton Springs. Do we get to see those places too?" Cathy asked, as they crossed another drearily bright avenue of paved walks and fenced-in islands of shrubbery.

"Miss, you fly back to San Francisco this afternoon. We don't have enough time and I don't have a car to drive you around."

"I totally forgot about that."

Evangeline had a weary look on her face when she paused and turned to look at Cathy. "Thanks for reminding me."

"Gosh, how touchy you are."

"Kat, I'm trying my best."

Cathy held both her hands up in mock surrender and said, "Okay, fine, whatever. Take me wherever you can take me."

They had lunch at a pizza parlor near campus, and afterwards they waited for a bus that would take them downtown. After ten minutes of waiting and fanning herself, Cathy said, "If you had a car, we wouldn't be waiting this long."

"If you had rented a car, you wouldn't be waiting this long," Evangeline shot back.

A bearded, red-faced man sat at the foot of a traffic sign clutching a heavy battered knapsack to his chest, pulling the collar of his filthy hoodie to his chin as though to take shelter inside his own clothing. Upon catching Cathy's eye, he smiled and whistled. It wasn't just his scruffiness that frightened her, but also the cheeriness with which he immersed himself in his own stench while singling her out. Why was it so difficult in this country to snuff out desire in men who had nothing?

Cathy looked away and folded her arms across her chest, eyeing the cars that sped past her, envious of the distances they could go. A grackle swooped down on her, opening its pointed beak to release a screech, and she ducked and screamed. The red-faced man cackled, asked for change.

A blue metro bus finally came into view and when its door swung open, Evangeline brushed past her and boarded the platform, inserted a few bills, collected their tickets and handed one to Cathy without saying a word. Cathy followed Evangeline into the bus, and Evangeline looked away as Cathy planted herself in the seat beside her. Nothing Cathy did, it seemed, could bruise Evangeline's calculated calm – even her anger was performed with care, as though she had practised these gestures in the event of a quarrel. Cathy knew that what Evangeline wanted from her was an apology, but this was something Cathy wouldn't give to her that easily. If Cathy were to be honest with herself, she'd admit that it was an apology from Evangeline that would quell her own anger – an apology for accepting this shoddy life and forcing it upon her.

Cathy gazed at the scenes that rolled past like pictures in a View-Master toy. She wanted to see something different in this town, something that would astonish her. Although the dome of the State Capitol Building impressed her with its rosy massiveness, many of the things she saw were familiar to her: the churches, the parking garages, the chain restaurants of the downtown area, the abundance of cars on the road. This was all Evangeline was capable of showing Cathy in this musty-smelling bus. Her Spartan lifestyle reminded Cathy of her own shoddy apartment and the cheap clothes she was forced to wear, and she was exasperated by the way in which Evangeline compensated for her present poverty with an optimism that Cathy didn't share. Evangeline was convinced she knew where her life was going – she had told Cathy that her dream was to be an academic, and Cathy imagined her surrounding herself with people who shared her naivete of the world at large. It was these people who could afford to snub the modest American Dream of material comforts, a dream that was less delusional and easier for Cathy to embrace, for it required little from her aside from optimism in the freedoms she already had.

There was one desire she found easy to fulfill in this sprawling country and it was the weightlessness she felt as she traveled across America by plane. But then again, she had to touch the ground in cities that were beginning to look increasingly alike, cities whose scrubbed cleanliness only served to remind her of the closer affinities she shared with the polluted, monsoon-drenched streets of Manila.

"I'm sorry if I can't drive you around," Evangeline said in a hard, sarcastic voice.

"There's nothing we can do about it," Cathy said, feeling the dryness of her throat.

When they had crossed a bridge and reached an eclectic row of one-story shops, Evangeline pulled the window string beside her, and Cathy stepped aside and followed her lead as they got off the bus. She took Cathy to a curiosity shop called Uncommon Objects, where Cathy noticed an abundance of doll heads and framed photographs of white, blushing babies. She looked at their price tags and gasped at the quoted figures.

"You can just imagine how much money we'd make if we raided our houses back in the Philippines and sold off all the worthless junk our grandmothers kept," she said.

"Nobody sells their heirlooms back home. Family property is family property," Evangeline said, staring at a Victorian baby doll in a yellowing eyelet dress.

"Imagine how creepy it would be if that white baby stared at me from my wall," Cathy said, pointing at another baby picture.

"Pretend she was your daughter in your past life. Maybe that would help."

Cathy grinned. "If I could get away with it," she said between her teeth.

In another corner of the store, a narrow-waisted, Victorian-style lace dress hung inside an open wooden closet, and Cathy stood on tiptoe as she took it down. She draped the bust over her chest, allowing the skirt to brush the floor. "I'd love to wear this for Halloween, but I'm too short. The skirt would drag behind me."

"It's *trail* behind you, not *drag* behind you." There was a slight, mocking lilt in Evangeline's voice.

"Whatever," Cathy said, returning the dress to the closet. She turned and made her way to the door without waiting for Evangeline to catch up.

"You're the one doing the dragging, not the skirt," Evangeline said, following Cathy through the aisles of the store.

As Cathy pushed the glass door open with her side, she took out her phone, logged onto Yelp, and when she caught a signal, checked into the store.

"What were you doing that for?" Evangeline asked, when they had stepped outside.

"Just checking into this store on Yelp," Cathy said. "It's too weird for me not to review it."

"You write Yelp reviews?" Evangeline asked, amused.

"It's my new hobby." She slipped her phone into her faux leather purse and with a quick, purposeful gesture zipped her purse shut. They walked down the street and when Evangeline spotted a bookstore, she pulled open the glass door and held it as Cathy entered.

Evangeline seemed to know what she wanted, for she gravitated immediately towards a bookcase near the shop window, pulling out books by Susan Sontag, Michel Foucault, bell hooks – theorists who wrote in a style that seemed, when Cathy had been in college with Evangeline, to be intentionally hermetic. The tactfulness with which Evangeline kept mum about the books she read or the ideas she had encountered was, for Cathy, vaguely condescending. Cathy wandered around the bookstore reading graphic novel blurbs, avoiding the thick, hardbound books – ambassadors of a lost era when readers like her weren't too impatient to bypass the challenge of a prolonged read, when they could impose upon themselves a stasis that promised few rewards.

As she stood before a bookshelf near the back of the store looking at a paperback copy of *The Great Gatsby*, Evangeline sneaked behind her. "And who reads these Yelp reviews?" Evangeline asked, her sarcasm couched in a sickly sweet voice.

"People who could use my opinions about these stores," she said. "At least there's some use in what I write." She looked at the cover of the book Evangeline was clutching to her chest and said, "Not everyone's smart enough to waste their time reading useless Lacanian theories."

Evangeline smiled. "If you put your intelligence to good use a little more, you wouldn't be stuck writing Yelp reviews."

"I'm intelligent enough to know what's useful," Cathy said, brushing past her and making for the shop's front door.

She hadn't realized until she had stepped into the fresh outdoor air that she needed Evangeline to find her way back to the apartment where she had left her things. She wished she had predicted this moment so that she could have left Evangeline's apartment with her rucksack on her back, but how could she be capable of preparing for disorder when it was in her nature to create it? She watched Evangeline through the window of the store paying for the book she had found, smiling at the cashier as she received her change. It was impossible to knock down the windowpane that separated the two of them without hurting Evangeline. Evangeline was already hurt, she could tell, but the windowpane had not been broken.

Evangeline pushed the shop door open, clutching her purchase, and gave Cathy an icy look. A group of women twice their size in cowboy boots and baby-doll dresses passed between the two of them. If Cathy looked just like them, she could've merged with their pack instead of confronting the anger of the person who was, in this town, her only friend.

"We're going home," Evangeline said, pointing at the bus stop at the other side of the road.

Back in the apartment, Evangeline called a cab service as Cathy packed her rucksack, and when her taxi arrived, Evangeline gave her a final, perfunctory hug.

"I'm sorry if I was rude to you. We're still friends, aren't we?" Evangeline asked.

"Of course." In America, the word *friend* meant anything.

"I wish you happiness in whatever you choose to do. I'm not bullshitting, Kat. I mean it."

"Thanks for the sincerity," Cathy said, breaking away from Evangeline's stiff embrace.

If this scene were taking place in Manila, she would've been walking towards her cab amidst car honks, wailing babies, lines of dripping laundry and the footsteps and laughter of passers-by. In their homeland, there were too many noises, smells and sights to distract them from the silence of inevitable partings. It took a trip to America for them to realize that they had parted long ago.

On the plane back to San Francisco, she closed her eyes as the ground released her into the weightlessness of the Austin sky. There was no need for her to look out the window – she had seen it all and sought only release from the heaviness she had begun to feel when she parted with Evangeline. It used to be that she brought a notebook with her whenever she went on a trip so that she could unburden herself on paper during long flights such as these. But in her effort to travel light, she began discarding the things she had no use for, and after a few more trips her notebook – like many of her previous necessities – had lost its use. Maybe it was this weightlessness of mind that she truly wanted, for only indifference could truly extinguish her longing. She'd have to will this indifference for now. Sooner or later, it would come to her naturally. She'd be like a bird taking flight.

THE AUTUMN SUN

It didn't matter to Tony Suarez why he had come to Newark that September of 1998. All he knew, or cared to know, was that the University of Delaware had granted him a fellowship to pursue a PhD, and that he had decided to take it. He knew it was another piece of bait held out to him by the American Dream, and he was always too embarrassed to ever admit harboring such a fantasy. But it was an opportunity to do something else, to see that other part of the world that remained unfamiliar to him. The labyrinths of math offered him a space where he could lose himself, but he wanted to live what he saw in his mind and to see its reality, perhaps, in another land.

But was that possible? On Friday nights, as he sat at his apartment window, beer in hand, he wondered if there was such a thing as change, and if he had ever changed at all after all those years of drifting and feeling his way without the help of the roads his father had built. He had come a long way from his hometown in the mountains and was glad he had, but he couldn't help being overwhelmed.

For instance, he didn't expect that the pangs of loneliness, as he walked those clean paved streets and passed those mighty brick buildings on campus, would cease so soon. It was probably the cool autumn air of his first few months that had tempered desire, if it ever was there. The cold suffused everything, even the bright autumn leaves, even the light that touched them.

But it was in that autumn he met Socorro again. It was then that all those lost memories surfaced, all those illusions he had tried to let go.

He was on his way to the cafeteria one November morning, his gaze on the ground, following the leaves that cluttered the tiled path. Deep green had given way to the fairer colors of dappled red, orange and yellow. It seemed as though these leaves had assumed a certain transparency, enough at least to reveal the mapping of their veins.

She could very well have been any woman who happened to resemble her, but just before the cafeteria door swung shut, he spotted those features his memory had attached to Socorro all those years ago. Dark wavy hair, creamy brown skin, eyelashes fluttering. Not as vibrant as before, but awakening nonetheless a comforting familiarity.

He became aware of the resonating crunch of fallen leaves under his shoes and the swift, almost subtle urgency of his steps as he walked towards the door. Now, for the first time in weeks, he was fully aware that he was going to have lunch, and that he intended to do so. But what lifted him out of his mind's cold stupor was something he couldn't fully comprehend: the sound of her voice. At the line, it rose above the amorphous buzz of the hall.

"Tony?"

He turned. It was her.

She had visibly changed in the years they were apart, and that austere, finely chiseled face he gazed into belonged perfectly to the dining hall in which they sat. It seemed, in her muted expressions of joy, that she had absorbed the cold of the landscape in every muscle of her face. Age had tempered their youth, he guessed; now that he was older, the passion her smile could have ignited when he was seventeen had mellowed into the warmth of recovered friendship. If she still harbored resentment towards him, it didn't show. He listened intently as she talked about settling down in Newark, teaching English in the university and getting married.

"So, how are you adjusting?" she asked.

He shrugged. "I don't know. Guess I need some more time to get my swing back."

"So it's homesickness beginning to sink in."

"I guess. But I don't dwell on it too often."

She smiled and gazed out the window at the flitting leaves.

"I'm here anyway, so if you need anything just give me a ring." Her voice was husky, but Tony liked it. He found it warm.

"It's a nice town," he said.

"It's so beautiful I sometimes forget home."

"I'm actually beginning to forget."

"Watch out for that. Forgetting makes things even harder for us." She laughed. "So, how's Baguio now?"

He smiled. "It's not exactly the place you'd like to return to."

Her eyes were pensive. "What have they done? I can't believe what my mother writes in her letters."

"It's what happens to all towns." He tried a comforting expression, but he sensed, in the way she smiled back, that he had hit a raw vein. "It's people's fault, most of the time."

Tony couldn't find any term to describe the city of his youth. Fallen, yes, but not quite so: the slums growing from its cracks could be taken as a crude sign of the city's resurgence. As for the narrowing streets, he felt it was a sign that things were returning to normal, that houses could rise as quickly as houses had crumbled down. He had grown up thinking that his hometown, nestled among pine trees and rolling hills, would last forever.

The earthquake had shown him that nothing could last. By then he was a freshman at the University of the Philippines and too far away from Baguio to see it taking place. All he knew was that the earthquake had destroyed all roads leading to the city. The telephone lines were clogged, and no one at his dorm could phone home and expect the call to go through. The television crews that were flown in could only show them images: roads cracked open, entire buildings reduced to rubble. Baguio was obliterated, and that was that – Tony had to accept whatever news there was.

It was then he first met Socorro, a pretty freshman who filled the silence with conversation. She worried about her family even more than he did, but as she'd always say, they had nothing else to lose but hope. It was the only way they could reassure themselves, futile as it seemed to him later on. When they found out that her father died, pinned beneath a collapsed wall at the university where he taught, nothing seemed to lift her from despair.

Now, in another time and place, Tony wondered if there was anything hiding beneath her dark pupils, or if it was merely his imagination they awakened. Her eyes seemed to gaze from an inconsolable blackness of long ago.

"Where do you plan to go after your doctorate?" she asked.

"I don't know." He cast his gaze around the hall, settling on hers.

He got to know his way around Newark, beginning with Main Street, where all the interesting nooks and crannies of the town were located. He discovered the ice cream parlor, where high school girls often hung out in the afternoon; the Main Barbershop, where a haircut cost twenty bucks; the No. 1, a Chinese diner he often ordered dinner from; and Margarita's, which served the best pizza in town. There was a Catholic Church at the end of the street and a Methodist Church in the middle. The Methodist Church – which stood pinkly aloof, bright and Disney-like among squat brick store buildings – particularly amused him. On Sundays, through the open door of the church, he'd see little girls in pink frothy dresses and adults in their best dresses and suits. Coming from a Catholic country, he had never seen such a show of opulence in churchgoers before.

Across the street from the Methodist Church was a bakery whose window he'd occasionally glance into. It was a clean place, furnished with wicker chairs, wooden tables and, as he found out one cold Saturday morning, cheap coffee. He stepped in, and a burly, cheerful man behind the glass case greeted him.

After paying for his cup of coffee, he took a seat beside the window. Outside, the gray light marked the edges of buildings. The church steeple calmly struck its sharp-edged point against the sky. People flowed into the silent current of the street, too self-absorbed to step in each other's way.

The door swung open, and he looked up. It was Socorro. A soft squeak of leather trailed behind her as she walked towards the glass display case. His eyes followed her lips as she gave her order: two loaves of rye bread and a box of blueberry muffins. The man behind the counter asked how her day was going as he slid the glass case open.

Her eyes wandered around the shop as she waited. She saw Tony by the window, raised an eyebrow and smiled. He nodded, lowering the cup from his lips. She paid, took the large paper bag in her arms and walked towards him.

"Never thought I'd meet you here," she said, taking the seat opposite. She took off her black overcoat and draped it over the back of her chair.

"Nice place. Do you come here all the time?"

"I buy our bread here. They're quite good, aren't they?"

"Best coffee I've had in weeks."

"So life's that bad?" She grinned.

"Not really. Only the coffee."

They sat there in silence. She pressed her elbows against the table and glanced restlessly around the room.

"I'm happy we've met again, you know," she said, finally resting her eyes on him.

"It's been a relief," he answered. "To know that someone here actually knows me, I mean."

"And after so many years."

He smiled in embarrassment.

"You never told me what happened to you."

He leaned back. "Everything's been said."

She laughed. "Haven't you ever quit keeping things to yourself?"

He shrugged. "What's so interesting about me?"

"Anything that will make me sure that I still know you."

"I was teaching in Manila." He paused. "And I was engaged until last year. That's all."

"Oh."

He waited for her to speak again, but she kept her silence.

"Strange that I meet you again here, at this shop," she said, finally.

"Why?"

"I met my husband here."

It had been her first month to teach at the university, she said, and she hardly knew anyone in town. She was buying bread when the man waiting beside her at the counter told her that he had ordered the same thing.

He had a look in his eye. Made her feel special, perhaps, and she probably needed it. There was a smile on her face Tony hadn't seen in a long time, that light-hearted, genuine smile he had almost left forgotten under the musty piles of memory. Her husband was a chemical engineer and worked at the DuPont plant near Wilmington. He loved secondhand bookstores, just like her, and they both went to Catholic mass.

"You mean you go to church?" Tony asked.

"Yeah."

"You said back in college you'd never step into a church again."

She laughed. "Not until I found out that I needed it."

"When did this dawn on you?"

"When I realized that I was needlessly driving myself insane when all I had to do was to listen to God speaking to me."

"Couldn't imagine you saying that before."

"Why not?"

"Didn't you say religion was the opiate of the masses?"

She laughed again. "There are things to be learned from propaganda too, you know."

"Well, it probably wouldn't work if it didn't make some sense." He tried to smile.

"You're so right."

They were silent.

"I wonder if my mother still hopes I go to church," he said.

"Why wouldn't she?"

"I don't know. I've probably shrugged her off so many times that she doesn't bother to ask anymore."

"But mothers are persistent too, you know."

"I wonder why she doesn't seem to give up. When she called last night, she even put my dad on the phone."

"So she has to push to get you two talking?"

"I guess."

~

As a boy, one of the family activities Tony enjoyed the most was the Sunday drive through John Hay and South Drive. His father would be at the wheel, wielding authority in his own quiet way. He knew every nuance in the curves of those pine-lined roads, and the trip would be so smooth that Tony would almost forget that he was in the backseat of a car. For him, it wasn't just a car ride, but a moving picture on all sides.

The old man was living in a dream of roads and exploits, and he'd often unreel this during these trips. He'd often say that Tony, his eldest, had a good head on his shoulders, and that the boy would replace him as head of the city works. That was enough to make Tony happy and to make him listen. But that patiently forceful voice only dulled one's attention as the years passed. It was just too hard for the mind to trail those words, Tony would recall; he was too drawn to those scenes behind the car windows that slipped so quickly away.

He always told himself later on that he was never the type of person who could stay in one place, and the idea of taking a desk job and working with the same people in the same town never quite appealed to him. Often, as he stood before his students at the University of the Philippines, he felt that he had no other choice but to rattle away the theorems and formulas he had learned in school. He figured that the options other people chose were just as amorphously strange. He always repeated to himself his high school math teacher's words: *A sheet of paper can't accommodate the shape of the universe.* Neither can any surface, if one explores the quantum possibilities of nature.

"Do you know what concentration means? God damn it, it means sticking to the wheel. It doesn't mean sailing through another galaxy in your head and driving the car into a tree," his father said to him the summer after his first year in college, when his father taught him how to drive.

It wasn't death Tony was driving to. He was driving to other worlds.

∽

When they stepped out of the bakery, he spotted a small brown bicycle parked near a sidewalk post. He was amused to find out that Socorro used it to get around town. She had gotten used to riding a bike ever since she was in graduate school, and since it got her from one place to another, she said, she preferred it to anything else.

"I like feeling the wind blowing around me. It's something you miss out on when you're in a car," she said.

"You sound like a movie script."

"Hey, there's no harm in being cliché."

"I can't disagree with you."

She smiled, boarded the seat and rode away.

He stood there as her bike sailed swiftly down the street. She steered it so smoothly it almost disappeared under her; it seemed for a moment as though she were merely skimming the space above the ground. He knew, though, that it was the bike that bore her up through the air that stirred her hair – towards, perhaps, the bliss of near weightlessness.

∼

They had grown up in the same town, but never met before college. Baguio wasn't that small a city anymore, and it definitely wasn't the small town his aunts and uncles romanticized. He had met Socorro elsewhere. He often heard that the world was too small, but he believed that there had to be some design that led one event to another, that connected disparate lives. They had both chosen to study in Manila, and there they met.

He thought studying in Manila was a chance to set out on his own. He had somehow lived a separate life from others, but this break from his parents gave him space to structure a life that only he could lay claim on. Some lives, it seemed, couldn't be shared with others. For how could you share the experience of being free with people who had never felt it? He listened to his cousins talk about losing their virginity, but when his turn came, it was the emptiness of that high that he remembered the most: that final, blissful, break from emotion.

If he could only forget Socorro's silent brooding over the crumpled sheets and her anger when she found out later that he couldn't return her love, there wouldn't be this need to circle around his guilt. If he could only efface her from his memory, he would be living his life instead of doggedly following her steps.

He and his roommate in Newark had saved enough money to buy beer and turkey from the supermarket, and had a decent Christmas dinner while watching TV. Later that night he phoned home. His mother answered and thanked him for the sweaters he had sent. Surprised that the package had arrived early, he asked how she liked hers. It was what he expected to hear, that she hadn't gotten such a beautiful sweater in years.

The day after Christmas, he stopped by his cubicle in the library to pick up some books he had left there. On his desk was a water-filled glass ball with a miniature house inside. There was a note stuck to it.

Tony, think of this silly gift as another decoration for this boring office. We passed by Woolworth the other day and I grabbed this without giving it much thought. Maybe it will amuse you. I was going to buy you a book by Stephen Hawking but I don't know what you've read by him. Or if you still read him at all. Anyway, Merry Christmas. Soc.

He took it in his hands and slumped down in his swivel chair, leaning back while wondering why she had given him a toy. Slowly, he turned it upside down and turned it upright again, gazing at the artificial snowflakes that drifted slowly, through the water, onto the house's roof. "The witch's house of candy," he said to himself, peering at the ornate, sugary details.

When they became friends, he felt it was because she expected him to stick it out with her after the earthquake. She needed comfort, and he felt too guilty to abandon her. It was also an urge to heal her wounds, not only for her sake, but for his own.

He liked her company and didn't have the heart to break off the friendship they had already forged. Her companionship seemed to be part of the Baguio of his past he had missed out on in his youth. He had her attention whenever he talked about what he read by Stephen Hawking; she seemed happy whenever he listened to the poetry she read to him. When Nirvana hit the airwaves, they both listened to the new music, and with her he felt the sudden urge to break away from his quiet, domesticated past. He had never seen such fire in a girl before. Strangely, nothing had made him feel as safe.

He had probably wanted her to expect too much from him, but when he needed her to stop, she didn't know how. He didn't dwell on things the way she did; he saw how much more it hurt to revel in all that madness than to enjoy it from afar.

He knew he wanted something from her, but it wasn't love. It was the freedom love seemed to offer.

∽

It was in February that he saw her again. They ran into each other one afternoon, and she offered to buy him coffee. He obliged her, and they started walking. It was then that he noticed the change.

The snow was beginning to melt, exposing the grass underneath, and he found the cold more tolerable. He could hear the slight crunch of salt when trudging down the walkways on campus and the sidewalks downtown. It's to keep people from slipping, Socorro told him.

"It's almost spring," she said, glancing around.

Her cheeks had filled out the past months he hadn't seen her. They were flushed.

"I know. I can feel the pressure."

She laughed. "Me too. I have a whole pile of papers to mark."

He took a cigarette from his overcoat pocket and lit it.

"You have something to tell me, don't you," he said, exhaling smoke.

"Yup."

"You've gained weight."

"Yeah."

"You're pregnant, aren't you?"

She smiled at him. "Does it show?"

"I'm not supposed to do this then." He chuckled, dropped his cigarette and crushed it with his shoe.

"When will you ever quit, Tony?"

"When I get pregnant."

They laughed.

"So what do you want it to be, a girl or a boy?" he asked, watching his breath dissolve softly into the grayness.

"Doesn't really matter. Whether it's a he or a she, I'll be happy."

"Thought of any names?"

"God, we still don't know. Dan jokes that if it's a boy we'll name him Daniel Junior, but we have to be more imaginative than that."

"For Chrissake, you ought to be. You're bringing new life to this world."

"I was thinking of the story my dad told me, about how I was supposed to be named."

"How does it go?"

"Well, the original plan was to name me Dante if I came out a boy, and Beatrice if I came out a girl."

"How did Socorro come up?"

"My grandma, my mother's mother, had just died. My mother was mourning. So when I was born, she asked my dad if I could be named Socorro instead after my grandmother."

He paused. "Makes sense."

"I would've preferred Beatrice though."

"Don't you want to be named after your grandmother?"

"Well, it's nice, but I would've liked Beatrice." She paused. "When I was a little girl, I hated Socorro."

"It's not a bad name. Sounds heavier, but not bad."

She sighed. "I just don't like the idea of reminding my mother of my grandmother."

"She probably wanted you to."

She put her gloved hands in her overcoat pockets and squinted. "I'm her daughter, for God's sake."

They were both silent.

"My petition for her was granted. She's coming here in August," she said, finally.

"That's great."

"With Dad gone, she's what I have left."

The bell tower sounded, it was five in the afternoon. They were approaching an open square, where students in small, scattered groups milled around.

"And maybe," she continued, "when she sees me now, she'll see how good a mother I'll be."

"There's no doubting that."

She folded her arms and bowed her head.

"We all learn how to live," he said.

"Live and let live. You realize it after you're twenty-five."

"It's hard to realize." He breathed in, and the bitter air traveled down his throat.

She was confiding in him, and it seemed she had finally forgiven him. The only thing he needed now was more time to commit to something. He wasn't sure if he'd settle in town for good. The American landscape opened itself to possibilities, and to explore them one had to travel easy. He could pick any road, drive without stopping and end up somewhere in California. That was the beauty of the American road system – there were no dead ends, only transits. And there were no dead ends in Newark either, only roads opening themselves to each other. He didn't need to drive down them all to know where they led. Even the paths people took every day led to one another. It was a life everyone tacitly led. But where they were all headed was what he couldn't guess.

Spring had come. The snow had melted, and the sharp bite of cold in the air gave way to the gentleness of emerging colors. Dogwood trees bore white and pink flowers, and other trees began to bring forth new leaves. In the morning he could hear chirping at the window. There was a tree beside his unit, and waking up with all those birds chirping brought a lightness to his mornings. One morning a crashing sound woke him up. Later, they found out that the son of an international student couple from the apartment across the parking lot had tried to hit a bird with his slingshot. The window glass had to be replaced.

The window by his library cubicle overlooked an open walk, and some days he'd see her going by. She'd often be professionally brisk, sometimes too brisk for him to catch a glimpse of her belly, but when he had a chance, he'd notice the flush in her cheeks. Eventually, her growing belly weighed down on her jaunty stride. From afar, Tony could see no strain, only a loving slowness.

Once, on his way to class, he met her again. In a sudden movement that surprised him, he passed his hand over her belly. She didn't seem to take offense, only smiled and took a few steps back. He could paint that scene over and over again in his head if he wanted to – that quick glance over her shoulder as she walked away, the gentle slope of her shoulder turning radiant, the light, scattered by the leaves, touching the surface of her belly. He wondered how smooth women's bellies were, how elastic to the growth of things that couldn't be seen.

He could never tell what was going on in her mind. He could only watch her from afar.

The Fourth of July was celebrated amid the summer heat in the streets of the town. In the morning there was a parade through Main Street, and the people who watched waved their paper flags in enthusiasm as the Newark High band played "God Bless America" and "The Star-Spangled Banner". Tony found it a solemn affair, for there was no pushing or shoving around, only the dignified happiness of many who stood and waved. In the afternoon the main roads were closed to traffic, and stalls lined the sides of the streets. There was a friendly, welcoming hum, but it wasn't the boisterous, far-reaching noise of the fiestas back home. An occasional pierced teenager walked down the street with other freaks in tow – only children took notice of them, staring and pointing.

Tony had stopped at one stall to look through a rack of vintage magazines when he spotted Socorro milling around at the other end of the street. She was looking through baby things and knick-knacks when he crossed the street and called her name.

"Hey," she said, a warm smile flashing momentarily across her face.

"What brings you here, all by yourself?" he asked.

"Dan and his colleagues are having a kiddie chemistry show around the corner. They're doing the routine for the third time. I decided to take a walk."

There were shadows under her eyes, tinges of grayish blue on surprisingly pale skin.

"It's nearing August," he said.

"It scares me."

"Come on, you shouldn't say that."

"Okay, maybe excited and scared." She paused. "It's my first, of course."

"There's always a first time."

"And the first time's the hardest, they say."

He couldn't come up with an answer for that.

"I know it will turn out okay, but I just can't stop worrying. Anything could happen," she said.

"In nature, there's danger."

She paused. "What?"

He gave her a sidelong glance. "Anything could happen. But you'll turn out all right."

"How am I supposed to know what could happen?"

He let go of an agonized sigh. "Just think it will turn out fine, okay?"

A bubble machine had been placed in the middle of the road, and children were playing and dancing in the clear, soapy sea it created. A young girl with blonde curls twirled around, arms outstretched, catching bubbles. They walked towards the sidewalk in silence and stopped to watch.

"Beautiful little girl, isn't she," Tony said quietly.

"If my daughter looked even just a bit like that," she said, glancing at him, "you'd adore her, wouldn't you?"

He looked at her. "So you know now?"

"Yeah. Ultrasound." She paused. "She could look like me, or she could look like Dan. Or she could look like both of us."

"Beatrice." The name escaped his lips.

"Yes. Beatrice."

The day was beginning to dim, yet the bubbles flashed even more under the light, popping upon the slightest contact with their clothes.

He popped a cigarette into his mouth. "You must miss your childhood."

"Of course."

"Do you miss home?"

She glanced at him. "Especially."

He took a drag. "I still remember those trips through John Hay."

"And those steep roads, and the pine air."

"I could hardly breathe the last time I was there. My lungs can't stand the altitude."

She looked at him. "I thought you cured your asthma."

"With this?" He held out his cigarette. "It only makes things worse."

"Why don't you quit, then?"

"Wouldn't make any difference." He took a deep drag and exhaled. "Besides, we all die anyway."

She shook her head. "You've never changed. You're still just as macabre."

"Can't endure change. It makes the heart break."

"Have I changed, Tony?"

He looked at her and he realized, upon eye contact, just how much her beauty filled him with sadness. "Everything has, Soc."

She laughed. "That's easy to say when you have no commitments."

"Do any of us?"

Her eyes lingered on his face. When would she turn away and lose that persistence, if it was ever there? He wasn't sure if he imagined it. The truth was that he felt removed from this life of hers. A life of children, fathers and mothers, of hopes he couldn't quite understand but which he tried to appreciate – as if these could fill that silence that had sprung from the gaps and misunderstandings between them. She hadn't asked anything from him, even if her eyes lingered on his face.

"When we were young, we let things slip past," she said. "Forgive me, but I've had a hard time accepting that."

"I know. I was an asshole."

"No. You were just being honest. We weren't capable of loving then."

They fell silent, and then, in a voice that broke, she finally said, "I have to go." Turning away, she covered her eyes. Darkness claimed her, softening the edges of her figure as she walked away.

All he could do then was let chance take its inexorable course. There was nothing left to do but stand at a distance; that desire to rework things in the mind, he realized, was a waste of time.

It was impossible to deny the feeling of helplessness when he found out that Beatrice died, but it happened, and nothing else could be done.

He found out one day late in August from a friend at the English Department. The infant's heart was weak, and for weeks they kept her on life support. When the doctors told the couple that there was no chance their daughter would survive on anything else, they had to give up.

The funeral was scheduled on a Saturday morning. The obituary in the local paper contained no decorative prints, only an announcement of the child's death and the schedule of the wake and funeral. Its bareness caught his eye, a calm space opening itself up to him. Death's only consolation, it seemed, was silence. And yet that withdrawal spoke of a certain urgency he again had to respond to.

He could only feel his own helplessness as he watched Beatrice's small white coffin being lowered into the ground. Desperation couldn't heave her from the black pit that was to be her home. She had left the world before he could have seen or spoken to her, and nothing existed between them to justify any feeling of loss. He was always a spectator in this drama, and would remain one.

If there was any purpose left for his being there, it was for her mother. Socorro had never gotten over her father's death, and now she had lost a child. What more was bearable to lose? He couldn't understand her calm aplomb throughout the funeral, especially as the child was being buried. Tony couldn't even tell if she was crying becuase her sunglasses were too dark.

He took his chance when the ceremony was over and the funeral crowd had dispersed. She was alone when he approached her.

"How are you?" he asked.

"I can't cry more than I can."

He nodded.

"I just feel too empty to feel anything. I don't know when this will ever stop."

She glanced at him, and he could see, through her sunglasses, her eyes looking straight into his.

"Maybe emptiness would help, for the time being."

It was the only advice that he could give her.

As she walked away, arm in arm with her husband, he thought that even love couldn't fill that emptiness. How could they love without wanting to regain what was gone, what could never be possibly there? Desire filled them with too much pain, but if they attuned themselves to this change, nothing else would matter; the body was ripe for release.

He walked on, seeing her and her husband disappear from view, and heard a crackle from under his shoe. He stopped to look at what he had stepped on. It was a maple leaf, orange and dry, veins visible enough to lead his eye from the stem to the cracks his shoe had made, towards edges that spread outwards. It was too soon to be autumn, he thought, and glanced up at the tree from where the leaf fell. Indeed, there were only some orange and yellow leaves among the green. They seemed to hold the midday sun, even as the light penetrated their thinness, setting them aglow. At times, even their edges disappeared in the blinding light. It seemed like a chasm, opening his gaze to a finer radiance.

MARICEL

At dismissal time, one would spot six boys taking their sweet time as they swaggered towards the gate. Sometimes they stood, legs apart, in a circle in the middle of the walkway; they'd definitely be in the way if you wanted to get out sooner, for that was what they wanted. They had their shirttails out, in defiance of the school's dress code. They were proudly aware that others envied their insouciance – they yawned, looked at those who looked at them and winked. One of them had a gold chain dangling from his earlobe, and he'd toss his head as though his fancy earring couldn't catch enough light. He had rotten teeth and a high-pitched voice. Maricel didn't like him. Rather, she liked the boy who stood at the head of the circle: the fair, dark-eyed, broad-shouldered boy who made her blush.

"Hoy, Miss Byuteepul!" this boy yelled at her one cloudy September afternoon, as she and her kabarkadas walked past them on their way to the gate. As if on cue, his friends started hooting. This was the part she didn't like. She didn't want their attention, only his.

"Get out of our way, punyeta!" Nadia, Maricel's kabarkada, spat out.

"Hoy, ugly, he wasn't talking to you, so back off," the boy with the chain dangling from his earlobe yelled back. He swaggered towards Nadia, and thrust his face in front of hers.

"Why, who do you think you are?" Nadia muttered, narrowing her eyes.

"You think you can talk to me like that, eh? You think I don't hit girls? Maybe you want a black eye as big as the one I gave my girlfriend."

Donna, another girl belonging to Maricel's barkada, touched Nadia's shoulder. "Let it go. He's a Tumbleweed."

"Let's just get going, Nadia. He's not worth your time," Maricel said. A crowd of students in uniforms had gathered around them, their bodies smelling of sweat and curiosity.

Nadia waved her kabarkadas away. "This isn't any of your business. This is our fight."

Just then, the fair, broad-shouldered, dark-eyed boy pulled his friend away. "Hey, don't start a fight with these ladies. We don't do that kind of stuff, right?" he said, flashing a smile at the girls.

Nadia sneered. "Just admit you're both pussies and leave us alone."

He glanced at Nadia, then raised his palms and backed away. "Hoy, peace ha. We don't want a fight. All we offer you is peace. Peace!" he exclaimed, waving the peace sign near her face, as though he were explaining something new to a child.

"Yeah, that's exactly what we want. Thank you!" Maricel said, putting an arm around Nadia's shoulders and pulling her towards the gate, while Donna tagged along behind them.

When they were past the gate, Nadia grabbed Maricel's wrist, squeezing it.

"What do you think you were doing in there, butting into a fight you weren't a part of, eh?" Nadia whispered, twisting Maricel's wrist until she cried out.

"I'm sorry, I won't do it again, please let go, please," Maricel begged. Nadia's hands were small, but strong.

"And you, Donna, you're just as worthless," Nadia said as she pushed Donna's cheek with her free hand. Donna whimpered and looked away.

Maricel breathed hard and swallowed, as if this could make the pain a little more bearable. Nadia chuckled, dropping Maricel's wrist. Gasping, Maricel brought it to her chest, squeezing it with her other hand.

"Do you think you're beautiful? Well, miss, you're not. You're so ugly!" Nadia hissed into her ear.

A teacher glanced at their group, raised an eyebrow and kept walking.

The closer she was to her family's apartment, the louder their voices became – harsh, raspy, masculine voices, jostling and mingling as night settled in. She could identify her brother's voice: a deep and solid baritone he used for barking orders or invectives, and rarely for endearments.

"You should have seen him the other night," Jojo, her brother, said. "Drunk after two beers! Who gets drunk after two beers?" A ripple of laughter through the group.

They were gathered in front of the sari-sari store a block away from their apartment, smoking and passing around a shot of cheap gin and a bag of pork rinds. She looked away as she walked past them, careful not to encourage Jojo's friends with as much as a nod or a look.

The buzz of the television mingled with the sputter of cooking oil as Maricel walked through the front door. Her mother had returned a few months ago from Israel, where she had worked as a housekeeper and sent her monthly earnings home. Now that she was finally with them, she kept the TV blaring as she cooked, dusted the living room, washed clothes, talked on the phone and slept. When she had been away, Maricel and Jojo lived with their unmarried aunt, a bank teller who was out with her boyfriends much of the time. Maricel had gotten too used to the silence of her aunt's house; this constant blaring made her anxious and walled in whenever she came home from school.

"There's fried fish and sliced tomatoes," her mother said. "Rice is in the pot. Eat whenever you want." She ladled oily slices of fish into a serving bowl and left them to cool on the dining table.

Maricel went to her room to change. She could hear channels being switched as she unbuttoned her white blouse, unzipped her checkered uniform skirt and pulled on a pair of sweatpants and a T-shirt. When she returned to the kitchen, her mother was sitting before the TV, legs folded under her bottom, cigarette in hand.

"Ma?"

"Ow."

"Let's eat."

"I'll eat after I finish this show. Just go ahead, child."

As Maricel ate, she watched her mother suck on her cigarette, exhale plumes of smoke and tap the ashes into an amber-colored ashtray with the words "San Miguel Beer" printed in bold Gothic script. Maricel still couldn't bend her wrist, and she used her good hand to hold the rice scooper. She wondered how long her mother's savings would last, and if her mother planned to look for a job.

The door swung open and Jojo ambled in. He placed his hands on the back of the living room couch and leaned in as he took in the moving figures on the television screen. "I can never watch a basketball game here because of your telenovelas," Jojo said, straightening himself. He gave Maricel a cursory glance, and it was only when his eyes landed on the platter of fish did he start walking in her direction.

As Jojo took a plate from the dish rack, their mother spoke. "Mang Ernie has a TV in his sari-sari store. I see you watching games there all the time. I wonder why you complain."

"Because I want to watch the games at my house sometimes." Jojo slammed his plate on the dining table, right across from where Maricel sat.

"Try paying the rent and doing chores. Maybe then you could think about doing whatever you want in my house."

"Oh, so this isn't my house anymore?"

Maricel got up, brought her plate to the sink and switched on the faucet. Aside from listening to the sound of running water, there wasn't much she could do to block out their voices.

Her mother took another indulgent drag, and after exhaling, said, "As long as you're not paying the rent, Jojo, it isn't."

"You're a bitch, Mom."

Maricel retreated to her bedroom before her mother could come up with another tart reply. She lay face down on her bed and buried her head in her pillow, trying to imagine the silence of long ago before her mother had returned, when her own life wasn't enclosed within these cramped spaces.

∼

Nadia and Donna hadn't been her only friends. Back in elementary school, there was Jamie, whose friendship seemed as impossible as the house she inhabited. She could still remember the silence that filled the living room of Jamie's house; it wasn't hollow, but ghostly, as though a living soul had been ensnared by the house's stillness. Objects stared at Maricel when Jamie took her hand and led her beyond the front door: an old phonograph gathering dust in one corner of the living room, a leafy plant in another corner, two watercolors of the same desolate forest, a box of colored glass balls at the center of a driftwood coffee table, ceramics and carvings displayed on the divider in the wall, and two huge bookcases crammed with books. The only books in Maricel's house were a Bible and a phone directory. She wondered why people would want to read so much.

She came here every afternoon with Jamie, after school. She'd stare in awe at Jamie's Barbie dolls, stored in a glass case in Jamie's bedroom. Jamie would take them down, one at a time, and sometimes shake them from side to side in Maricel's face singing "Isn't she pretty? Isn't she pretty?" while Maricel blocked her face with her hand to keep the doll's hair from getting into her eyes. There was Police Officer Barbie with her black cap, snappy white blouse and black miniskirt; Bridesmaid Barbie with her pink, polka dotted train and puffed sleeves; and Miss Philippines Barbie with her tiny tiara, butterfly sleeves and silvery tube skirt. Maricel's body was developing faster than Jamie's, and the dolls, when undressed, seemed to tease her about the future that was growing inside her. Boys leered at her as she walked down the corridors of her private

Catholic elementary school, while Jamie ignored them, twittering away about the latest book she had read. Jamie had the skinny body of a boy and was too absorbed in books and movies to pay attention to the boys in their school. Maricel, on the other hand, didn't have enough books at home to distract her. As she sat in class, she returned the looks of these boys, and was suddenly conscious of how her training bra was biting into her flesh, squeezing at breasts that wouldn't stop growing.

Jamie's father – a tall, quiet, bespectacled man – was always at home whenever Maricel visited Jamie's house. He asked them about school while he prepared peanut butter and jelly sandwiches for them. When he wasn't talking to them, he'd be in his office next to the dining room, typing on his computer. Jamie said he was a sportswriter – he wrote PR for rich and famous people too, she added with a flourish. Maricel nodded and pretended to know what "PR" meant so that Jamie wouldn't laugh at her. She sometimes wondered what her own father did – Jojo once told her that he was in Manila, but if she looked for him, she wouldn't know where to go.

Jamie passed the City Science High School test when they were about to graduate from sixth grade. By then, Jojo was going to the public Central High, and Maricel knew she was going there too. Her mother's contract in Israel was about to end, and it wasn't as if they had money left to keep sending Maricel to private school. Maricel didn't mind, except for the fact that she wouldn't be seeing Jamie as often. They agreed to call each other every day, and they did, at least during their first two weeks as high school freshmen.

"Friendship never dies," she told Jamie over the phone, and Jamie said, "Isn't there a better way of saying that? That's so cliché."

Jamie was spending more time with her new friends at the Science High, smart kids like Jamie who lived in leafy neighborhoods Maricel had never been to. In one of their phone conversations, Jamie teased her about not knowing the meaning of an English word that Jamie had tossed at her like the Barbie dolls that Jamie allowed her to play with, before taking them away from her. Maricel didn't bother to remember the word after she hung up that night. She didn't have to be reminded that she wasn't smart enough, or rich enough, to be Jamie's friend.

When Jamie didn't call for two weeks, Maricel picked up the phone, and hesitated before dialing Jamie's number. She couldn't get past the third digit. It seemed that Jamie had already realized, long before she did, that these calls weren't worth their time.

∽

It was another Monday, another general flag ceremony. They had just finished singing the national anthem and school hymn, and they knew it would take at least half an hour more for Dr Manalo – the principal – to leave the podium. Maricel's classmates were taking off their jackets and holding them above their heads to shield themselves from the heat. Citizen's Army Training officers in white T-shirts and khaki pants stood side by side on either end of the quadrangle, keeping students corralled under the cloudless sky.

The section lines had dissolved now that people had found their groups. The hip-hoppers stood with their legs apart, showing off their baggy pants and unbuttoned polo shirts. The Igorots, dressed in corduroy bell-bottom pants and silverpointed cowboy boots, threw angry glances at the crowd, and stood in tight circles as though holding a secret loathing for those who didn't belong to their tribe. A group of lipstick-wearing girls stood in a circle, passing around a compact powder case and taking turns powdering their faces. Maricel spotted Jojo's barkada from a distance pacing around in idle circles, wiping away the sweat on their foreheads with the sleeves of their uniforms, while chatting with a bored-looking group of girls. Dr Manalo's voice floated above their heads, failing to penetrate the hum of their voices.

"Let us give a big round of applause to the Baguio City Central High School!" Dr Manalo's voice thundered from the podium. This was the school band's cue to play a quick, sloppy marching tune.

It was then that Maricel spotted the fair, dark-eyed, broad-shouldered boy.

He seemed to be telling a story to his friends, because they listened to him with rapt attention as he accompanied each punchline with movement. He moaned, twirled his finger in the air, swayed his head from left to right and bent backward, dodging an imagined attacker. Maricel wondered what the story was. As if he had read her mind, he spotted her in the crowd, and smiled.

She was barely following the story Donna was telling her. Donna's stories became more unbelievable every time Maricel listened to them, and today, it was about a girl from another high school who had been brainwashed by her cousin.

"He locked her up in a closet for an entire weekend. When they opened the closet," Donna whispered, "she had drool all over her clothes. She couldn't speak but her eyes were open wide."

"So she became inutil?" Nadia asked.

"Well, what else? She wasn't moving."

Their voices trailed away, dissolved in the heat. Maricel's eyes wandered, passing over the sea of anonymous, unremarkable faces. Once or twice her gaze fell on Dr Manalo, whose wide smile flashed at them like a searchlight. Maricel could hear the sound of the principal's voice but couldn't make out the words.

Nadia nudged her. "Hoy." She grinned when Maricel turned, and said, "You're not listening."

"Yeah," Donna said. "Why weren't you listening?"

"Hey, sorry, I was just—"

"Looking for someone in the crowd?" Donna teased. She and Nadia doubled up in laughter. Nadia grabbed Maricel's arm, grinning as she dug her sharp fingernails deep into Maricel's flesh.

Just as Maricel was about to cry out in pain, there was a commotion at the far end of the quadrangle, and Nadia dropped Maricel's arm. Everyone turned to see what it was. Maricel craned her neck to see above the heads in front of her. She recognized the broad-shouldered boy's green plaid jacket flapping in the wind as he dashed across the garden at the right end of the quadrangle and jumped over its low iron fence. That corner of the quadrangle was unguarded by Citizen's Army Training officers; their commandant shouted orders as students cheered. The boy turned, raised a fist in triumph, laughed and ran off.

"Show-off," Nadia muttered.

His laughter rang in Maricel's ears as they filed back to their classrooms. She trailed Nadia and Donna while they made their way through the crowd, and as she was about to lose them, she felt a tapping on her shoulder. She turned, and the boy with the gold chain dangling from his earlobe grinned at her. He thrust a note into her hand, winked and disappeared into the crowd.

Maricel slid the note in her skirt pocket and waited. At recess, she entered the girls restroom alone, and waited in line until she had a stall to herself. She locked the wooden door behind her, took the note from her pocket, unfolded it and read.

You are invited to a meeting of our proud organization at four o'clock this afternoon at Sunshine Park. Our organization boasts of over 200 members and is a powerful group in our school. Our leaders have chosen you to join our elite ranks, and we expect you to be there.

Noel Flores
Supreme Leader, Tumbleweeds
Maricel, I'm waiting for you.

The note was handwritten. He knew her name. His penmanship was astonishingly elegant, the last line a hook pulling her away from the sea of faces in her school. The word "Tumbleweeds", written in Gothic letters, had spread like a worm across these bathroom walls during the last couple of months, and had found her finally in this rank, mud-stained bathroom stall.

When the afternoon bell rang, Maricel rushed out of her classroom before Nadia or Donna could wait for her to join them in their walk to the main gate. She ran all the way to the park across the street from school, and almost bumped into a group of jacket-clad tourists from Manila who pointed their camera lenses at the towering pine trees and flowerbeds that lined the paved walk. Scarved Igorot cleaning ladies with tattooed arms puttered about with their brooms and dustpans, munching on betel nuts while sweeping up food wrappers and plastic cups. Concrete benches painted to look like halved pine logs lined the paved square, and students in uniforms sat on the pavement, surrounding the dark-eyed, broad-shouldered boy – Noel – who stood in the middle of the circle. Jacket-clad boys in caps and sunglasses flanked him. Girls wearing hoop earrings and lip gloss sat facing him, and threw suspicious looks at Maricel as she approached the group.

"Who is she?" a girl with scrunched-up hair and gold hoop earrings asked.

The boy with a chain dangling from his earlobe stood up, lowered his sunglasses and upon recognizing Maricel, said, "I invited her, Celia. She's cool."

"Shut up, Makoy. *I* invited her," Noel said, and nodded at Maricel. "Welcome."

He resumed speaking as she took her seat behind the group. A girl in the second row turned to look at Maricel, and dragged her ringed middle finger down the bridge of her nose. Maricel chose to ignore her, fixing her eyes on Noel.

The afternoon sun turned his fair skin into gold. His voice rose, fell and tumbled forth, and he cast his words over them like a solid, sturdy net.

"The Yellow Belters stole our spot at the Athletic Bowl. If it weren't for you stupid wussies, that spot would still be ours. What are you, chickens?"

He jabbed his finger at them and moved it from left to right as his voice reached another hard crest. She was amazed by how he held their attention at the tip of his finger, which radiated whenever it was touched by light. He set his eyes on her, and she felt his dark pupils girding her, pulling her in.

They dispersed when the meeting ended, the girls walking to the jeepney stop in one group, the boys to the graffiti-covered archway at the north entrance of the park in another. She watched both groups, too timid to join either of them. She felt someone tapping on her shoulder, and turned to see Noel.

"Thanks for coming," he said.

"Thank you for inviting me," she said, trying not to stammer.

"I wanted to recruit you for a long time. If it weren't for that nasty friend of yours, we would've approached you sooner."

"You mean Nadia?"

"Her name's Nadia? Name's too pretty for a face like that."

He brushed her cheek with his finger. Her face grew hot.

"I was just looking for an excuse to see you. I couldn't come up with anything else."

"You're kidding me."

"No, I'm not." He shook his head, cast down his eyes and kicked a pebble away. "Can I talk to you sometime?"

"When?"

"We'll see each other again. I'll find a way."

He brushed her arm with his palm, jogged away and joined his friends, who hooted and offered him high fives. She wished Noel could take her away with him, right then and there – but she had to wait for his signal, for permission to follow his lead.

Jojo was sitting on the living room couch, strumming a tune on his guitar, when she got home. As she walked to her room, he drove his thumb down the strings, paused and asked, "Do you know where Mom is?"

"No."

"The bitch." Jojo frowned. "For all we know, she has a new boyfriend."

She stopped. "So what if she has a new boyfriend?"

Jojo clasped his guitar. "What about our dad?"

"If he wanted to see us, he would've looked for us long ago."

"If she disappears for good, I'm not looking for her."

He gave the guitar strings a swift, upward brush, and then continued to play. Maricel clasped the straps of her backpack, trying to follow her brother's thoughts in the riffs he played. Ever since he found a barkada in high school, he rarely spoke to her, except to ask her about their mother or the next meal. Maricel never had the answers to his questions. To him, she was probably another useless fixture in the house, like the Hello Kitty clock on the wall, the small Santo Niño in his golden robe, the silk carnations on the dining table, gathering dust.

"If I disappeared, would you look for me?" Maricel asked.

Jojo stopped strumming and looked up. "What kind of question is that?"

"I don't know. It just crossed my mind."

"You're not thinking of running away, are you?"

Maricel hesitated. "Maybe not."

Jojo strummed a riff and looked up at her again. "If I were you, I would've left this place sooner. But I'm not you. It's your life, really."

"So that means you wouldn't look for me."

Jojo winced and scratched his head. "Stop bugging me. I don't know. Like I said, it's your life, and I don't want to get in the way."

"Don't, then."

Jojo picked up the remote, and the TV screen flashed at him like an opened eye. "If Mom doesn't come home now, I'll die of hunger."

She walked to her room and shut the door.

∼

The week wore on. She went to school every day, sat in her assigned seat, watched her teachers form words with their mouths. The walls of her classroom were closing around her; the endless chatter that filled the damp corridors followed her like a tidal wave that drowned her, filling her ears until she couldn't hear anything else except Noel's voice.

"Something's on your mind," Donna said at recess one day, as Maricel, Donna and Nadia stood in line in front of the fishball stand beside the entrance to the school cafeteria.

"Tell us your secret, puta," Nadia said, nudging Maricel awake.

Maricel turned to look at Nadia, and felt herself tremble as she said, "Call me puta again, and I'll slap you."

Nadia raised an eyebrow. "Excuse me. Was that an empty threat I just heard?"

"It's a warning, and it isn't empty."

Drops of spit landed on Maricel's face as Nadia laughed. "If it wasn't for me, you wouldn't have friends in this school. Those kids in our section would've messed you up really well. Oh, but now you can disrespect your poor friend Nadia, since you've just learned that boys would do anything to have a glimpse of those melons, eh?"

Nadia placed the tip of her finger on Maricel's nipple. By impulse, Maricel slapped her. Nadia cupped her cheek, eyes widened in shock, and before she could raise a fist, Maricel bolted.

"Hey, I'm not done with you! Be ready, punyetang puta ka!"

As Maricel ran, she searched the school grounds for a familiar face and was met with stares. She thought of hiding in the restroom stalls, but she'd have to wait in line before she could shut a stall door behind her. She thought of the alleyways behind the makeshift classrooms, but she remembered the construction worker who called her a sexy little thing a few weeks ago when she was alone and looking for a shortcut to her classroom after arriving late to school. She had to get out of this campus, maybe hide somewhere in the city. As she ran down the corridor to her classroom to get her things, she spotted Noel's swagger and green plaid jacket. He turned and stood, legs spread, blocking her way.

"Hey, hey, hey! What's with all the running?" Noel asked.

Maricel stopped before him and put her hands on her chest, catching her breath. "You have to help me, please."

"Someone chasing you?"

"Sort of. I just have to get out of here before Nadia finds me."

"Oh, so you were in a fight." Noel chuckled and took her by the arm, leading her down the corridor. "I knew you had some fire in you."

"She didn't know who she was dealing with."

"From now on, you won't have to run away from anybody. We're here to protect you."

"Thanks." Maricel swallowed. "I haven't seen you in this building before."

"Well, I haven't been to the freshman building in a while."

"Since you were a freshman?"

"No, not that long ago. I come to visit friends, once in a while," he said, stopping and fixing his dark eyes on her.

"Who were you visiting?" she asked.

"Just someone, but I don't know if she wants to be my friend."

Both of them smiled.

"I was getting bored, and I felt like taking a walk," he said.

"I wanted to take a walk too."

"So that makes us a pair."

He straightened himself and gazed into her face as though he were her teacher, waiting for her to respond to a question he'd just posed.

"We can leave this place if you want to," he said.

"Please."

"I'm not coming back after we leave. But you can if you want to."

"I can't come back."

"Of course. That's why I'm taking you away."

"Let me get my bag."

"I'll wait for you." He put his hands in his pockets and nodded as she made for her classroom door.

Traffic thickened as they entered the downtown area. The Baguio Chinese School – a navy blue building – cast a bulky shadow over the busy street. The acrid smell of day-old urine filled Maricel's nostrils as they passed the eucalyptus trees that flanked the entrance to Burnham Park. A skinny child blocked their way and shoved a pail of nuts into their faces.

"Little boy, not now. We don't have money," Noel said, before sliding a cigarette into his mouth.

"Please, kuya, please buy," the boy whined.

"Didn't you hear him? He said we won't buy," Maricel snapped. The boy gave her a hurt look and sprinted away.

"God, you have a temper," Noel said, before lighting his cigarette.

"Those kids just get on my nerves."

He pulled out his cigarette, and exhaled. "You're just as scary as your friend."

"Really?"

"I used to be so scared of you I wouldn't approach you."

"I'm a nice girl. You just don't know me enough."

"That's why I like you. You're a mystery to me."

A wooden swan floated on the man-made lake, carrying forth the nervous giggles of a group of nuns. Noel led her to a row of squat, narrow eateries at the other end of the park, and they shared a coffee-stained linoleum table with a pair of sullen jeepney drivers who slurped down their steaming bowls of watery rice mixed with pig entrails. Aside from the aproned women who stood behind pots of food and collected used plates and cups, Maricel was the only girl in the eatery. But Noel said this was his favorite place to go for lunch, and she felt safe with him.

"Things usually get better when we've tested you," Noel said, mixing the caldereta on his plate with his rice.

"What do I have to do?" She waved away a fly from her Coke bottle.

"You'll have to prove your loyalty, just like the rest of us once did."

As he said this, he placed his hand on hers, and gave her a look of reassurance.

"You look scared," he said. "Don't be. I'm on your side. I'll make it easier for you."

"You would?"

"I was the one who recruited you, so why would I make things harder for you? Besides, I'm the 'Supremo'. Everyone respects me."

In the dim light of this soot-filled dining hall, his eyes seemed gentler. His voice carried a comforting weight that enveloped her in its warmth.

"Let's go," he said, nodding. She stood up after him and followed him outside. Flies settled on their plates, sipping the leftover juice of their meals.

"I live nearby. Would you want to come over to my place? My mother's at work. We'll have the house to ourselves," he said, taking her hand as they crossed the road.

"Can't we just hang out at the park instead?"

Noel laughed. "Cel, we're still in uniform. If a teacher catches us, we're dead."

"But why do we have to go to your house?"

They had reached the other side of the road. Noel stopped and gave her a puzzled look.

"Don't you want to see my place?"

"I don't know."

"But I thought we were friends," he said, letting go of her hand.

"Yeah, of course we're friends. I'm just feeling nervous, that's all."

"You don't trust me."

"No. I'm just not used to this."

"Fine. Go home. I thought we were cool, but it looks like we aren't."

He turned and began making his way through the midday crowd.

She never came home this early – what would her mother say if she walked through their front door at this hour? She couldn't go back to school either. Nadia was waiting for her, and no one would protect her now, not even Noel. She hadn't been careful, and now she was losing him.

"I'll come with you!" she yelled. "Please, don't leave me here!"

He turned and walked back to her. "Why didn't you say so earlier?" he asked, putting an arm around her and pulling her along.

Used clothes stores spilled onto the sidewalk. Battered leather bags and stuffed toys were heaped in cardboard boxes that flanked the entrances to these shops. Tired blouses hung in rows, their faded drooping shoulders knowing a firmer past, and hanging from plywood walls were winter jackets, dresses and the occasional sequined gown. Girls with empty stares sat near the entrances of these shops, listening to afternoon telenovelas on their cheap Chinese radios.

Noel led Maricel to a side street and they passed a few more stalls. The peeling facade of the Bayanihan Hotel cast its shadow on the sidewalk, darkening the greenish liquid that trickled down the gutters. Young boys clad in greasy rags darted through the crowd, dipping their hands into blind beggars' cups. Veiled Muslim pedlars filled the air with their shrill, nagging voices. Wet clothes hung like heavy flags from the windows above.

They approached a narrow wooden doorframe and clambered up a staircase that creaked under their feet, entering a small hallway lit by moth-stained incandescent lamps. Children darted past them, battering the floorboards with their feet as they ran into the street. There were doors on each side. A radio blared from one of them, a baby screamed from behind another. They passed a few more doors before stopping in front of one. Noel pulled out a bunch of keys from his pocket, picked through them and inserted one into the doorknob. A woman in heavy makeup and shorts stood in the doorway across from where they stood, trailing them with her eyes as she drew a cigarette to her lips.

The door opened with a creak. In front of them was a worn velvet couch, facing a glass coffee table and a small television set; a long plastic shelf on the left, holding plastic figurines and dusty stuffed toys; a kitchenette on the right, near the window, covered by an oily lace curtain; and, beside the kitchenette, a row of unevenly painted doors.

"Anybody home?" Noel called out, sauntering across the apartment before turning back the oily curtain with a finger. Stopping in the middle of the room, he put his hands in his pockets and said, "You can put your bag down. I want you to sit on the couch."

Maricel approached the couch with caution, and as she sat down, the smell of old cigarettes and sweat rose from the cushions like an invisible cloud. She felt a pang of loneliness as her eyes traveled around the room. Noel watched her as she placed her backpack on the coffee table and folded her hands in her lap, as though he had witnessed this scene before, and had rehearsed his part long before Maricel knew hers.

Noel took a seat beside her and placed an arm on the back of the couch, behind Maricel. The noise of the street floated up to the room as he placed a sweaty hand on her shoulder.

She had spent so many of her days just being afraid. Thinking about the future seemed like a luxury she had enjoyed when she was younger, when her mother wasn't around, when she had more time for herself, when she could come to Jamie's house and make Jamie's Barbie dolls enact the life she dreamt of having. Without her knowing it, she had laid to waste her own future. Here it was before her: a drab room in a drab city.

He leaned over and kissed her on the cheek.

She thought of the doors along the corridor outside this room, and how equally hopeless, perhaps, the rooms behind each door looked on the inside.

His hand moved down, to where her collar was, and he unfastened the top button of her blouse.

"Don't." The word came out in a dry whisper.

He unfastened another button and looked up. "Don't worry."

She pushed his hand away and stood, taking her backpack with her. She fixed her eyes on a plastic wall clock as she pulled her backpack straps over her shoulders, straightened her blouse and buttoned it up.

"You need my help, Maricel."

"I have to go home."

"We have members across the city. They all listen to me. If you want to get home safe, you'll need my help."

As she turned, she spotted a vase on the coffee table. It was tall and heavy enough.

"You don't strike me as naïve," he said, spreading his legs wide. "You must've heard of the things we do. We protect our friends, but we're not kind to our enemies."

"What's going to happen?" she asked.

He winced, crinkled his nose. "You don't trust me. I'm sorry Cel, but I have a reputation to protect."

He rose from the couch and followed her as she backed away from him. He put his hand in his pocket and jingled the keys that were inside. "I was just trying to help you."

"Please don't hurt me."

"If you just trust me, I won't hurt you," he said.

Her heart was pounding. She brushed one of her backpack's side pockets. There was a pencil in there. That would do, for now. As she pulled it out, gripping it, he grabbed her wrist. The pencil fell from her hand. She screamed, and he clamped his left hand over her mouth, using his other arm to shove her to the wall. He was tall and strong, and she felt the air in her lungs go out of her as he leaned against her body.

His right arm tore across her chest, ripping her blouse open. Buttons fell to the floor. His other hand was pressing down on her mouth, and she yanked her head back before sinking her teeth into the skin of his palm. His hand tasted of salt and dirt, and she bit down until she could taste his blood. He yelled and pulled away, gasping, and she stomped on his foot, ran to the door, struggled with the doorknob and swung the door open.

She shoved a little boy aside as she ran down the hallway. The ashen glow of the light bulbs trickled down the staircase, illuminating the doorframe that seemed, as she pulled her torn blouse over her chest, like the end of a long tunnel.

On the jeepney home, she trembled as she fixed her hair and wiped away the blood from her lips with the back of her hand. Her blouse kept falling open, and she held it together with a closed fist. When other passengers stared at her, she looked away. She'd return home and pretend that nothing happened. That wasn't difficult to do; no one at home asked her questions whenever she returned from school. Home was a place where time remained constant – nothing changed, or propelled her towards the future.

Male voices peppered the air as she approached the front door of their apartment. When she opened the door, Jojo and his friends were gathered around the kitchen table, laughing, jeering, slapping each other's backs. Jojo was too distracted to even notice her, and she was thankful for this. A cloud of cigarette smoke hovered above his head, and empty beer bottles littered the table. Her mother was seated on the living room couch, eyes glued to the TV screen.

Maricel was too tired to come up with excuses for being home early, so when her mother looked over her shoulder, she braced herself for a scolding.

"You're playing hooky too?" her mother asked.

"We were dismissed early today," Maricel answered.

"What happened to your shirt?"

She hurriedly grabbed the lapels of her blouse and pulled them together. "The buttons fell at school."

There was an explosion on TV, and her mother turned. This distraction was all Maricel needed. "Oh my God, is Lucie dead?" her mother asked, nervously tapping the ashes of her cigarette into her San Miguel Beer ashtray.

Sitting beside her mother wasn't too difficult. They didn't need to talk – the sound of the TV was enough to fill the silence that came between them. The background music swelled when a body was pulled from a burning car, and her mother brought her hands to her open mouth.

"Ma?" Maricel asked.

Her mother's eyes were glued to the screen. She hadn't heard her.

"Ma. What's the story of this show?"

Her mother's hands fell to her lap. Just as Maricel was about to give up, her mother began to speak. "It's about a girl who was exchanged at birth with another girl at the hospital where she was born. Her real parents are rich, but the poor parents of the other girl raise her. The other girl grows up rich and bullies this girl when they meet at school. I wonder why they killed the spoiled girl. She was mean, but she wasn't that evil—" Her mother winced as Jojo and his friends broke into song.

"Can't you shut up? I'm thinking!" her mother yelled.

They stopped singing, and Jojo yelled, "If you don't want to hear us, turn up the volume!" before waving at his companions to continue.

Her mother pointed the remote at the TV screen and pressed the volume key, drowning their laughter in music. Their singing grew louder, jostling with the sound of dialogue and weeping.

Without taking her eyes from the screen, she yelled, "When I was in Israel, I couldn't watch Filipino telenovelas. My boss watched TV all the time too, but the shows were all in Hebrew. I really had to come home."

"Did you miss us?" Maricel yelled back.

She took Maricel's free hand and squeezed it. "You should watch TV with me more often," she yelled. "You're always in your room and I never know what you're up to."

Maricel nodded and tried to concentrate as she fixed her eyes on the TV screen. But she soon found herself pulling her hand from her mother's grasp and rising from the couch, taking her backpack with her. She forgot about her blouse and it fell open, exposing her bra.

"Hey, sexy!" one of Jojo's friends yelled.

She froze, and the fear she'd felt earlier that afternoon – and even before that – came rushing back like a cold wave. It had stalked her through the city, all the way to her home. Pulling her blouse closed, she turned to look at this boy. He licked his dark lips, winked at her, laughed. What was it that this boy wanted, that Noel, and all boys, wanted from her? They all had that same look, that same leery voice.

Jojo grabbed him by the collar and dragged him out of their apartment. Maricel ran into her room, shutting her bedroom door behind her before Jojo could call her a slut. The sound of the front door slamming vibrated through her body, a hollow instrument that could only register a painful, regretful emptiness. She dropped her backpack on the floor and leaned against the door, closing her eyes. They were hurting – it was hard to keep them shut. She opened them, and through her tears she saw her twin bed, her collection of thrift store teddy bears on the shelf above and the lone window that faced the gray wall of their neighbor's house. It was a small, often suffocating room, but it was a good place to hide and cry; her chest heaved as she climbed into her bed, burying her face in her pillow. The noise outside her door drowned out her sobbing, and she cried until she was exhausted. Afterwards, when she was strong enough, she sat up and wiped her face with kleenex.

Her wrist was still hurting, and she rubbed it. She would need to ice it, in case she had to use her fists when Noel and his friends came looking for her at school the next day.

INHERITANCES

When Andrew received his mother's call, he was unbuttoning his shirt in front of his bathroom mirror, savoring the lazy, pleasant buzz that lingered in his head. He'd spent the evening drinking and sauntering down the warm, noise-filled streets of Makati with friends who could drop everything at a moment's notice to celebrate his good fortune on a Tuesday night. His breath reeked of alcohol, his clothing smelled of cigarettes, and he was annoyed about having to shower when all he wanted was to crawl into bed and into the arms of the girl he had brought home. But Nina, who laughed as she unbuttoned her blouse, had told him that a shower would do him good. He took her slow disrobing as a sign she'd join him, but she made no promises. He had gotten this far with her and wasn't in the mood to argue.

When Andrew's phone buzzed against the vanity table, the first thing that occurred to him was that there had been an emergency at the hotel, and that, as his boss's new right-hand man, he had to be there to clean up the mess and soothe frayed nerves.

"It will be more work, but you'll be adequately compensated," his boss had told him that morning, his large hand squeezing Andrew's in a strong, friendly grip before letting it go. Andrew was, of course, the perfect man for this kind of promotion, because no one else at the premier hotel where they worked understood a guest's needs as much as he did. Like him, the men and women who checked into this hotel sought refuge from the lives they led, a place where their needs could be met with no strings attached. What they sought was freedom, which they never had in their homes or workplaces, for it was a hotel that provided ease, an escape from other people's expectations. From the people working behind the reception desk to the chambermaids who emptied their guests' wastebaskets in the morning, he always reminded new hires that the people who walked through their doors were their guests, no matter what their last names were, what their skin color was, what they did for a living, how their accents sounded or even how they held their silverware. The last thing their guests wanted when checking into this hotel, he told them, was to be judged.

But it wasn't his boss, it was his mother's number flashing on his phone screen, and for a moment, he hesitated before taking the call. He pushed the bathroom door shut when he sensed the panic in her voice, before walking away from the door and towards the sink.

"It's your father," she said, sounding like she was about to cry.

"What happened?"

"He's very sick."

"Have you talked to Carmina?" His elder sister, Carmina, was a doctor and lived an hour away from their parents.

He could hear her taking a deep breath before she said, "He locked himself up in his room and won't open the door. He thinks the cops are coming for him."

"Ma, what's going on?" His mind cleared as he spoke, not because he wanted to know what his mother was talking about, but because what she had just said made absolutely no sense to him.

"It's been happening," she said, hesitating, "for a week now. I didn't want to tell you because I was sure you'd be worried. You know how disappointed he was when he failed the bar this year, don't you?"

"Ma, you should've talked him out of it."

"I tried, but you know how stubborn he is. It's been his lifelong dream. I couldn't just say no."

"You could've told him that it doesn't matter to us. At his age, he should be tending to his garden." This was what his father excelled at: putting pressure on himself, even when the people who knew him were too busy getting on with their lives to mind his failures.

"If you were here, you could've helped me talk him out of it."

There was a faint, hesitant rapping on the bathroom door, followed by Nina asking him if everything was all right.

He put a hand over the receiver and said, "It's my mom." He pressed his phone to his ear as Nina pulled away from the door, and a chill overcame him as he was enveloped anew in a world he thought he'd left behind.

The nightmares started three weeks ago, his mother said above the static, just after the bar exam results were released. His father didn't find his name in the list, and two nights later he started crying out in his sleep.

"I tried comforting him, but he wouldn't go back to sleep. Then the next day he started telling me to lock the gate and the door because the cops were after him. He wouldn't let me leave the house, even when we ran out of food."

"Did you tell Carmina?"

"I told her everything."

There was a pause.

"And what did she say?"

"She said she couldn't bear to see him like this."

"Goddamnit," Andrew muttered under his breath. He was aware that his sister's marriage was on the rocks, but the old man was her father, and his parents hadn't mortgaged their house to send her to medical school so that she could avoid them when they were ill. "But he's her father," he said, pounding his thigh with a clenched fist.

"I called for an ambulance about an hour ago. They're in the driveway, but your father ran into our room to hide. He thinks they're the police. He won't open up. I'm afraid he's going to hurt himself."

"Am I supposed to go there?"

Baguio was at least a six-hour bus ride from Manila. With luck, he'd get a midnight trip from Cubao, and it would be morning by the time he reached his parents' house. He was angry with Carmina for refusing to help when she was just an hour away, but the more he thought of her, the more he understood why she couldn't go. What did his mother expect him to do once he was there? Like his sister, he was afraid. If strangers couldn't talk his father into opening his door, neither could he.

"You have to come. I'm begging you. You're the only person who can help us now." He knew he couldn't argue with her any longer. Her voice was breaking as she spoke.

Nina was waiting for him on the living room couch when he opened the door. She had taken one of his robes and wrapped it around herself. Although the sight of her waxed legs falling out of his robe would've excited him earlier, he couldn't will himself to feel anything aside from embarrassment when their eyes met. He leaned against the wall, staring into the darkness of his sparsely furnished living room, waiting for the appropriate feelings to come rushing to him. Her bare feet padded towards him, and he froze at the touch of her fingers.

She was only a friend from work – they were hardly a couple. But he took her hand in his, afraid that she'd leave him if he told her the truth.

"It's my dad. I have to go home."

~

Andrew wouldn't be in Baguio for another few hours, but if his father attempted to take his own life in his room, at least his mother wouldn't tell him later that he didn't do anything to prevent it. He fell asleep on the bus and when he woke, the sun was rising, pouring its rays over mist-covered mountains and rice paddies that surrounded his hometown. He was almost home and felt a soft glow of hope spread within him as he looked out the window, almost forgetting why he was sitting on a bus on his way to his father's house.

He checked his phone and saw that his mother had texted him at two in the morning, saying that the ambulance that had come to pick his father up had left and would return the next day.

As his bus entered his hometown's empty streets, he rang the hospital, asked for an ambulance and called his mother from the bus station to tell her he was on his way.

An ambulance was waiting at the gate of their hillside home when he stepped out of the cab. Two orderlies in white suits were chatting and smoking in the shaded tree-lined driveway when he unlatched the gate. One of them had what appeared to be a straitjacket draped over his arm and nodded at him as he walked past them.

"You been here long?" he asked them, and they smiled sheepishly as they dropped their half-finished cigarettes on the gravel and put them out with their white shoes. The front door slammed and his mother, with her hair unkempt, came rushing to his side. She clutched his arm as they entered the alley of shrubbery leading to the front door. "Are we going to let them smoke in our yard too?" he asked.

"Don't worry. Your dad won't notice."

His head was heavy with sleep as he strode past the tiny, dark living room and his mother's slick-tiled kitchenette. He walked up to his father's closed door, glanced at the laminated photograph of Saint Thérèse of Lisieux pinned to the wood, sighed and knocked.

"Dad, it's me. It's Andrew."

The old man stirred. "Is that you, *anak*?"

"Yes, Dad. It's me."

His father unlocked his door, poked his head out and asked timidly, "Is the coast clear?"

The hairs on the nape of Andrew's neck stood on end when his father grinned.

His mother rushed to them. "They've left, dear."

"It's just us, Dad," he said, sliding an arm around his father's frail body and giving his mother a quick nod.

She met his glance, took the old man's hand and said, "It's a beautiful morning, Arturo. Why don't we take a walk?"

Andrew held the front door open for the three of them, glad that the shrubbery his father planted by the door years ago kept the orderlies hidden from view. Footsteps crunched against the gravel, and he could feel his father hesitating, pulling away from his grip.

"Agents," his father whispered.

"It's just Carmina. She's home," Andrew said, in the most nonchalant tone he could muster. The two orderlies marched towards them, side by side, unfurling a straitjacket between them.

Andrew brought his arms around his father's waist, while his mother gripped the old man's wrist with both hands. His father whimpered and tried twisting himself out of Andrew's embrace, and their eyes met before he moaned in a voice that sent chills through Andrew's body.

"So you're with them now."

One of the orderlies was holding a syringe, and he stabbed the needle into the old man's arm while Andrew held him. After some struggle, Andrew's father collapsed in his arms, and Andrew pulled him up while the two young men fastened the jacket's belts around him.

"Thank God," Andrew's mother said, wringing her hands, while Andrew released his father into the arms of the orderlies. His arms ached, and he sank onto the front step as he watched them take his father away. Two more orderlies were coming through the gate, pushing a stretcher between them.

Andrew rose and took his mother's hand as his father was loaded onto the stretcher.

"I told him you were coming, and he waited for you," his mother said, as they followed the group of orderlies through the open gate.

"And I tricked him."

"There was no other way."

∼

The doctor on duty assured him that the windows of the General Hospital's psychiatric ward were equipped with metal bars "as a necessary safeguard". His father had convinced himself that he was being brought to jail, and being brought to a room with bars would only confirm this belief. Andrew asked the bespectacled, baby-faced doctor if there were alternatives to this arrangement. The doctor tilted his balding head and laughed as though to commiserate. He then suggested a private rehabilitation center on the outskirts of town.

"It's a beautiful place, with rolling lawns and lots of space for walking and exercise. Although, you'll have to spend a lot more if you want to put him there."

His mother was filling prescriptions at a nearby pharmacy, and they stood right beside his father, who lay sedated in bed.

"I think they left brochures for us. I can get one for you, if you're interested."

"Thanks."

The doctor's sneakers squeaked against the faded linoleum as he opened the door and strode down the hallway.

Andrew thought of what his mother had told him as they sat at his father's bedside, watching his father's bony chest rise and fall beneath his thin hospital gown. "He kept dreaming that you, Carmina and I were locked in our rooms. He'd wake up in the middle of the night, yelling at me for not opening our doors to him."

As he sat beside his sedated father, waiting for the doctor to return, he recalled the sound of his father pounding on his bedroom door. No longer was he an adult, sitting beside his father's hospital bed; instead he felt small enough to crawl under his bed with his plastic Spider-Man as his father yelled at him through his bedroom door in a crazed voice that made him shiver. The memory faded just as quickly as it had overwhelmed him when the doctor, holding a brochure, asked him if he was all right.

The picture of an ivy-covered brick inn on the cover of the glossy brochure intrigued him. The private room featured inside had high ceilings, a single bed, a nightstand, a bookshelf and cushioned flooring. It had a window that overlooked an open lawn. He noticed the latticed grills.

He checked the prices listed at the back of the brochure and made his calculations. Much as he believed that a person like his father, a retired high school principal, had every right to receive care in a place like this, he also knew that privacy, comfort, fresh air and individual attention came at a price.

His mother stepped inside the room, and he rose from his chair, telling her he had to make a call. In a balcony shaded off from the street by a bamboo grove, he dialed Carmina's number. She picked up after four rings.

"Where are you?" she asked, with an air of authority that was typical of her but threw him off, nonetheless.

"I should be the one asking you that."

"I'm in a meeting."

"Do you know that Dad's in the hospital? And that he wouldn't come out of his room until I came home from Manila?"

"I'm really sorry. I just wasn't up to it."

"I wasn't up to it either. But I'm here and you're nowhere."

"I just can't see him like this. I'm in a daze."

"Oh, come on, ate."

There was silence on the other end, and then he heard her sniffling.

"My husband has another woman," she said, her voice cracking.

"What's that got to do with this?" he blurted out. He soon regretted saying this, for she erupted into sobs.

"None of you care about how I feel," she sobbed.

"Ate, you have to calm down."

"How can I calm down?" she wailed into the phone. "My father's sick and my marriage is falling apart."

"That husband of yours has cheated on you three times. It's time for you to leave him and come help our father."

She quieted down, then asked, "What's the name of your attending physician?"

"Doctor Paragas."

"I went to med school with his sister. Tell him that."

"And how's that supposed to help?"

"He'll treat Dad better if he knows his sister's my friend."

He glanced over his shoulder at the hallway and spotted a jaundiced young man lying in a gurney. The young man's skin clung to his bones, and he returned Andrew's stare with glazed-over eyes. There was no way he could spend another hour in this harshly lit building, filling his nostrils with the nauseating scent of bleach used liberally to mask the sour smell of illness and death.

"I'm putting Dad in a place where he'll get proper care and he might just recover from this. It's going to cost a lot of money. But you and I are going to share in the expenses. If you aren't going to contribute your share, I'll tell Ma you did nothing."

"Guess I have no right to say no."

"You don't," he said, and hung up.

∽

He sat in the ambulance that took his father to the rehabilitation center, holding his mother's hand as they watched his father's face twitch and grimace in his sleep. He could almost picture the old man being pursued in his dreams by the same policemen who haunted him during his waking hours. They accompanied his sleeping father as nurses wheeled him into his new lodgings, Andrew wanting to make sure that the room they put him in was what the brochure had promised. Afterwards, he took a quick look around the grounds and the activity room, and signed some forms, settling the bill at the front desk as his mother spoke to the institution's attending psychiatrist. He took his mother out for lunch afterwards, wrote her a check and brought her home in a taxi. No one could say now that he didn't care for his father, especially not Carmina, whom he barely had the chance to speak to and likely wouldn't go out of his way to console.

Afterwards, as he leaned back in his bus seat on his way back to Manila, his eyes lingered on the groves of pine trees clinging to the mountainside, which slowly grew sparse as the bus slithered down the two-lane road into the lowlands. He remembered the pine trees his father had planted around their yard years before he was born, and how they towered over them all, casting shadows on him as he had walked down his father's driveway that morning to fetch him from his room. When he was growing up, these trees had grown tall enough to shield their house from view. His father drove him and Carmina to school and back, oftentimes pointing out that the trees kept them safe from the prying eyes of intruders. Neither he nor Carmina had playmates from the neighborhood, and the one friend he brought home when he was in elementary school was soon sent away after his friend blurted out a cuss word while they played sipa in the yard.

When he returned to work the next morning, he found a cream-colored box on his desk with a Post-It Note shaped like a chef's hat stuck to its corner. "If you need anything, please let me know. Your friend," it read. A chuckle escaped from his lips when he read the phrase, "Let them eat cake!" embossed on the lid. He opened the box and found three rows of pastel-colored macarons inside. He popped one in his mouth and let it melt on his tongue as he sank into his swivel chair and leaned back.

He pulled out his phone from his pocket, typed out, Dinner tonight? and sent it to Nina.

Minutes later, she answered, I get off at 8 tonight, but I can fix you dinner downstairs. If you can wait for me, I can meet you. What would you like?

He hadn't been thinking clearly the night his mother called, and hadn't refused Nina's offer of a ride to the bus station. It was eleven at night when they set out in her Golf, and they sped down Epifanio de los Santos Avenue in silence, their eyes fixed on the dusty, littered highway as rickety city buses barreled past them. She glanced at him when they stopped at intersections, and when he met her eyes, she smiled. She'd then glance at the road, knowing perhaps that it wasn't the best time to intrude.

Salmon. Cook it whichever way. Will be downstairs at 8. I'll tell Chef Luis not to nag you.

Thanks. I need that.

Thanks for the treats.

Hope they're still fresh.

The grilled salmon served to him that night at the hotel café was juicy and fresh in the middle and glazed with sugar and wine sauce. He was finishing up a glass of sauvignon blanc when a young lady in a Tintin T-shirt and jeans walked up to his table.

"How's your meal?" It was Nina.

"You startled me," he said, putting down his wineglass.

"It's the lighting," she said, pointing at the shaded lamp in the middle of the table. "Makes me look like a little girl."

"This was so good," he said, pointing at his empty plate with his fork.

"Thanks." She pulled up a chair beside him, put her elbows on the table, rested her chin on her palms and fixed her round eyes on his face. "How's your dad?"

"Not bad," he said in haste, then, "Are you hungry?"

"I had an early dinner. But thanks, anyway."

She had round cheeks, a small chin and long-lashed eyes that narrowed into slits when she smiled. Her face had been heavily made up when they first met at a friend's birthday party, and in the smoky, strobe-lit interior of the pulsating nightclub where they danced, he thought she was beautiful. He couldn't catch her name above the music's thumping, and so she took him by the hand to the restroom, where she planted a soft kiss on his earlobe and whispered, "It's Nina." While they kissed, his hand wandered up her dress and found a naked, round breast to fondle. She gasped with pleasure when he stroked her nipple with his thumb, and as it hardened to his touch, she grasped his hand through the material of her dress and with a drunken smile said, "Not yet." A name like Nina was easy to remember, but when she wore her sous-chef's uniform to a meeting the next day, she wasn't as easy to recognize. Only then did he take notice of her at work, as he imagined what she looked like underneath all those clothes.

He smiled at her and asked, "Do you want to get some fresh air?"

Ayala Avenue, in early June, was quiet and balmy at nine in the evening. The terraced fountains at their workplace had just been lit up, creating a watery, illumined stairway that guided Andrew's gaze upwards towards a starry, cloudless Manila sky. He walked past this fountain almost every day on his way to work and back to his apartment, but the sight of shimmering water cascading down these steps had a comforting, almost magical effect on him as he held Nina's hand.

Bentleys and Lamborghinis had become a common sight on the streets of the central business district in recent months. Whenever he walked home, his eyes lingered on these cars that sped past him, observing the way their polished bodies captured the faraway gleam of offices and hotel rooms several stories above, flinging their gathered light across the street at pedestrians like him. The executives he lunched with claimed these were boom times, and he could believe them, judging by the number of people booking rooms at the hotel, as well as the number of foreign businessmen checking in. Young executives like him were the future of this country, he was told at the gala dinners he was invited to. He found solace in this thought, telling himself that he was part of an economic revolution, that people like him weren't alone in thinking this, that the Makati business district wasn't just an island of glass and concrete rising from a sea of shantytowns and garbage-strewn streets.

The rustle of palm leaves filled his ears as Nina talked about being homesick in New York, where she had been just a year before, and about wanting to come home to a warm night like this after having survived a particularly harsh winter.

"I was dating a guy I went to culinary school with. After we graduated, I thought of staying on because of him. Horrible, competitive guy, but I was stupid and in love. Then one night, after I came home from an interview that did not go well, he joked that I could be his maid if I really wanted to stay in America." She gave his hand a slight tug and laughed. "Did I make you mad?"

"I would've punched the guy," he said.

"You're cute," she said, giggling.

"But I meant it," he whined. But she was laughing, and for reasons he couldn't understand, he started laughing too.

He placed his hand on the small of her back when they stepped inside his building's elevator, and when they entered his unit, he pulled her waist towards his and kissed her. She dropped her purse and rested an arm on his shoulder as her mouth opened to his, and when he asked if he needed to shower first, she whispered in his ear, "I want you now."

He had thought of her throughout the day, and as he carried her to his room, lay her down on his bed, pulled off her Tintin T-shirt and unclasped her bra, he realized that what he truly wanted was oblivion. He wanted everything in his life to disappear: his job, the stupid, ugly face of an angry guest who claimed that her mink coat had been returned by their in-house cleaners "with a nick in it", the antiseptic smell of hospital corridors, the childish twinkle in his father's eyes when he opened his door to him, asking if the coast was clear. All he wanted was Nina, her body and the look in her eyes as he entered her, pulling him in. He plowed her and clawed at her breasts, suckling them, seeking to bury himself deep inside her warmth until there was no escape, going gentle when she laid her fingertips on his chest and said, "Andrew, you're hurting me."

He laid his head on her stomach afterwards, and when he apologized for being rough on her, she tucked a lock of his hair behind his ear and said, "Something's bothering you, that's all."

He wanted to tell her about his father's madness but fought the urge. He chose to think of the subtle, surprising flavors of the dinner she had made for him, how they lingered on the tongue, and how his mother's cooking would never compare to hers. He remembered the taste of his mother's bland vegetable stew which he hated, and then it all came rushing back to him: the memory of his family eating vegetable stew for weeks because they couldn't afford anything better, because his mother was the only one working and his father had left his job because he wanted to review for the bar, which he would go on to fail for the second time. He spoke of this memory as she stroked his hair, and he felt he could tell her everything, no matter how absurd his stories were, because she was listening. He had started this story and had to tell it to its end.

Once he had gotten so hungry that he pinched some money from his mother's purse and used it to buy corn chips at school. "I put the bag of chips in my backpack and nibbled on them all day between classes. I forgot to throw away the bag before coming home." He remembered his father barging into his room while he was studying for a test, belt in hand, pulling him onto his bed before whipping him, while his mother watched on, begging his father to stop because it was just ten pesos. "She told him anyway even if she knew he'd beat me," he said. "It was the day after the bar results were released. He failed, you know. My dad probably felt super when he found out his son was also a thief."

"But it wasn't your fault."

"It set me straight though. From that point on, I never stole again."

"But you were hungry."

"Wasn't an excuse for stealing." He looked into her eyes, which were filled with shock and sorrow, and said, "At least he took his failure like a man. He went back to teaching, didn't complain about his life, even if we never got rich. We managed. That's one thing about him I admired."

She closed her eyes as she shook her head. "What he did to you was wrong."

He raised his hand to stroke her hair, laughed and said, "I don't know what I would've done if you weren't there the other night."

In a low voice, she asked, "What happened?"

He sighed. "He had it in his head to try taking the bar again now that he's retired. And guess what, he flunked it again." He looked into her eyes to make sure she wasn't pulling away from him as he spoke. "He got really depressed. He was having a nervous breakdown when I saw him yesterday."

She stroked his forehead and said, "You poor thing."

He felt a sharp pain rise up in his throat as he said, "I'm not like him though. I'm not crazy."

She slid beside him, and the touch of her arms sent a convulsion of grief through his body. He lacked the strength to keep the sobs at bay, and fell apart as she drew him close to her breast.

"I hate my father."

"I know," she cooed. "And it's all right."

"He shouldn't have had children. He shouldn't have had me."

"Don't say that," she said with a wry smile.

Streaks of sunlight fell on his face when he woke the next day. His bedroom door had been left open, allowing the faint sound of a running shower to reach him as he lay in bed. He checked the clock on his nightstand. It was almost seven. As he pulled the sheets away, he faintly remembered a hand resting his head on a pillow, fingers tucking his blanket under his chin and the touch of a woman's lips on his forehead as the rest of his body eased itself into slumber.

∽

"You've worked so hard. You should treat yourself to a new car," his boss told him over lunch one day. "Take out an auto loan. Get yourself something new. We're paying you well." It was a gentle way of saying, *You can't impress our clients with that old clunker of yours*, meaning his eight-year-old Mazda. Although he had thought of getting a new car when he learned of his promotion, his father's medical bills had to be settled, leaving him with just enough for some basic luxuries.

"It's not a Lamborghini but listen to that engine," he said to Nina. They were speeding up the wooded hilly roads of Tagaytay in his newly purchased secondhand Audi convertible, the roof folded down on a pleasant Saturday morning.

"It's already a sexy car, silly. We'd get kidnapped if this were a Lamborghini."

"I'm glad I can't afford one," he said, turning briefly to watch her shaking her hair loose from its chignon.

"When my brother was kidnapped, he was just driving our family Pajero," she said, leaning back in her seat as the wind whipped through her hair.

"Good God!"

"I know. It was horrible. But he made it out alive thanks to my parents."

"And you still came home, despite that."

She raised her hand to feel the wind. "This is home."

They spent much of their time indoors as typhoons lashed their city during the rainy months and monsoon rains flooded the streets. There were nights he spent at her apartment in Salcedo Village, where she had a fridge stocked with strange health foods and the occasional hotel kitchen leftover. When the streets were flooded, she spent the night at his pad, which at the height of a storm was a ten-minute drive from the hotel. They made love while typhoons whipped rain across the city's sky and slammed it against their windowpanes. He kept a bottle of her favorite shampoo in his bathroom, and she kept a bottle of his aftershave on her vanity counter. While dressing for work one morning, he found her Tintin T-shirt piled with her underwear and pajamas in his dresser.

He pulled it from the drawer, breathed in her scent, refolded it and returned it to its pile.

His mother texted him with updates on his father. He's getting better, she said. He wasn't imagining policemen and judges anymore, and he was beating other patients at Scrabble in the rehab center's game room.

At least he's good at something, he texted back.

He's content. I hope he stays this way when he's well.

He'd have to stay crazy for that to happen.

Don't call your father that.

His father came home in October just as the skies began to clear. The long weekend of National Heroes' Day was coming up, and his mother called in the middle of the week, inviting him over to lunch that Saturday to celebrate his father's return. Carmina and her daughter would be there, she added.

"I really don't see the point of going," he murmured, burying his face in the nape of Nina's neck as they lay in bed.

"You really don't want to know how your father's doing?"

He kissed the down at the base of her neck. "This means I can't come with you to visit your parents."

She sighed as he rested his hand on the curve of her waist. "If you go see your father, I'll make marzipan for him."

"He doesn't even know what that is."

She gave his thigh a playful slap. "Then he should try my marzipan before he tastes a crappy store version."

∼

His Audi's engine purred softly beneath his feet as he set out for Baguio at sunrise. If he drove instead of taking the bus, he could take the new freeway that bypassed the traffic-choked farming towns dotting the old, two-lane highway. The sky was clear, and he drove with his roof down as he sped past swampland, mango orchards and statues of the Virgin Mary perched on lone rocky hills. The freeway sliced through swaths of rice fields, and birds flying by the roadside raced him as he sped on. The engine did not complain as he navigated the steep, twisting two-lane road that slithered upwards into the Cordillera's interior. A chill set in as he drove on, and he knew he was home when he drove into a thin fog curling down the mountain slopes. As he switched on his fog lights and unfolded the roof of his car, he spotted a lone, scraggly pine tree clinging to a barren mountain slope, right beside a billboard advertising a country inn with sweeping views of pine forests and meals served with fresh baguio strawberries.

His father's pine trees cast shadows on his car's leather seats as he pulled into the driveway. His mother had opened the gate for him and was pushing it shut when he switched off the engine, unbuckled his seatbelt and leaned back in his seat.

"Well, this is new," his mother said, walking towards him. He stretched, feeling a subtle ache creeping up his neck. He took off his sunglasses, placed them on the dash, cracked his door open and reached for Nina's marzipan in the passenger seat.

He stepped out and kissed his mother on the cheek before handing the pie to her. "And you brought dessert too! Is this from the hotel?"

"No, but it was made by a sous-chef who works at the hotel. She's a wonderful baker." He closed the car door behind them and as his mother stared at the pie said, "It's called marzipan, a kind of cake made with crushed almonds." He pushed the lock button in his trouser pocket and the car made a loud, decisive chirp. "Nina made it especially for you."

"Your girlfriend?"

He smiled. "Yeah."

A look of relief crossed her face and she said, "Well, it was wise of you not to bring her here."

He lowered his voice to a whisper as he said, "So he's not yet well."

"Oh, he's gotten better but you know," she said, waving her hand around and smiling with her mouth closed. "It will take time before he returns to his old self."

Parked at the corner of the driveway underneath his father's guava tree was the old Ford Sierra that Carmina inherited from their father after her wedding, which Rico, Carmina's husband, had painted a garish green. It glowed in the shade of his father's guava tree, like a radioactive frog with headlights for eyes.

"Is Rico here?" he asked, since it was Rico and not Carmina who knew how to drive.

"Of course." She gave him a short firm nod.

"You do know what happened between them, don't you?"

"What was I supposed to do, turn him out? Besides, your father likes him. If I told him to go away, who knows what your father would do."

The screen door slammed, and Rico waved at them as he approached.

"Nice car!" Rico called out.

"Thanks," Andrew said. "It's secondhand." His body tensed, as though preparing to bolt, and he fondled his car key in his pocket as Rico pumped his other hand. Rico wore a striped golf shirt that may have fit him a year before, but was now stretched tight over his belly.

"Doesn't look secondhand," Rico said, wiping his bottom lip with his thumb and forefinger as his eyes wandered up and down the Audi's silver body. He whistled, grinned and said, "Mommy was just telling us that you got a promotion. I got a promotion at the hospital too, but you know how it is with us nurses in this country. They barely pay us a living wage."

"I'm sure you're doing all right," Andrew said. As they walked towards the house, he took his phone out of his trouser pocket, typed, My sister's husband is back, acting like nothing happened. He just called my mom "Mommy". God's playing a sick joke on me, and sent it to Nina.

The old man's eyes remained fixed on the TV screen, even when Andrew stepped inside. His squarish face, which was once chiseled, with a healthy tan owing to hours spent under the sun pulling weeds and hacking at tree branches with his bolo knife, was now soft and pale, almost blubbery. He had obviously regained the weight he had lost. He was wearing a T-shirt that advertised a brand of ibuprofen, and he sat on their tiny living room's bamboo bench, sandwiched between Ruth, Carmina's five-year-old daughter, and Carmina, who was flipping through a faded copy of *Vogue* with a young Cindy Crawford on its cover.

Confetti and balloons rained on a weeping game show contestant as a group of bikini-clad girls gyrated and sang in the background. "Itaktak mo, itaktak mo," Ruth sang, her small pitchy voice trailing the thin falsettos of the dancers.

"Ruthie, ask for a blessing from your tito," Rico said, closing the door behind them. Ruth jumped down from her seat, head bowed, and approached her uncle. Andrew felt the enormity of his hand as the little girl took it, and his hand barely grazed her forehead before she let go and returned to her seat. Carmina glanced up from her magazine, fixed Andrew a bored look and said, "Hi Drew."

"Hi, Carmi."

"Arturo," his mother said, setting down the pie on the round dining table that separated the living room from the kitchenette.

His father's eyes darted around the room, searching for her, and when he found her standing behind the bamboo bench he asked, in a childlike voice, "Are we eating yet?"

"We will, soon. Andrew's here. You've been looking for him since yesterday, remember?" she said, pointing across the living room to where Andrew stood right by the front door.

The old man's eyes lit up. "You came!" he cried.

Andrew smiled. "Yes, I did."

"He even brought dessert," his mother said. "Something his girlfriend made."

But his father wasn't listening. His eyes had returned to the TV screen.

"He does that a lot," his mother said as she opened a cabinet and pulled out a stack of dishes.

Ruth leaned her head against her grandfather's side, and the old man gingerly placed a hand on the girl's shoulder.

"I didn't know Charmaine baked," Rico said, taking a seat beside Carmina.

"Different girl. Her name's Nina," Andrew said.

"And this girl cooks?"

"She's a sous-chef."

"Sus-chef?"

"Sous. Assistant."

"That's French, isn't it?"

"He's blushing," his mother said, giggling as she set the table.

"If she can cook well, you should marry her."

"Thank you for telling him that, Rico," his mother said. "He's thirty-two years old."

"Oh, come on, Ma."

"It's true. Your dad and I won't be here forever."

"Mommy's right," Rico said, stretching an arm on the back of the bamboo bench before placing his hand on Carmina's shoulder. "Life isn't just about work."

"Marriage isn't for everyone," Andrew said, wishing he could wipe his brother-in-law's smarmy grin off his face. Perhaps Rico sensed this, for he gave a nervous laugh, turned to look at the food-laden table and said, "It smells delicious, Mommy."

"Andrew," his father said in a soft voice. Everyone in the room turned to the old man.

"Yes, Dad?"

His father's eyes lit up like a mischievous child's.

"The last time I saw you, you were drunk," his father said.

"When was this?" Andrew asked, alarmed.

"Before they brought me to the hospital," his father said, "You were staggering. Like this!" His father spread his arms and swung his head from side to side before bursting into a fit of giggling.

Carmina turned around in her seat to face their mother and asked, "He hasn't taken his pill yet, has he?"

"Which one?"

As Andrew made for the restroom, Carmina said, "The blue one, the one that controls his hallucinations. Don't worry, we'll go through all his pills later."

After relieving himself, Andrew switched on the sink faucet only to hear a dry whistle escape from its spout. Sighing, he uncovered the plastic drum beside the sink and used a plastic dipper to rinse his hands. He dried his hands on his mother's yellowed terry cloth towel and checked his phone. He had a new message from Nina: It'll just be a couple hours. You said so yourself. Take a deep breath. Don't kill each other! xoxo

Thank God she isn't here, he said to himself, before texting back, Hope everything's going well on your end. I love you. He kneaded his throbbing temples with his fingertips, looked in the paint-speckled mirror, blinked his tired eyes and stepped outside.

Lunch was the usual celebratory fare: chicken and vegetable pansit, fried chicken, vegetable lumpia, pork adobo, a bowl of wet, lumpy rice. Rico told jokes that Andrew had heard from his barber in Manila, praised his mother-in-law's cooking and was first to pass a dish when the old man wanted something. "Everything tastes good, Daddy?" he asked, and the wrinkles in the old man's face deepened as he smiled and nodded in assent.

When the sound of forks and spoons clinking against china filled the silence that fell upon them, Rico mentioned the recent news of a Filipina maid who had been raped and killed in Saudi Arabia. Andrew could feel himself wincing inside, especially when his mother, who had heard about the woman in the news, started describing the young lady's injuries. He was trying to think of something else in the news that could steer the conversation away from this gruesome police report, when Rico himself changed the topic by talking about his life in Saudi Arabia, where he had worked as a nurse for two years.

"It's burning hot in Saudi. I had to drink three gallons of water a day just to stay alive," Rico said, mixing the sauce of his pork adobo with his rice.

"Were there many Filipinos in the hospital?" Andrew's mother said, deboning the fried chicken on his father's plate as his father looked on.

"Yes Mommy, there were many Filipino nurses and doctors at the hospital where I worked. We're running their hospitals and building their roads. Those Saudis don't work at all, they just hire us to do the work for them."

Carmina raised her glass and said, "Rico told me a story about a truckload of toilet bowls. The Saudis didn't know what was in the boxes they were unloading, so they just tossed these boxes of toilet bowls out of the truck!"

"Imagine Mommy, a truckload of toilet bowls all gone to waste!"

So, you finally found your crowd, Andrew thought, using one of his mother's party napkins to wipe away the grease on his lips.

"At least in the Philippines, we all get a good education," his mother said. "They may have oil but we are educated."

Switching to English, Rico said, "At least in Philippines, we knows English!"

"Is that right?" Andrew asked, folding his napkin.

"Of course, yes! In Philippines, we knows English more!"

"Okay," Andrew said, his laughter nearly escaping his mouth as he spoke. His mother gave him a look of reproach from across the table. Carmina ate her food in silence, while her daughter twirled her noodles with her fork, humming a tune.

The old man had piled a mountain of rice on his plate, and he stared at it in bewilderment, muttering to himself as he clutched his fork and spoon. His mother put a hand on his shoulder and asked, "Would you like anything, Arturo?"

"Daddy, do you need anything?" Rico asked in a loud voice. "More meat to go with all that rice?"

"I think he heard you," Andrew said.

His father brushed off her hand, scooped a ball of rice with his spoon, pushed it near a piece of chicken and lifted the spoon to his mouth.

"I knew you could do it, Daddy," Rico said.

"No one said he couldn't," Andrew said, annoyance edging his words.

As though Rico hadn't sensed this, he turned to Andrew with a warm, guileless smile and said, "Say brother, you work at a luxury hotel, don't you?"

"That is correct."

"If you work at a hotel, relatives get discounts, don't they?"

Andrew drank up the last of his soda, raised an eyebrow and said, "Yes, that's one of our perks."

"Hey, Carmi, wouldn't it be cool to spend a night there?"

In a tired voice, she asked, "And when will we have the chance?"

"You could take leave. Or we could do it when you visit Manila for one of your doctors' conferences. Andrew can make it happen. Di ba, Andrew?"

With a fork, Andrew pushed the remaining pansit noodles on his plate into a pile. "I can extend my discount privileges to my sister."

"But Ruthie and I can come along too, can't we."

He met Rico's look and said, in a firm voice, "Just my sister and her family."

"Thanks," Carmina said, with an apologetic, seemingly commiserating smile. "We appreciate it."

"We weren't asking for anything else," Rico said, stabbing a chunk of pork with his fork.

"I was just making sure," Andrew said.

"Making sure of what, Drew?" Carmina said, putting down her fork and spoon.

He couldn't stand the pretense any longer. "I was making sure that he wouldn't abuse the favor. This hotel isn't just some roadside motel he can check his mistresses into."

Rico wiped his mouth with his napkin, tossed it beside his plate and said, "Carmi, do you want me to leave? Because it seems like your brother doesn't want me here."

"No, you sit down. This is your home too." She turned to Andrew with a scolding look and said, "Let's not fight. It's Dad's party, not ours."

He laughed, rolled his eyes and said, "You weren't even here when he needed you. And now that he's sort of well, you can be his doctor again, acting all concerned and sorting his pills."

"She helped too when you left," their mother said, while his father brought another piece of chicken to his mouth.

"At least Rico and I visited Dad in the center."

Andrew could hear his own voice rising as he said, "But I brought him there. I made all the arrangements."

"Well, thank you for that, but you could've also visited him while he was getting better. He didn't get one visit from you."

"I was the one who thought of visiting Daddy," Rico chimed in. "We were there for him."

"Yes, it was Rico's idea," Carmina added, giving Rico's hand an affectionate squeeze. "Without him, I wouldn't have gotten through this."

"I played Scrabble with your dad," Rico said, rubbing Carmina's hand with his thumb. "He's gotten really good."

"I beat him every time," the old man said, pointing his fork at Rico.

"That's true," Rico said, nodding. "He beat me fair and square."

"Of course he'd beat you," Andrew said, laughing. "You can barely speak English."

A look of disbelief crossed Carmina's face as she asked, "What is your problem?"

"Can I have dessert?" Ruth asked. Andrew's mother smiled at her and said, "Your tito Drew brought a pie for us. It's a special kind of pie, isn't it, Andrew?"

"But I beat him," his father whined, fear creeping over his wrinkled face as the room fell into a hush.

"Of course you beat him," Andrew said, in a voice that sounded astonishingly insincere. "You beat him on your own terms."

"I did, I really did," his father whined, and his face crumpled as a tear rolled down his cheek. Their mother rushed to his side, holding his shoulders as his body heaved.

"Look what you've done," Carmina said, as Andrew stared at his lap, too afraid to say anything more.

Andrew lay on the lumpy, sagging bed of his childhood room, waiting for sleep to come as he stared at the mildewed ceiling. He had raised his hands in surrender as he rose from his chair at the dining room table, claiming that the long drive up to Baguio had worn him down and that he wasn't himself. His mother had been rubbing his father's shoulders in an attempt to soothe the old man, and wouldn't look up when she said, "Drew, you need to lie down and rest. You can use your old room if you want to." He was too embarrassed to defy her after all the trouble he had caused.

He had looked inside his closet before going to bed and found his comic books, sweaters he had long outgrown and even his old school uniforms. Moth-eaten blankets formed an amorphous mass on the floor beside his bed, while his mother's old fashion magazines were stacked in a neat pile beside them. The entire room seemed to be covered in a film of dust, and his old comforter smelled of must and age. The kapok fibers used to stuff his pillow gave off a sour, aged scent as he turned to his side. He thought of the years that lay between his departure for Manila after graduating high school and this brief, upsetting visit. Years had passed since he lay in this bed, under these covers. His life had taken off in Manila, while time stood still in this room. He never spent the night at his parents' home whenever he came to Baguio, preferring to check into the Camp John Hay Manor whenever he had business in this town, so he could understand why his mother hadn't dusted and aired his room. What he couldn't understand was why his mother hadn't gotten rid of objects that were of no use to anyone still living in this house. Surely a poor kid could wear his old uniforms and sweaters, and a poor family could keep themselves warm during the winter months with just one of his fleece blankets. Her old *Vogue*s wouldn't bring her up to date with the latest fashions, and he was surprised to find that she hadn't given his comic books away to the newspaper-and-bottle collector who occasionally passed through their neighborhood. It was almost as if she had been waiting for her little boy to come back to his room. Perhaps she expected him to lock himself up, pull on a sweater, crawl under his blankets after a scolding – or beating – and console himself by reading about *Planet Opdi Eyps*, a land where monkeys wore human clothing and went on all sorts of adventures.

The cloud of strain he had left behind seemed to lift as silverware clinked against plates and the sound of laughter and conversation penetrated his closed door. His mother was offering Nina's marzipan for dessert and Rico volunteered to cut the cake into equal slices, claiming he was good at math. Slices were passed around and his mother remarked that the cake was good, while Ruth asked if she could have ice cream with her slice. He could hear the relief in his mother's voice as she said to the child, "Yes, you like chocolate ice cream, don't you?"

Carmina protested, saying that too much sugar would be bad for the child. But their mother brushed away her protests by saying, "It's only once in a while."

"You're spoiling her," Carmina said. Neither Carmina nor he had had ice cream when they were growing up. *Sugar is bad for you*, their mother used to tell them, echoing what their father used to say about dessert.

"I can indulge myself in a little spoiling, can't I?" their mother responded.

His muscles ached when he woke to the sound of dance music and the bored, nasal voice of a TV announcer rattling off a list of prizes: flat screen TVs, Samsung Galaxy Notes, washing machines, a year's supply of Surf fabric softener. He breathed in the smell of kapok as he rubbed his eyes. He checked his watch. An hour had passed; it was two in the afternoon. The heaviness in his head had lifted. He got up and checked his phone.

He had a text from Nina, sent an hour earlier. It's different when you're not around. I love you, it read.

After combing his hair, smoothing the creases of his shirt and putting on his shoes, he stepped outside. He saw his father standing at the dining table, fumbling with a knot on top of a bag of green mangoes as Ruth watched on.

"When I was just a little older than you," he said to Ruth, finally untying the knot, "we used to climb the mango tree of our neighbor's backyard and steal as many mangoes as we could before the old man who lived in that house chased us away with a bolo knife. When my father found out what we were doing, he gave me a good whipping!" He took one mango in his left hand and allowed the fragrant fruit to rest in his palm. Ruth grinned at her grandfather, perhaps expecting him to offer her a peeled mango. Andrew watched on, wondering why his father's tenderness had to skip a generation.

"Do you want to eat those mangoes, Dad? I can peel some for you," Rico called out from the bamboo bench, where he sat with Carmina. When his eyes met Andrew's, Andrew lifted a hand and said, "Sorry man."

"Apology accepted," Rico said, with a quick lift of the chin.

"I can peel these mangoes myself. Why, do you think I can't do it?" the old man said.

Upon hearing her father, Carmina sighed, put down what she was reading and approached the dining table.

"Mila, give me a knife," their father said, as their mother dried her hands with a tea towel.

"Mom, don't," Carmina said. Their mother glanced at her and then at Andrew, pursing her lips as she wrung the towel in her hands.

He repeated, "Give me a knife."

Andrew saw the sad desperation in his father's eyes and said, "Mom, give him a knife."

His sister stared at him in shock and hissed, "Have you lost your mind? You know he'll hurt himself."

Their mother backed away, like a frightened child. Andrew walked to the kitchenette, rummaged through the drawers and took out a knife. "He wants to peel his own mangoes," he said, turning to Carmina. "Let him do it." He took his father's free hand, pressed the knife's handle into his palm, closed his hand and stepped back.

His father whispered, "Thank you," and started slicing the top of the mango he clutched with his left hand, gripping the knife inwards, towards himself. A strip of green skin fell to the table, exposing the mango's firm yellow flesh. He set the blade against the edge of the mango's unpeeled flesh, sliding the blade to the mango's pointed tip. His wife took a plate from the dish rack and offered it to him, and he set the naked mango on the plate. Rico rose from the bamboo bench and approached the group that had gathered around the old man. He stopped beside Carmina, who took his hand and gripped it as she stared at her father in fear. The old man took another mango and sliced into its flesh, exposing a paler yellow underneath. He set this peeled mango on the plate and took another one. Ruth took a strip of green skin and licked its fleshy inside. Carmina snatched it from her hand, tossed it on the table and slapped Ruth's buttocks. As Ruth cried out, their father peeled his third mango, stripping it away and exposing a darker, wetter yellow. "This one's overripe," he declared, just as the knife slid from his grip, cutting into his skin.

"Now look what he's done!" Carmina said, rushing to her father's side and taking the knife from his hand.

Their mother was frozen where she stood and said, "I couldn't tell him to stop. He insisted."

Andrew put an arm around his father and pulled him close when he wailed in pain. "It's all right, Dad. At least you tried," he said, rubbing his father's arm, wishing his father could stop shaking.

Rico slipped into the bathroom and returned with bandages, scissors, cotton and alcohol. Dumping these on the kitchen table, he waved the women away, pulled out a chair and forced the old man to sit down.

Rico pulled a piece of cotton from the bag he held, and soaked it in alcohol. "Daddy, you should be more careful with knives. They can hurt you," he said, taking his father-in-law's hand and rubbing the alcohol in. The old man yelled and tried to pull his hand away, but Rico's grip was strong. "There, there. Don't do that. I know it hurts, but this is good for you," Rico said, in a sickly sweet, singsong voice. The old man's hand fell limp, and he shook with weeping.

Carmina shook her head, looked at Andrew, and said, "This is all your fault. What did you want to prove, anyway?"

"He needed to peel those mangoes on his own," Andrew said, meeting his father's teary gaze with a steady look. "That wound isn't deep. It's going to heal."

LEAVING AUCKLAND

Maya was fast asleep in her loft when Paolo rose from his air bed, his thin travel blanket falling away from his knees. The wind had pulled him from the depths of sleep – it was the kind of wind that sounded like a wailing child when it made its way into his dreams. Now that the brief warmth of summer had given way to the chill of autumn, this howl had become an insidious coming and going in his ears, reminding him that he wasn't used to this sound, that he was far away from home.

Although Maya's twin bed could fit them both, Maya struggled to sleep beside him, so they ended up buying an air bed for him early on in their relationship. Before going to sleep they'd lie parallel to each other in separate beds; him asking her about the dreams she had, her asking him if he was warm enough. Secure in his love, she fell asleep before he did, leaving him to ponder over the love he offered her. It was when she was asleep that his loneliness crept in, driving a wedge between them in the dark. In the morning, after every second night he spent with her, he'd fly back to Auckland, leaving her alone in the solitude of her Wellington apartment with the promise of his return.

He approached the window and put a finger between the venetian blinds, peering into the darkness at a city that slept. The Victorian houses that rose from the flanks of Mount Victoria glowed in the night, asserting their Englishness in the middle of the South Pacific. New Zealand was a blank slate to the builders of this city, a land one could fashion whichever way one wanted, and to Paolo, these houses spoke of an earlier time, a time from which he and Maya were far removed.

After he and Maya had made love in her loft for the first time, he descended her stairs, looking out her window and into the deepening summer night before exclaiming, "This is paradise!" From her loft, Maya laughed – she was a writer, unimpressed by clichés. She was used to this view and its foreignness, in the same way that she had become used to other views in other foreign cities far away from the land of their birth. Paolo hadn't even left his adopted land to visit her and yet these quaint Victorian homes – so different from his parents' squat bungalow in Auckland – taunted him with their permanence, with the stories they possessed but didn't tell. Tonight he felt as though he floated above these pitched rooftops, sailing above the wind that crashed into windows and howled through cracks that had been left unrepaired. As much as he tried to feel the ground beneath him as he walked these city streets, he felt as though he were invisible even to this town's ghosts.

In Maya's case, she had chosen to live on the fourth floor of a modern apartment complex, buying herself a nice view of the hills and houses. A view was all she needed, for she didn't intend to settle here for good. Paolo wondered how a person could ever feel at home in a place that one had no desire to claim as one's home – he guessed it was Maya's rootlessness that allowed her to live in a city where he felt adrift. He looked up at Maya, asleep in her loft, the grills of its banister fashioned like a net that cradled her from harm. She had lived alone, in too many foreign places, for too long. She was used to this solitude more than he was.

∼

"She's the daughter of my former boss in the Philippines," his mother had told him, after asking him to clean out his room for another guest. These people were always from the Philippines, and he always knew what to expect. They all showed up at his mother's doorstep, lost and bewildered in the new country, and his mother took on the task of helping them get their bearings. She made sure they knew the right word for a fancy kitchen implement or a part of the house, just so they remembered who they should listen to if they wanted to survive in this new land. She had been as clueless as they were when she had first arrived, but now she was in charge – and she wouldn't let any of these transients forget this. Paolo wasn't sure what grated upon him more, the authority his mother assumed when speaking to these new arrivals, or the deferential attitude her guests took on when dealing with her. Despite being teased for their ignorance, they all called her Auntie. His guess was that they couldn't help it – many of them had arrived in New Zealand alone and were seeking a surrogate mother to chastise them as they found themselves unmoored for the first time in their lives.

Paolo had been away from the Philippines for so long that he had become a foreigner to the ways of these guests, and he found himself unable to appreciate their servility when confronted with his mother's demands: to help rake up the leaves in the backyard, to wrap Christmas presents, to scrub the pots and pans. One guest had scrubbed the rubber coating off a brand new set of cookware, mistaking it for dirt. His mother found their ignorance entertaining, in the same way that she found their predilection for praying before meals and singing karaoke afterwards, comforting. None of these characters defied his mother's expectations, which was why she allowed them to sleep at her house. Their actions were too familiar and predictable to disrupt what seemed like a series of pre-arranged relationships. They were Filipino, they were newcomers, and they all needed her help.

"You don't mind letting her stay in your room, do you? She's a young woman who's coming all the way from Wellington – we can't allow her to just sleep on the living room couch." It was impossible to say no to his mother as she would have already formulated an answer for him long before she made the request. She treated these young women like her daughters, and they all slipped into the same role she had tailored for them. In her household, at the very least, they played the part: covering their bosom with their hands whenever they had to suffer the inconvenience of leaning forward in front of Paolo or his older brother, Brandon, or nodding their heads in agreement when his mother bemoaned the fact that Kiwis never went to church. They were all dalagas who guarded their virtue in the same way his mother held fast to her expectations of every woman who walked through their door.

"You'll take her to your salsa class too, won't you? Her parents are in the States this year and she can't afford to see them, the poor thing."

His mother was at it again, believing that a night of salsa dancing would make him seriously consider his mother's candidates for a future daughter-in-law. The last guest he brought to a salsa party – upon his mother's request – had fixed a frightened stare on his shoulder as he rested his hand on her waist and urged her to relax. He was puzzled when he started receiving texts from her the week after she returned to university, asking if he was free and whether she could visit him at the Mexican café where he waited tables and taught salsa classes. How could he tell her that there was nothing between them – that he was just trying to be nice to her because her nervousness around him made him nervous too? This was what many Filipino girls refused to understand: he gave every woman his all on the dance floor, but he had no interest in dating a Filipino girl. They all gave meaning to every touch they received, and while this kind of innocence likely appealed to men back home, he found it exhausting and pitiful.

But their new visitor from Wellington had an American accent and didn't speak in halting English, unlike her predecessors. She had lively, intelligent eyes and was unafraid to begin a conversation with him as he washed the dinner dishes. As she sat on a barstool before him, she talked about her journey by train from

Wellington, and remarked that Kiwis were as nice as – or even nicer than – Texans.

"Pardon me for saying this, but I never knew that Filipinos could live in Texas," he said, watching her pull back a lock of curly hair from her round, delicate face.

She laughed. "They're not all that bad. Not all of them are gun-owning Jesus freaks. Then again, I lived in Austin, the sane part of Texas."

His mother, by this time, was ensconced in the living room with a distant aunt who occupied the upstairs guest room. His aunt was a dour-faced woman from California whom he had never met before, whose cackling laughter was eerily similar to his mother's. They were reading jokes aloud from their smartphones about the new Miss Universe, a Filipina with long legs, slender arms and a German last name who nearly lost the title by accident after the contest's bumbling, overexcited host mistakenly named Miss Colombia the winner. Paolo didn't like this Miss Universe, perhaps because his mother seemed to like her too much for his taste.

"What do you mean by sane?" he asked the American guest. Her name was Maya, and she was nowhere near as tall and statuesque as this year's Miss Universe, but she expressed no interest in beauty pageants, and didn't seem to be the type to do so.

"You know what I mean. It's the reason you're afraid of Texas."

Even though her face had yet to shed the puppy fat of her youth, she gave off the confidence of someone who had lived overseas before and was no longer in awe of the foreign. Fear, he knew from experience, was often disguised as awe.

He brought her to the salsa class he taught the next evening and watched her gravitate towards the bar. She ordered a drink as he guided other girls through beginner moves. The confident worldly woman he had met at his mother's house the previous evening was now awkward and shy, and he wanted to pull her back into the swarm of happy dancing bodies to show her there was no need to be afraid. After dancing with some of the regular girls whose curves and rhythms he had already grown accustomed to, he took Maya's hand and guided her through the basic steps. She knew how to sway her hips, but she kept glancing at her feet, laughing nervously as he lifted her chin.

"Don't look at your feet. Connect with me," he said. Her lips parted as he said this, giving him the impression that she was a genuinely interested student. She was listening – or rather, her body was – and following his lead as he made ninety-degree turns and coaxed her into a spin. She relaxed into his arms as he dipped, then caught her at the end of a song. "I want to do that again!" she said when a new song came on. She was unguarded for a beginner, which was why she was picking up the moves so quickly.

"In a year, you'll be spinning on the dance floor," he said as they stepped aside to watch the after-class dance party unfold. She smiled in disbelief, and he wondered whether she had caught on to his flirting.

A word of Tagalog slipped from him as they walked down a narrow street to where his car was parked, and she reassured him as they climbed inside, that he could speak the language again if he wanted to. "You speak such good Tagalog, I'm envious," he said to her on the drive home, wondering how she could hold onto the grammar of the old language while speaking English without the usual trepidation of a new immigrant. He couldn't admit to her that he once spoke Tagalog fluently, but had been teased in school for his halting English. He had decided to release himself from all those familiar expressions and cadences of speech that were holding him back, preventing him from expressing his thoughts in the language of his new home. How had she mastered English without losing her footing in their native tongue?

"I had no choice. My parents brought me back to the Philippines when I was nine years old. I was forced to learn," she said, as they sped down the expressway.

"You mean to say you didn't grow up in the Philippines?"

"Well I did, but I spent my early childhood in the States."

"Your English is really good, you know."

She looked away from him, and a note of impatience crept through her soft voice as she said, "Thank you."

Everyone else was asleep when they arrived at his parents' home and before she withdrew for the night, he brought out a bottle of wine and asked if she wanted a drink. He wanted to know how she ended up in New Zealand and whether she had arrived in the country alone. She took a seat on a barstool and, allowing him to pour her a glass, said she had responded to a job posting for an English subject librarian at Victoria University of Wellington. She had done a master's degree in Information Studies at the University of Texas because she thought it would lead to a job in America, not realizing there were too many library science graduates in America and not enough library science jobs. "That's what you get for insisting on doing something that's related to what you love when America thinks that you haven't compromised enough. I should've become a nurse instead," she said, laughing.

Before the librarian's qualification, she had earned a master's degree in Creative Writing, which she explained was a worthless degree as far as finding a job in the States was concerned. "It helped me become a better writer though, and I'm mainly a writer. Being a librarian is just a day job," she said, tapping her palms on the countertop to rest her case. He asked her what she wrote.

"Fiction, mostly. I'm writing a novel right now in my spare time."

"About the Philippines, or America?"

"It's about the Philippines, of course. I write about home all the time." And with that, she smiled into her glass of wine and took another sip.

"And now you're in New Zealand," he said.

"It looked like a nice place to live when I researched it. Far away from the rest of the world. Beautiful. Easy to get a work visa, especially if you have degrees from a Western country."

"Your parents probably miss you." He had been with his parents when he left the old country, and oftentimes wondered whether he would have had the courage to leave the motherland if he alone had to make the decision.

"We talk every day. My mum's on Facebook," she said.

"At least you talk to her. I barely talk to my parents," he said. He was sure his parents were fast asleep and that he could say this aloud. "Well we talk, but we don't really talk, if you know what I mean."

"That's sad."

This was his first Christmas in New Zealand after his return from Argentina, and he needed someone to commiserate with him, more than anything.

"I talk to my parents all the time," she said. "I tell them almost everything."

"So how long have you been away from home?"

"Six years."

"That's an awfully long time for someone who's close to her parents."

"Yeah, but you get used to it," she said, playing with her wineglass. Her story was not unlike the stories of those who came to their house to seek temporary refuge, and he was deceiving himself into thinking she was different. He was sure she shared their reasons for being here, even if she wasn't reciting the same script. She wasn't talking about how much money she could make in this country or asking whether he knew more about securing permanent residency. The people who came to visit his parents clung to these questions as though they were life rafts that would carry them to safety. This girl, on the other hand, did not share their fears.

"Life's great back home, don't get me wrong. But when you're a woman and you refuse to be tied to a single place or a single person ... they just don't get it back home."

"Tell me about it," he said, filling her empty glass without her bidding. "You're a girl who's lived overseas for so long. If my mum was your mum, she would've told you to be careful."

"That's why I'm keeping my distance from your mum." She laughed, downed half of her glass and said, "I'm sorry. She's your mum."

"That's all right. I know who she is."

Later that night as she got up to leave, he stood in her way and kissed her, catching her off guard. They were both drunk, it was Christmas, an old year was coming to an end and soon – he was sure – he was going to move out of his parents' house. In a few days this girl would be leaving. Her hand rested on his back as her tongue encircled his, and when his hand grabbed her breast, she pulled away and whispered in the mother tongue, "That's enough for tonight. Off to bed now."

∽

He was going to visit her in Wellington, he repeated aloud as they drove past houses with grilled windows and dumpsters with graffiti swirls on their lids. He took Maya's small slender hand as they both fixed their eyes on the empty streets of West Auckland, reassuring her when she questioned him that he meant every word he said.

When she left for Wellington a day after Christmas, he added her on Facebook. She then grilled him over Messenger about the girl in his profile picture, and he tried to explain that Juliette was his former dance partner and nothing more.

Judith says she's your ex, Maya responded.

He had forgotten all about Judith – a family friend – and how she and Maya had sequestered themselves in the sunroom at his parents' Christmas party. As his mother and aunt took turns with the videoke microphone, Maya and Judith leaned towards each other on his mother's wicker sofa, their eyes growing serious the more they spoke. Maya had gathered her information from shy, mousy Judith whose sliver of a mother hovered behind her whenever she showed up at a party. How could Maya trust the word of a girl who had never left her parents' home and knew nothing about the world? Judith was nothing like Maya. Judith was a girl; Maya was a woman.

Those pictures were taken two years ago, and she was my ex by the time they were taken. I use them to promote my dance classes. You have to understand, we were dance partners too.

The picture had been taken in the streets of Buenos Aires at Juliette's behest, since she wanted to have pictures to show her future grandchildren that she was a dancer in her youth. They had broken up by this time but still danced together, and he was at her disposal for a favor such as this. If they could deceive onlookers into thinking that they were still together, it would be because they were professionals. After every dance, he and Juliette returned to being the exes they were.

But she's your ex, and you still had her pictures up when you added me.

Baby, just because we were dancing together, doesn't mean we had feelings for each other. I know that non-dancers don't understand this, but you have to understand, he texted, wishing he could say this to her in person instead of allowing his words to speak for themselves.

The photographer Juliette hired in Buenos Aires knew just when to capture a moment of unrehearsed intimacy between them. When they danced, they could lose themselves in each other, and he could forget – at least temporarily – that she was often a closed book when they were not dancing. In the end, he was just her dance partner who enjoyed the privilege of dancing with her and nothing more. In the photo he chose for his Facebook page, his lips hovered close to her collarbone. His eyes were closed and her face was turned away. Whoever looked at the photo would only see the gentle slope of her neck, and her upswept blonde hair.

Maya said she would think about meeting him. The morning after, they agreed to meet in Wellington.

∼

If Maya only knew what his relationship with Juliette had been like, she would understand that he would never want to go back to

Juliette. It only dawned on him when he started living with Juliette, that Juliette felt for him the way a master felt for their servant, which was why there was always an argument over an unwiped stain in the kitchen or a conversation Paolo wasn't meant to overhear. He thought that she would make his world bigger when, really, she made him feel small.

However, Juliette did make his world big, if only initially. Growing up with his parents, he had become accustomed to certain habits of living. It was when he started going out with Juliette that he saw how unpolished his parents were. She was the first girl he dated who pointed out his mother's domineering ways to him, and the first girl who corrected his father when the old man tried to impress her with his mistaken assumptions about the French Revolution. She liked good wine, good food and good music, and the more he brought her to his parents' house, the more he felt embarrassed by his parents' lack of manners. He was ashamed by how his mother couldn't care less about using the word "please" to turn a command into a polite request, and by how his father made loud sucking sounds at the table even in the presence of guests. As long as he remained tethered to his parents' lives, his future with Juliette was doomed. Juliette would play cool, registering neither disapproval nor amusement, making him wonder whether she was being polite, or whether she simply didn't care enough to be involved.

∽

After he had booked his ticket to Wellington to visit Maya, he felt the ties that bound him to his parents slowly loosening, allowing him to plan, again, for a future that neither of his parents laid out for him. If Maya could lay claim to her own life, so could he.

While Auckland's flat sprawl pushed the city's suburbs away from its center, allowing them to become sleepy New Zealand towns in their own right as soon as the Sky Tower disappeared from view, the hills of Wellington kept its neighborhoods close, gathering the city in one tectonic sweep around a pool of water. This wasn't Paolo's first trip to Wellington, yet the city's cramped geography had never struck him as intimate or accommodating until this visit. Maya said she would meet him at a bus stop in front of Arty Bees Books on Cuba Street, where her apartment was just a ten-minute walk away, and he wondered whether he would have caught a glimpse of her building from his plane when it made its abrupt, shaky descent.

The plane was shaking when we landed, Paolo texted.

It's the wind, Maya texted back as he rode the airport bus into the city center. It's what makes landing in Wellington so rough. But you arrived on a good day.

She appeared before him in a lacy summer dress, all dolled up and ready for their first date. Her eyes smiled behind her sunglasses as they walked down Cuba Street, their arms encircling each other's waists. "Do you like Malaysian food?" she asked. He said he didn't mind it, although he hadn't had Asian food in a long time. In the noisy, cramped restaurant where they found a table, she high-fived him, allowing him to bring her hand down to the tabletop where he stroked her manicured fingers. If all went well, he told himself, she'd be his before he flew back to Auckland.

Like many Filipino girls, she was shy, and he fondly remembered how they had kissed in front of her bedroom door at his parents' house in Auckland, and how she had whispered in his ear that she wasn't ready. Yet she had invited him to lie beside her in her bed that night, which was an indication – however slight – that she might soon be willing. A Filipino girl would never allow a man she had just met to go this far with her. Unlike the girls in New Zealand he had previously dated – none of whom were Filipino – Maya was the perfect combination of demure and daring.

As they stepped onto her apartment building's rooftop deck, he could feel himself breaking through the surface of a dream into the reality of an endless Wellington sky. By getting on a plane to visit this girl, he had released himself into the world. She pointed at the

Victorian timber homes built on hills that rose around them, while he watched a ferry entering the harbor, leaving a trail of foam in its wake. Although he knew little about this city, he was with Maya and with her, he was safe. He lifted her doll-like face towards his and kissed her, delighted by the fact that he was a head taller than her. He could lift her easily and swing her around if he wanted to. This he did, and her screams of delight rang above the city's rooftops.

He brought her back to the ground and squeezed her again. She pulled away, asking him if he wanted to see more of the city, and he pulled her back into his arms, saying, "Not so fast." Since he had traveled this far to be with her, he wasn't going to let go of her that easily. "We aren't in a hurry," he said, as she pursed her lips and looked at him with mock resistance. He could tell that she liked her independence, but he had to convince her that, in his arms, she was safe.

"How are your parents?" he asked, as they walked down Cuba Street, past galleries, restaurants and vintage clothing shops, in the direction of Oriental Bay.

"They're fine," she said, and after a silence added, "Actually my mother's not talking to me."

"Is it because of me?"

"It's because I told her about your Facebook pictures before you explained things to me. When I told her afterwards that I accepted your explanation, she stopped talking to me." She frowned. "Don't worry. She does that a lot."

Maya made it sound as though her mother's silence was easy for her to take, but how could it be when she was an only child living alone in a foreign land? He had never intended to isolate her from her family, and he could tell by the way her eyes darted away from him that she was putting on a brave face.

"She compared me to my cousin who took her husband back after he cheated on her. I told her I'm not my cousin." Her eyes mourned as she laughed. "I disappoint her."

"This is all my fault."

"No, it's not. It's my fault for telling them about our problems before we resolved them. You have pictures with other dancers, don't you? I told her that, but she said she hoped it wasn't just some lame excuse."

He hadn't lied to her, if he were to be honest with himself – when those pictures were taken, there was nothing between him and Juliette.

"How's your mum?" she asked, her face brightening up.

"She sends her regards."

"Wow," Maya said, laughing. "We can't escape her, can we."

"Yes we can," he said, draping his arm around her shoulder as they waited for a pedestrian light to change. "We've already gotten away," he whispered into her ear.

They spent the rest of their walk talking about his mother's new guests: Filipino construction workers involved in the Christchurch rebuild, who had left their wives and children behind in the Philippines, and whose collective loneliness hung over them like a cloud until his mother bought them a cartful of beer. One of these workers had gotten so drunk that he wandered outside and was found asleep underneath a tree the next day.

Paolo didn't hold it against Maya when she laughed at these stories – he wanted to make her laugh – but she turned serious as the conversation turned to his mother. "She may have been nice to those blokes, but she wasn't too nice to me. She asked if I came here because I wasn't making it as a writer in the States," she said, raising an eyebrow in annoyance. "And whether I got scholarships to study in the States because they like Asians, the way universities supposedly do here. When I told her I've published my work in the States, she just laughed."

He was familiar with his mother's put-downs, having been subjected to these himself after he chose to pursue dancing professionally, but he was caught off guard by Maya's story. His mother had probably sensed that Maya had a little more spirit than the other girls who came to visit them, and wanted to put Maya in her place.

"I didn't know that. I'm sorry."

"It was horrible. It would've been the worst Christmas of my life if it weren't for you."

"She's not normally like that with intellectuals, that I can assure you." They had entertained guests in the past who were professors in the Philippines, but these were older men and women whose titles alone insulated them from criticism. Maya's parents were professors, but Maya was young and perhaps in his mother's opinion, just a lowly librarian with grandiose aspirations. While his mother – a secretary at a not-for-profit – spoke about the professors in reverential terms, Maya was just a child to her.

"She probably thinks of you like her daughter, which is why she's giving you unsolicited advice. I know it sucks because she does that to me too."

She laughed. "And I'm making it worse by dating you."

He pinched her waist. "Come on, she's not here. We don't even have to talk about her."

His skin began to burn underneath the harsh sun as they made their way to the bay. They found an empty bench near a swath of sand where men and women sunbathed, while children holding their parents' hands waded into the water. "You're a lot like them," he said, gesturing with his head towards the half-dressed Kiwis roaming the beach. "You like the sun. A Filipino would run for cover."

"Because they don't want to be dark," she said, resting a bare arm behind his back.

"You're such a white girl," he said, laughing. Since she was wearing sunglasses, he couldn't tell whether she was insulted or amused by what he had just said. "You speak like an American, and you like the sun."

"And you like that?" she said, with an edge to her voice that he hoped to soften with flattery.

"You're the first Filipina I've dated," he said.

"How come?"

"You're just different," he said, brushing her hair away from her face.

"You probably haven't met that many Filipinas."

"I have. And they're not like you."

"So you've just dated white girls all this time?"

"Pretty much."

"I'm the opposite. I don't date white guys anymore."

"Why not?"

"Well, the ones who dated me had a fetish for Asian girls." She rested her head on his shoulder.

"If it's any comfort, a girl once called me her caveman." He didn't tell her which girlfriend this was – he was with Maya now, and it no longer mattered.

"Oh my God."

"And I've had the parents of my exes say things to me that weren't nice."

"I went on two dates with one white guy in the States. On our second date, he asked if I'd be working in a factory if I had stayed in the Philippines. He seemed to find it sexy."

"What the fuck."

She draped her arms around his shoulders and said, "It was horrible. It would've been worse if we had sex. He pressured me and I said no."

"You should be proud."

"I'm just glad I'm with you."

Their conversation at the beach had given them a sense of comradeship that could result in physical intimacy, if handled correctly. They returned to her apartment, and he sat at her kitchen table while she prepared some tea. He looked at the stairs that led to her loft and had an idea: he would sweep her off her feet – literally.

She hadn't yet finished her cup of tea when he rose from his seat and lifted her from her chair. She smiled as she relaxed into his arms, and let her hands rest on the nape of his neck. For a split second, he held her above her thrift store couch before making a turn for the stairs. A look of fear crossed her face as she asked, "Aren't we going for the couch?"

He grinned as he carried her to her loft. It was a romantic gesture, and she was probably impressed by his strength. He hadn't scared her – she was just surprised.

She allowed him to unzip her dress and then pull down her cotton panties, moaning loudly when he went down on her. She then looked away as he pulled on a condom. "What's wrong?" he asked.

She gave a start. "Nothing."

Had he known she was a virgin, he would've taken his time. It came as a surprise to him, after having heard her proclaim that virginity was a myth while lying in bed at his parents' house. After he failed to enter her, she turned away, cried and admitted to him that he was her first. As he cradled her in his arms, she called herself a freak, and he wanted to shake her for belittling this gift she had just offered him. "It's not a big deal," he said. "In fact, I'm honored."

"Really?"

Rather than being revolted, he found her innocence endearing. "Why wouldn't I be?"

She was, in the truest sense, his. She insisted rather vehemently that she wasn't saving herself for marriage. "I just wanted to do it with a guy I liked," she said. She had seen the world, and yet she chose him.

∼

Dancing had taught him that if he were to understand how to put a woman at ease, he would have to observe the way she moved. At the tango milongas he led in Auckland, too many men thought that leading a woman meant pushing her too far. Really, a good leader listened to a woman's body, connecting with her as he led her across the dance floor. Women insisted on dancing with him at the weekly milongas because he made them feel comfortable, and they all found him nice.

He had been unusually lucky with women, and he attributed this to his willingness to listen. Giving a woman what she wanted was all about earning her trust and becoming the partner she wanted him to be. He had learned over the years that women couldn't resist having a man who was at their beck and call. They brought their defenses down, clinging to him long after his love for them had expired.

While studying geography at university, he met Juliette at a university tango club. She knew exactly how he wanted to lead her, and her body moved as though it were a complete extension of his. Her eyes betrayed neither excitement nor disapproval as they danced and when they spoke afterwards, her smile was just enough to disturb the calm surface of her face without giving too much away. She had a foreign accent and when he asked where she was from, he learned that she was an exchange student from Belgium. "You're a good dancer," she'd said, in a low voice. She made it seem as though she rarely gave out these compliments, being a skilled dancer herself who had danced with many partners before. He could sense a connection between them, or at least the potential for one.

She had chosen New Zealand for her overseas year, she said, because it seemed so different from what she was accustomed to. For her, New Zealand's landscapes felt too breathtaking to be real. And yet his world – consisting of university, dancing and his home life – was small compared to hers. He was unashamed to throw himself at her feet, showing up at her dorm to deliver a bouquet of roses, engaging with her in conversations about Belgian and French culture whenever they went out for coffee after dancing. She seemed to enjoy the attention for she didn't turn him down, yet he could sense that she wasn't easily won over. Did she truly enjoy his company, or was it the attention he lavished upon her that she found difficult to refuse? With her he could never tell, but perhaps she would reveal herself to him once he won her over.

Even when they finally made love in her dorm room, she wore the same smile on her face that betrayed nothing except amusement. She looked into his eyes as he entered her, guiding him in, and gasped when he hit a sweet spot before letting out a soft, approving laugh. He had gotten this far with her, and all he needed now was for her to open up and take him in.

∽

"My father once said he was worried that I've lived overseas for so long, I've forgotten what it's like to be Filipino," Maya said, as they sat in a pizza parlor just outside her apartment building. This was on his second visit, and the drizzle outside cast a haloed veil over the busy stretch of Cuba Street.

"Do you think you have?" Paolo asked. She had left the Philippines as an adult, and while he could understand her desire to return, it was hard for him to know for sure if he felt the same way about their country of birth.

"Yes and no. When I lived with my parents for a year before coming here, I really felt like I'd changed. Things just weren't the way they used to be."

"When I first met you, you didn't seem Filipino at all to me."

"That makes me sad."

He took her hand, which fit snugly inside his palm. "What I meant was that you're different. If you were like the other Filipinas I've met, you wouldn't be as fascinating."

"How am I so different?" The look on her face wasn't confrontational, but her eyes sought an explanation.

"You're open-minded. You have your own opinions. Heck, you don't believe the things that Filipinos usually believe in."

"Like church?"

"Yes, like church. And saving yourself for marriage."

She smiled. "Why should I believe that crap?"

"See? You don't believe things simply because someone told you to believe in them."

She pursed her lips in thought and said, "Unfortunately, that's very Filipino, no?"

"But whenever I visit you, I feel like I'm coming home," he said, drawing her closer to him. In this city, only Maya could remind him why he was here. Her boxy, narrow apartment where they cooked meals, made love and talked about the motherland felt like home. Wellington, on the other hand, with its narrow streets and Victorian and Edwardian facades, served to remind him that it was impossible for him to merge his personal history with its stony, ancient geography. Auckland constantly reinvented itself, welcoming immigrants like his parents to redefine its bland sprawling landscape, while Wellington held fast to a sense of Englishness that failed to speak to him, no matter how long he had lived in this country.

"I mean that. I only want to be with you," he said.

She smiled at his hand and squeezed it back.

After they made love in her loft for the second time that day, she rested her head on his chest and said, "Tell me how you became a dancer."

He often surprised himself by how vividly he could remember his childhood. He told her about a time when he was five years old: he and other children of staff members at the University of the Philippines were made to sing and dance to "I Saw Mommy Kissing Santa Claus" at a staff Christmas party. He joked that the performance ruined his childhood, since he was unable to get the image of his mother kissing a white man in a Santa suit out of his head. However, he enjoyed performing in front of people and when his family migrated to New Zealand, he was often asked to dance at Filipino parties, where he quickly became a star.

He was socially awkward at school and struggled with his English for years, but whenever he danced – whether it was with a girl or in front of an audience – people quickly forgave him.

"It was the one thing I was good at," he said as they lay in bed, watching the drizzle outside turn into a full-on downpour.

"Sometimes I'm not sure whether it's a career or a hobby. I have to get a real job soon – use that qualification I earned at uni. No one can be a dancer forever. The body surrenders eventually."

"That's the same way I feel about my writing," she said. "I sometimes wonder whether it's a career or a hobby. But it keeps me connected to home which is probably why I keep doing it."

"But you still chose to live abroad," he said, fondling her breasts.

"I'm free here," she said, smiling. "I don't get judged for being an unmarried female writer here. But it's hard too. I get lonely a lot."

"I wish I could come home to you more often."

She kissed his shoulder. "You could move here if you want. But I'm not asking for that." Or maybe she was.

∽

He and Juliette had been perfect for each other on the dance floor. They could read each other's minds and their bodies spoke the same language. Together they joined dance competitions and his mother videotaped their performances, showing them to the never-ending blur of guests who came to them for food and company. Although his mother barely spoke to him, she shared his achievements with her friends as though they were hers as well. And they were, for her choice to move her family to New Zealand years ago had given him the freedom to pursue a life he enjoyed. Ashamed as he was to admit this, he was sure that without his mother, he would have been no different from the new immigrants who came to visit her. He would have studied nursing or a technical course back home, knowing how he could only gain admission into this country if he assumed a particular role.

After watching his dance videos, the women asked, "Are you involved with each other?", "How can you touch each other so intimately without having feelings for each other?" He couldn't give them any categorical answers since the relationship that had developed between him and Juliette outside the dance studio was difficult to define. They were dance partners, he told his mother's guests. Nothing more.

But when Juliette finally agreed to be his date at a Filipino gathering, he knew she was his – or at least she would be in the eyes of his relatives and friends. She wore a white pantsuit that was neither too formal nor inelegant, and she was cool but polite as he introduced her to the elders and his childhood friends. She ignored the men as they stared at her, and she treated the women with civility as she took the hands they offered her and quickly let go. They all stood at a respectful distance from her whenever she graced their gatherings. They were all too shy to initiate conversation or ask if she liked what she had just eaten (she always ate like a bird at these parties). There was little else to talk about with her, having always kept to their tiny community that nurtured petty grievances and shallow insular talk.

At the expatriate parties she brought Paolo to, he learned that introducing himself as a tango dancer to strangers always worked as a conversation starter. He lent a sympathetic ear to these expats from South America and Europe when they complained about the dearth of culture in Auckland. "There is so much natural beauty in this country," they all said, "but it's so lacking in culture!" When they learned that he and Juliette were dance partners, they all suggested that the pair visit Buenos Aires, the birthplace of tango. "So much corruption but so much culture," they'd say, proceeding to compare cities they had visited like gourmands comparing fine exotic wines. "Paolo isn't just my dance partner," Juliette told them. When she introduced him as her caveman, he laughed along with them, just to show that he could take a joke.

"Can't you see that she's just playing with you?" his childhood friend Daniw asked, after cornering him at a Filipino gathering that Juliette was unable to attend. Paolo and Daniw had been close friends since their years at a Catholic boys' college, having banded together with other Filipino boys for protection. But Daniw knew nothing about Paolo's current life, and was clutching on to the last vestiges of their shared youth by offering unsolicited advice. Daniw had never dated someone like Juliette and had never, in fact, expanded his horizons beyond the boxing classes he took at a West Auckland gym. So how was he to know what was good for Paolo? Perhaps Daniw knew deep inside that Juliette would never give him the time of day – what with his acne scars and his coarse guttural manners.

"You're just jealous," was all Paolo could say.

"Whatever you say, loverboy," Daniw said, rubbing his pudgy nose as though to relieve a deep-seated irritation. "But don't say I didn't warn you."

He expected Daniw to give him the cold shoulder when he called him two years later, having learned from Juliette that she had cheated on him with a coworker at a French café.

"I thought you ought to know," was all she could say to him before she left the apartment they shared for her shift. Left alone to contemplate her words, he punched a wall and broke a few knuckles. Daniw drove him to the hospital, and as Paolo sat beside his childhood best friend, he was unashamed to cry.

∾

"They're all children. Thirteen years old, twelve years old, three months old, all dead on the same day," Paolo said. It was a warm February day, and the cries of seagulls pierced the clear silence around them, reminding him of how far away they were from the city as he and Maya stood at the gate of a small cemetery on Somes Island, in Wellington Harbour.

"Sad, isn't it?" Maya said, leaning forward to get a closer look. "They came all the way from England with their parents just to die here." According to the placard, the island had once been a quarantine station where many new immigrants died of the Spanish flu.

"Disease often claims the most vulnerable," he said. "Imagine what their parents would've felt."

"If their parents survived."

"Yeah."

This was a cemetery for children, he realized, looking at the ages of the dead. Like them, he was a child when he arrived in New Zealand with his family. Although his journey did not end with his death, he began to feel a strange pang of envy as he stood before their graves, as though the end of his childhood deserved some form of commemoration. When he and Maya were at the supermarket the previous day, Maya asked him if he liked gummy bears. She said her father bought them for her all the time when she was a child growing up in the States. Paolo winced, remembering a bag of gummy bears that a kind uncle had given him as a parting gift to eat on the flight to Auckland. It was his first time flying, and he finished the entire bag of gummy bears on the plane before throwing up into a sick bag.

These children had tombstones, while all he had was the lingering medicinal taste of gummy bears on his tongue.

The island trail took them through swaths of native bush. "That's a native cicada," he said, pointing at an insect with green flecks on its back. Maya had never seen a cicada before, and let out a childish "Eww" before he nudged her towards the tree trunk where the insect was perched. He grunted, "What 'eww'? It's just a cicada!" then handed her a taupata berry, telling her it wasn't poisonous. When she hesitated, he popped one into his mouth to prove he wasn't joking. He plucked off a leaf from a kawakawa bush and asked her to chew it, to savor its smoky spiciness.

"Has your mum talked to you yet?" Paolo asked, as he and Maya rested on a bench, eating their packed lunch.

"Not yet," Maya said, before she bit into the chicken and avocado croissant sandwich that he had made for her that morning. "This is delicious, by the way."

"I feel so bad for driving them away."

She chewed on her food and said, "They don't know you, that's why. Once they meet you, they'll realize how wonderful you are."

She snuggled up beside him and rested her head on his shoulder. "She'll come around. I know from experience."

She was carrying on as though it didn't bother her at all, and yet a few days ago she had called him crying because she missed her mum. "I'll be there soon," he had said on the phone. "I love you." He was her family now, whether he liked it or not.

"They know I'm an adult. I can do whatever I like with my life."

"If only I was as brave as you."

"What do you mean?"

He laughed. "What I meant is that I can't imagine myself living alone like you, in a foreign country, and carrying on without hearing from your parents when you've been close to them for so long."

"Don't worry, it's just my mum. And besides, I have you."

"If only I could afford to come here more often, I would."

"Long distance is so hard."

"It doesn't have to be long distance forever. I know you said you could move to Auckland and find a job there, but it would make more sense if I moved here." He took a swig from his water bottle, swallowed and said, "I have to move out of my parents' house sometime."

"You don't have to do it for me."

"No, it's for me too. I have to leave Auckland sometime." He still felt like a foreigner in Wellington, but he trusted Maya to ease his transition. If she could bravely live alone, perhaps he too could make that final step away from his prolonged youth.

"We aren't like other Filipinos who are opposed to living together before marriage," he said.

Her face brightened. "You could teach dance classes here."

"Or use my uni qualification to get a job in government."

After finishing their lunch, they trekked towards the island's summit, where he asked Maya to tell him the names of the fog-capped suburbs of Wellington that he could see from their vantage point. In time, or after a few more visits, he would know which suburb was best for the life they were beginning to plan. But for now, they could behold the city from a distance, allowing the silence of the island to insulate them from the complications of the lives they had left behind. Maya had a life to return to in Wellington, while Paolo had her. Wasn't that enough reason for him to move to Wellington – to be with her? He tried to push his misgivings aside as he took her hand and led her back to the summit's flank, where a network of World War II bunkers had once been built in case of a Japanese air raid. When they found a cobwebbed room for themselves underground, he pulled off her T-shirt and sucked at her small, pert breasts. As his lips traveled downwards, he told himself that the woman he loved was giving herself to him on this island, whether or not he abandoned his life in Auckland to live with her in faraway Wellington.

∼

Fellow dancers in Buenos Aires would ask Juliette if Paolo was gay. He's not coming onto girls, they'd tell her as they sat in the outdoor cafés of San Telmo, expecting Juliette to demystify his behavior on his behalf. "He's not gay, he's my ex," she'd tell them. He sat beside her, watching her field their questions about him as though she were his keeper. Her Spanish was better than his, and he could trust her to explain their situation to strangers in simpler terms – like the fact that they still lived together because they were unable to afford to live in separate apartments with the money they had saved for this trip. He was relieved to think that certain important events in his life, like moving to a foreign country, were beyond his control. He doubted that he would ever have gathered the courage to travel to Buenos Aires alone, and he was glad that they had planned this trip months before they broke up.

When they were not taking lessons together from the masters of tango, he would wander alone down the cobblestoned streets of San Telmo, past colonial buildings, flea markets and outdoor cafés where tourists encamped. He'd drop coins in the hats of tango dancers who performed in the streets, wishing to be possessed by a similar passion when he danced with Juliette. He'd return in a taxi to the apartment he shared with Juliette when his feet ached and he could no longer walk. Juliette was respectful enough not to bring male visitors to their living quarters, but if he found himself sitting at their balcony as she turned into their street at dusk, he would oftentimes hear her low and sensuous voice forming endearments in French that were not addressed to him. He had come to Buenos Aires to learn passion, and instead found himself building a fortress around his heart as their apartment door clicked open and Juliette's footsteps, quick and officious, disappeared behind a closed bedroom door.

He was just an immigrant boy who thought he would never have the chance to leave Auckland, but here he was, in the birthplace of tango, watching the sun set over the ancient rooftops of San Telmo. And yet this beautiful city he had yearned for while living in Auckland remained out of reach to him, even as he learned its language, danced to its music, felt its cobblestones underneath his feet and ran his hands over its ancient stone walls. He did not belong here, no matter how much he tried. He began to wonder whether it was Auckland he was pining for. If he were to be honest with himself, he was unsure where home was.

∼

Two days after their trip to Somes Island, as he sat before a computer screen in Auckland to talk to Maya, he thought of how their plans ceased to frighten him when a pane of glass and hundreds of miles separated them both. On the phone, or on Skype, all she asked from him were words. And words, as they spilled from his mouth, revealed more about him than he thought they would.

She spoke about a friend who threatened suicide after losing her brother to Typhoon Haiyan, and he found himself – with no hesitation – admitting to her that he had tried taking his own life four years ago. "I went to jump off the Auckland Harbour Bridge, but I ended up just sitting on the ledge until the police arrived."

"Do your parents know about this?" she asked.

"They never found out," he said, "which is why it seemed easy to do. You know how Filipino parents expect their children to be the perfect sons and daughters, just because there are more opportunities here. Well, my life was never perfect."

"No one's life is perfect," she said, her eyes growing sad. "You're too hard on yourself."

It was a palatable portion of the truth that he decided to share with her, now that she knew his family's story quite well. He found it somewhat amusing to remember how he used to contemplate death in his room, his thoughts having nowhere else to go, only for him to step outside to see his mother lounging in the living room, watching one of her Tagalog telenovelas. "The lawn has to be mown," she'd call out to him the moment she heard his footsteps. No matter how much he wanted to leave his mother for good, she always had a way of dragging him back into the life she had built for him.

On a warm December afternoon, he had parked his car at one end of the Auckland Harbour Bridge and walked down its footpath, until he had a full, expansive view of the sea. As he rested his arms on the railings, trying to look as inconspicuous as possible to passers-by, he wondered how difficult it would be for rescuers to find his body if it sank deep into the waters below or was eaten by sharks. Would his parents find a body to bury, or would they just have a tombstone for his name?

He had lifted himself up to the ledge, imagining his parents waiting on the shore as rescue teams combed Waitematā Harbour for signs of life, his mother wailing as they carried his waterlogged body towards her. The night before, he had imagined a calm, forgiving sea taking him back into its warm and watery womb. Perhaps his body, if it truly belonged to the water, was never meant to be washed ashore to then be buried beneath the ground. As he took a seat on the bridge's railing, the sea below churned, and container ships arriving from Sydney and other faraway cities sailed beneath him as he found himself unable to lose his footing in life.

It took an hour before the police came to pick him up. A stocky Pacific Islander constable drove him home, lecturing him throughout the trip about how Jesus had died on the cross for him and how all his problems could be solved if only he turned to the Lord. When they stopped in front of his house, Paolo waited in his seat, expecting the officer to walk him to the door and talk to his parents. But perhaps it was a busy night for the officer, for he turned to Paolo and said in his thick South Auckland accent, "Now you're in charge. Go and tell your parents what happened. I'm sure you'll do the right thing."

Inside his parents' house, his father was telling a story about his exploits as an army sergeant in the Philippines to a small gathering of guests. It was all his father had to talk about, having only reached the sixth grade before leaving his hometown in the mountains to join Marcos's army. His mother's smile was impatient yet tolerant as she sat in an overstuffed chair, having heard the same stories at every gathering where she gave her husband free rein to speak.

She glanced at Paolo when he stepped into their house. She said to her guests, "This is our son, Paolo," as the crowd of shy old men in leather jackets lifted their heads and nodded at him. "Have you had anything to eat? There are dishes in the sink. Can you take care of them?"

Paolo ran hot water over a pile of dirty dishes, which could have been the same pile of dirty dishes he had washed a few nights ago, and realized that as long as he lived, his mother's heart would remain unbreakable.

A few months later, he met Juliette.

Paolo's brief stint as an expatriate with Juliette in Buenos Aires had emptied his savings account. His parents weren't happy about his decision to live with them again, but nor were they upset. They were Filipino, after all, and many Filipino sons lived with their parents way into their adulthood. With them, he could live his life whichever way he pleased, leaving early for his job at a café in the CBD, coming home late at night from a salsa party or a tango milonga. He could avoid arguing with his father and being available when his mother needed a favor from him. Their relationship with him had always been quiet and distant, and he was amazed at how little had changed. There were chores to do around the house but otherwise they respected his privacy, as they always had.

To the women he met in dance studios and Mexican bars across Auckland, he was a darling who banished their nervousness as soon as he placed his hand on their waists and smiled into their eyes. They all loved him, even if all he gave them was a single dance until they met again on the dance floor. Only Maya could make him come home early in the evening, pulling him back into a house whose inhabitants tolerated his presence without asking for much in return. As Maya sat alone in her apartment in Wellington, waiting for his Skype call, he extricated himself from this crowd of adoring women, speeding down the expressway alone at night to meet Maya in his room, in front of a computer screen. Without the blare of Latin music filling his ears or the warmth of a woman's thigh as it brushed against his, he was a man confronted by the silence of his own thoughts, a son who had little else to offer aside from his presence in his mother's house.

Why did Maya depend on him, of all people, to quell her loneliness? There was not much he could offer her aside from his promise to return, and she held onto this promise like a prisoner awaiting probation. "When are you coming here?" she'd ask, draping her Chinese silk robe on her bare shoulders after having stripped and touched herself for him. He found it touching, the way she purchased lacy lingerie for these occasions; the way she parted her silk robe, baring the gold necklace that he gave to her on Valentine's Day at a time when he believed that she was his ticket to freedom. Tethered to him by the neck, she asked him what he wanted to see, what he wanted her to do to herself. She seemed more and more like an imprisoned girl who performed sexual favors for him in exchange for the keys to her cell. As he reached orgasm with his hand, his guilt exploded before his eyes when he saw how he had exploited a lonely, naked girl who shivered as she dressed, complaining about the autumn cold.

Perhaps she too was unsure of their future, and yet she awaited his calls, his visits. He didn't deserve her love and yet there it was. He contemplated the silences that followed their calls, trying to make sense of the uneasiness he felt as their relationship progressed. He could talk to her about anything, yet when their calls ended, he felt smothered by her hopes. As he put away his laptop and switched off his bedroom lights, he pictured Maya climbing up the steps of her loft bedroom, her faith in his love strong yet unproven.

In his tiny bedroom in Auckland, he lay in bed, and the silence of Maya's apartment in Wellington filled his ears, overwhelming the sound of cicadas outside his window. He had pictured himself leaving Auckland for good the first time he visited her in Wellington, but what he didn't imagine back then when he saw a life with her, was the constant state of exile she had learned to accept.

She was not in love with New Zealand. Although he knew that her bitterness stemmed from an accident she had a few months after she arrived in the country, he thought it was rather unfair of her to blame every Kiwi she met for what had happened. *It was just one stupid driver who made the mistake of turning into a street as she was crossing it*, he said to himself, but she seemed to believe that it was New Zealand's responsibility to shoulder her personal pain. "They're racists," she'd say to him, after claiming that the policemen who investigated the incident told her that she was to blame for what had happened. *Is that really what they said?* he wanted to ask her, pursing his lips as the question crawled towards the tip of his tongue. *Try going back to the Philippines,* he also wanted to say. *At least in this country, they'll pay for your medical expenses.*

He often wondered if she derived a perverse sort of joy from peeling away the scabs of her wounds to re-expose her hurt. Her mind would return to the past, as though searching for something she had dropped on the ground during the time of the crash. Perhaps it was a detail that would give her closure, or an artifact from her previous life. Whatever she was looking for, he didn't have it on him. She had survived, he wanted to tell her, and although her injured knee seized up every once in a while, she hadn't lost her life. What was there to reclaim, if she had lost nothing?

A text arrived just a day after he had decided to give himself a break from their Skype conversations, thinking that if these provided no clues as to whether he could leave Auckland to be with her, he would have to search within himself for answers. I don't feel safe, her text read, after he had eaten breakfast. Kiwi drivers are so reckless. I have to cross the street every day here, and every day I feel afraid.

He had lost patience with her, and texted back, I know how it feels to survive a traumatic event. When I was beaten up a few years ago, I kept looking over my shoulder afterwards. But it's unfair to blame all Kiwi drivers for a mistake that one stupid driver made. I know it hurts but don't make it worse for yourself.

Experience had taught him that forgetting was often the only way to recover. But now he had made himself her enemy and she wouldn't be silenced. She battered him with messages, comparing Kiwi drivers with American drivers, complaining about how traffic rules in New Zealand privileged drivers over pedestrians and about how the police had told her that she was to blame for what had happened to her. He realized that there was only one way to appease her, and it was by giving her express permission to open her wound fully to him. Something inside her was festering, and although he was tempted to look away, she would never forgive him for doing so.

When she answered his call, he asked her how she was and told her that she could tell him anything. This was her story, not his, and he was relieved that this duty required little of him aside from lending an attentive ear. There was hesitation in her voice, as though she had been brought to shame by his kindness. She started at the very beginning, on a rainy evening in June, when a black car turned into the street she was crossing and stopped when she raised her hands and screamed. He had heard this story before but could hear the anguish in her voice this time, the powerlessness of her scream as the man behind the wheel decided not to see or hear her, but to drive straight into her. She fell on the car's bonnet and then fell onto the ground when the car reversed. The driver was a gray-haired, businesslike man who pulled over and got out of his car, asking if she was all right. His car was brand new and he was wearing a nice winter coat. As soon as he approached her, the bystanders who had helped her up started chastising her for not being careful enough, as though they knew automatically who to side with. A girl who had asked her if she was all right glanced at the driver, took a second look at her and said, "It's fifty-fifty, you know. Both of you are at fault."

She had expected the police to be more compassionate, but instead of allowing her to recount her version of the incident when they took her statement over the phone, they fed answers to her, as though they had already drawn their conclusions about the case. "The car was five meters from you when you stepped off the pavement. Is this correct?" the constable asked her before she could sift through her memories. Later, a senior officer would scold her when she spoke of her injuries, silencing her by saying, "Don't call yourself a victim. You're not a victim. You should've been looking."

Hours later, she would receive a call from a man who identified himself as "the driver" asking her if she was all right. When she told the man on the phone about the nightmares she had, the man giggled and said, "What I meant to ask was whether they found injuries on you when they brought you to hospital. Injuries on your body, I mean."

She went to the police station the day after receiving this call, demanding an explanation, only to be told, "We aren't obligated to protect your details because you're not a victim. Didn't we tell you that you and the driver are equally at fault?"

Paolo remembered the night he had been mauled outside a bar in South Auckland. He had never thought of reporting the incident to the police, for what was a Filipino boy doing late at night in a neighborhood infested by Islander gangs? To the police, there were no distinctions to be made between him and the men who robbed him and left him for dead – they were all troublemakers who happened to pick a fight with each other in a neighborhood where brown boys picked fights with each other all the time. He hadn't put much thought into his decision not to go to the police but as Maya's voice broke, he realized that while he had lived in New Zealand long enough to accept his invisibility, Maya – a newcomer – had not yet come to terms with this difficult truth.

The police station's superintendent – whom Paolo imagined to be a smug, avuncular, gray-haired Kiwi – insisted on meeting Maya for coffee after he had been forced to issue an apology on behalf of the junior officer who had given her number to the driver of the car. At the university coffee shop where they agreed to meet, the officer grinned when she complained about how the police had taken her statement. He bought her a flat white and commiserated with her before adding, "Since you're equally at fault for what happened, you are liable to the driver in case his car sustained damages."

"My God," Paolo said, feeling sorry and angry all at once.

"They didn't care," she said, as she began to cry. "My life didn't matter to them at all."

"It all makes sense now."

"I'm sorry for blaming it on New Zealand. It's your country."

"Come on, you didn't make me feel bad at all. I just thought at first that you were being unfair to them. I'm not a Kiwi, all right. Just because I grew up here, doesn't mean I'm Kiwi." He oftentimes said this in the company of his European expatriate friends who called Kiwis uncultured and unsophisticated, but with her, he said it with pride.

"But you've spent almost your entire life here."

"That doesn't mean I'm Kiwi," he said, knowing that with her, he could always come clean. "I don't mean that in a bad way, but I can't call myself a Kiwi."

"I'm glad you didn't break up with me over this," she said, cheering up.

"Why would I break up with you over this? You have a good reason for being angry." He thought of how living alone made a person's mind return to the wounds of the past, to the source of the mind's unresolved pain.

"Don't hesitate to call me if you need someone to talk to."

"I love you," she said, in a voice full of gratitude. Among all the women he had dated, only Maya could make him believe this.

"I love you too."

At least he had listened to her story, which was all anyone could do.

∼

Paolo had spent so much time postponing his trip to Wellington that he felt chastised by the cold air when he stepped through the airport's sliding doors on a windy morning in March.

Maya was coughing when they met outside her apartment building, and in the lift she complained about how the sudden change in weather had made her sick. He had arrived at a bad time.

"You should be taking care of yourself," he said, as he dropped his bag on the floor of her unit and allowed her to lean against his chest.

"But I wanted the apartment to be clean before you arrived." Sure enough, the apartment was clean, except for the flip-top lid of her rubbish bin that bore traces of food. Hadn't she noticed this? She coughed into a crumpled tissue and said, "I'm so sorry that I'm sick. I ruined your weekend."

"It's good that I'm here so that I can take care of you." He waited for the tenderness he once felt for this girl to return to him, but he had postponed this trip for so long that he felt as though he were holding a stranger in his arms.

As he peered outside her window, he saw the same Victorian houses he had seen in the middle of summer, a cold autumn light defining the sharp edges of their turrets and peaked roofs. A gale whistled through her window, making her building shake. "This building is safe, isn't it?" he asked.

"It's earthquake-proof," she said, matter-of-factly.

He found himself yearning for space inside her small apartment as he helped her prepare lunch. He had never felt this strange about his previous visits, but today he felt as though he had wandered into this woman's apartment in this strange city without any particular purpose in mind. If there was a question he had meant to ask her during this visit, he had forgotten what it was. She was likely unaware that the question ever existed.

But he played the role of the dutiful boyfriend because he didn't know how else to pass the time. As far as she was concerned, he was keeping her company, buying groceries and medicines for her, scolding her for not wearing a scarf to protect her neck from the cold wind, asking her at the Vietnamese restaurant to finish her pho. Just one more day, he said to himself, and he'd be back in Auckland.

On the afternoon before his departure, she put her arms around him as they sat in her bed, and said, "I miss you."

"But I'm here."

"When you're here with me, I think of how you're going to leave me, and it makes me sad."

He laughed, unable to muster an answer that would satisfy her.

"That's what my mother tells me whenever I visit her," she said, resting her head on his shoulder.

He thought of the silence he left her with whenever they parted, a huge, cavernous silence that haunted him as he lay in bed in

Auckland at night. He wanted to deserve her love, even if he had none of her strength.

This was a life she had chosen for herself, a life of changing addresses, in which one had to believe in the future, despite one's missteps.

The southerly winds kept him awake as Maya fell asleep that evening, secure in her belief in his capacity for love. He rose from his air bed, allowing his travel blanket to fall away from his knees. There had been a time when he felt safe with her, when he believed that her love alone would carry him away from Auckland, away from his parents and their unchanging expectations. He peered outside her window at a city that had grown familiar to him without shaking off its foreignness. It was wrong of him to expect Wellington to warm up to him when it faced the southerly winds, as though wishing for self-annihilation.

He pulled himself away from her window and returned to bed. He closed his eyes, listening to the wind's howl. He was a child again, lying in bed inside his parents' house in the Philippines as typhoon winds whipped their city, downing powerlines and slapping rain onto windowpanes. The walls of his family's house were thin, and their roof could be blown away if the winds were strong enough. In Auckland, he had found himself missing those cold windy nights back home, in which he imagined himself in a ship that rocked back and forth in the middle of a storm. After they left his childhood home in the Philippines forever, he would never feel as safe.

He envied that child who was unafraid of the wind's relentless howling.

NOTES ON THE TEXT

Comprised of many regional languages, Filipino is the most commonly spoken language in the Philippines. The stories in this collection richly reflect this harmonic blend. Below are the Filipino words peppered throughout *Love and Other Rituals: Selected Stories*, and their meanings, as agreed with the author.

adobo – a stew-type dish typically made with chicken or pork and other staple ingredients like soy sauce, bay leaves, peppercorns and garlic

aktibista – activist

anak – child

aswang – a Filipino mythical creature (similar to a witch)

ate – older sister, but also used to mean older female

baklas – plural of "bakla", meaning gay or a homosexual man

barkada – a group or gang of friends

bolo – a type of long or jungle knife, similar to a machete

caldereta – a beef stew cooked with tomato sauce. Various vegetables are included in this dish such as potato, carrots, bell pepper and olives.

dalagas – plural form of "dalaga", meaning young maiden

delicadeza – no finesse, tact or refinement

di ba – "isn't it"

don/donya – a term to address a person who is wealthy or perceived to be wealthy. Don is masculine, donya is feminine.

hay – the sound of a sigh

hay naku – a common phrase someone uses to sigh in exasperation, such as "oh my goodness!"

hija – daughter

ikaw naman – "oh come on"

inutil – incapacitated (in the context of "Maricel")

itaktak mo – shaking while pouring until nothing is left (the lyrics of a popular song)

kabarkada – a member of a group of friends

kuya – older brother, but also used to mean older male

lang – only or just

lolo/lola – grandfather/grandmother

longganisa – a local sausage or chorizo

lumpia – a type of Filipino spring roll filled with various ground meats and mixed vegetables

malunggay – moringa, a plant native to parts of Africa and Asia

manananggal – one of the best-known mythical creatures in Filipino folklore

manang – title for older sister in Ilocano, one of the regional languages of the Philippines

mang – a familiar title of respect for a man

matangos – pointed

na ba – "na" means now or already; "ba" signifies that the preceding word/phrase is asked as a question

naku – "oh my". An expression of shock, disappointment or anger.

naman – a word to emphasise the phrase surrounding it

na rin – too or as well

ow – an expression someone may use when they are distracted

pamangkin – a genderless term that means niece or nephew

pandesal – a soft, fluffy, slightly sweet bun

pansit – a general term for traditional stir-fried noodle dishes in Filipino cuisine. There are many types of pansit based on the type of noodles and ingredients used.

payaso – clown

po – a word of respect used when speaking to someone older

pok-pok – a colloquial name for a sex worker or somebody (usually female) who is sexually promiscuous

punyeta – a vulgar expression of frustration. When directed at a person, it is like calling someone an asshole.

punyetang puta ka – "fuck you, fucker"

puta – whore. A term of abuse.

sari-sari – variety

sayote – also known as chayote or choko, an edible plant from the gourd family

senyorito/senyorita – master or young gentleman; little miss/mistress or young lady

sige – okay

sinigang – a soup or stew defined by its sour, savory flavor; tamarind is often a key ingredient. This dish is served with various proteins.

sipa – a traditional sport similar to kick volleyball

sus – "oh my gosh". Derived from the phrase "susmaryosep", which is a shortened form of "Jesus Mary Joseph".

taho – a street dessert made with silken tofu, simple syrup and tapioca pearls

tama – correct

tampo – distancing oneself due to offense or dislike

Tanduay – a brand of local rum in the Philippines. A Tanduay girl calendar is a calendar with provocative pictures of women promoting Tanduay products.

telenovela – a general term for soap operas, whether Filipino or foreign

tinola – a chicken dish cooked in a ginger-flavored broth. It is often made with sayote, green papaya and either moringa or green chili leaves.

tito/tita – uncle/aunty

ulam – a meat, seafood or vegetable dish accompanied by rice

yaya – nanny

PERMISSIONS

Permissions have been obtained to reprint the stories in this collection, which first appeared in the following publications: "The Feast of All Souls" in *The Masters Review*, "Love and Other Rituals" in *Thin Noon*, "Playing With Dolls" in *Day One/Amazon Publishing*, "Stopover" in *Five Quarterly*, "The Autumn Sun" in *The Philippines Free Press*, "Maricel" in *The Fictioneer*, "Inheritances" in *Your Impossible Voice* and "Leaving Auckland" in *failbetter*.

ACKNOWLEDGMENTS

They say it takes a village to raise a child, and in my case, I have benefited from the generosity of many villages in many different places who helped me find my voice as a writer, and who have provided the time and support necessary for me to develop the stories in this collection.

None of this would have been possible without my father, the late Francis C. Macansantos, a poet, fiction writer and essayist who was my first writing mentor. Unlike many writers and artists who see child-rearing as a hindrance to their art, you understood how important it was to welcome me inside the sacred space in which your poetry came forth into the world. When I started expressing interest in literature and writing, you were not discouraging at all, but recognized this light within me that had to be nurtured and cared for. You set the highest standards for my work while also being my biggest fan, and your faith in my gifts gives me the fortitude to withstand the challenges of a brutal business. You live on in my work and in the life I have created for myself, Papa – thank you.

This book would not have completed its journey to publication without my mother's tireless faith and support. My mother, Priscilla Supnet-Macansantos, always believed in a world that had a place for the stories I wished to tell. I would like to thank her for sustaining all the nurturing spaces that have enabled me to continue creating. Thank you, Mama, for reminding me that writing is a real job, and that my life is not wanting as it is.

I began writing fiction in earnest thanks to Jose "Butch" Dalisay's undergraduate fiction workshop at the University of the Philippines Diliman, which he steered with a firm but compassionate hand. It was his openness and generosity as a mentor that allowed me to truly fall in love with the art of storytelling, and to trust that voice inside me that wanted to tell all these stories about the places where I have lived. Emil Flores, Celeste Flores-Coscolluela,

Carlos Aureus, and Paolo Manalo of the University of the Philippines Diliman also served as caring and compassionate mentors to the young and insecure writer that I was.

Most of the stories in this collection were written during my time at the Michener Center for Writers at UT-Austin, which will always have a special place in my heart for opening doors that I once could not imagine walking through. I owe a huge debt of gratitude to James A. Michener, whose generosity of spirit has enabled emerging writers like me to enjoy three years of fully funded writing time in a nurturing and supportive environment. I would like to thank Elizabeth McCracken, Michael Adams, Jim Magnuson and Oscar Cásares for taking a gamble on me, and for continuing to believe in my talents even when I struggled. Thank you to Elizabeth McCracken for your life-changing wisdom and sustaining faith, for being one of the strongest advocates of the first good story I wrote for your workshop, "The Feast of All Souls", and for making me feel so welcome in your office that I could talk about anything and everything for hours on end. Thank you to Michael Adams for your gentle and fatherly mentorship, which trained me to read my own work with diligence and care. Thank you to the other wonderful mentors who have played a pivotal role in my career: Allan Gurganus, Brigit Kelly, Anthony Giardina, Tomaz Salamun, Cristina Garcia, Gabrielle Calvocoressi, Margot Livesey. The varied perspectives you all provided me for navigating the long and difficult path of creativity will always remain valuable to me. To my classmates, friends and comrades in arms, including Greg Marshall, Chad Nichols, Mary Miller, Antonio Ruiz-Camacho, Jeff Bruemmer, Brad Kelly, Chanel Clarke, Matt Moore, Iheoma Nwachukwu, Alen Hamza, Hsien Chong Tan, Fiona McFarlane, Karim Dimechkie, Leanna Petronella, Brian Oglesby and Sarah Saltwick: many thanks for carefully reading and responding to my work, for the shared laughter and stories over drinks, and for the sense of belonging that has continued to sustain me in our lonely profession.

I would also like to express my gratitude to the International Institute of Modern Letters at the Victoria University of Wellington for continuing to provide me with the funded time and support I needed to continue honing my voice. Damien Wilkins, you are one of the sharpest and smartest readers I have ever had – thank you for your clear and incisive comments on my novel, and for giving me the time and space for my writing to mature. Thank you too for allowing me the time to work on "Leaving Auckland" even if this wasn't part of my PhD project. I am grateful to the community of writers surrounding me during my time at the IIML, for the friendship, conversation and laughter, as well as for the care with which you have handled my work and given feedback: Peter Cox, Justine Jungersen-Smith, Nikki-Lee Birdsey, Kate Duignan, Miles Fuller, Airini Beautrais, Gigi Fenster, Catherine Robertson, Therese Lloyd. To my Aotearoa bff, Whitney Cox, thank you for the play and movie dates, and for all the lengthy and meaningful conversations about books, life, writing and exes while walking around the Botanical Gardens or eating at Royal Thai and Little Penang. Laura Borrowdale, thank you for reaffirming my belief that sex has a place in literary fiction. Bekky Thorne and Brendan Daniel Sheridan, thank you for keeping in touch long after I had left New Zealand. Thank you to Chris and Margret Cochran of Wellington, New Zealand, who generously lent me their cottage in beautiful Martinborough for two self-directed mini-residencies. Thank you to Aotearoa, New Zealand, for your inspiring landscapes and people that have made their way into my work and heart and will remain there for years to come.

Just when I thought I would not have a place to stay in Austin, Texas, Arnold and Prescy Ornido generously welcomed me into their home, and together with Rela Manigsaca, helped me find lodgings that were conducive to creativity. In Wellington, New Zealand, the Zabala family went above and beyond the call of duty to help me get settled in. Wherever I have lived in the world, the

Filipino community has always been there to assist me in building and sustaining a home away from home.

I would not have had the fortitude to withstand the challenges of a writer's life if it were not for the early encouragement and support of editors who selected my work for publication in literary journals. I would like to thank Lauren Groff, who chose "The Feast of All Souls" for inclusion in the inaugural volume of *The Masters Review*, as well as Kim Winternheimer for her helpful feedback and edits; Morgan Parker at *Day One*; Hadley Sorsby-Jones and the team at *Thin Noon*; Thom Didato and the team at *failbetter*; Vanessa Jimenez Gabb, Crissy Van Meter and guest editors including Patty Dann who chose "Stopover" for publication in *Five Quarterly;* Lynsey Morandin and Madeline Anthes at *Hypertrophic Literary;* Keith J. Powell and Stephen Beachy at *Your Impossible Voice*; Paolo Manalo of the *Philippines Free Press*; and the team at *Unsolicited Press*. Special thanks to Jaroslav Olsa for selecting "The Autumn Sun" for translation into Czech. My immense gratitude to *Glimmer Train* for recognizing "Leaving Auckland" and "Stopover" with finalist and honorable mention, which gave me a huge morale boost early on in my career. Thank you to Keith J. Powell for nominating "Inheritances" for *Best of the Net*, and to the team at *Longform* for featuring "Stopover" as an editor's pick. I am also indebted to Cirilo Bautista of *Philippine Panorama* and Krip Yuson of *The Evening Paper* for being early endorsers and publishers of my work.

I could not be more grateful to Sybil Nolan and Katherine Day at Grattan Street Press for picking out my manuscript from the slush pile and connecting with it in the most beautiful way possible. Just when I thought that this book would never live in the world, you reminded me why these stories matter, and why they should reach the widest audience. Sybil, you are the first person who told me that you read the book twice, and hearing that from you made my heart sing. Thank you to the editorial team at Grattan Street Press for reading and editing my work with so much care and attention, for lending an attentive and compassionate ear when I came to you with my own suggestions and concerns, and for making these stories so much better than when they first came to you.

I am indebted to the artists' residencies that provided me with the restorative gift of time and space to write my stories and meditate on life and art: Hedgebrook, the Kimmel Harding Nelson Center for the Arts (which generously hosted me twice), the I-Park Foundation, and Storyknife Writers Retreat. The friendships I have made at these residency programs have continued to nourish and sustain me. Thank you to Judith Podell, Susanne Pari, Rowan Hisayo Buchanan, Leah Schnelbach, Sara Ammon, Jaim Hackbart, Elizabeth Shores and Jake Hebbert for the long walks and rejuvenating conversations. Lydia Blaisdell, David B. Smith and Priscilla Stadler connected so meaningfully to my work during my recent stay at I-Park, and for this I will always be grateful.

Edith and Edilberto K. Tiempo of the Silliman Writers Workshop mentored generations of writers in the Philippines, including my parents – especially my father – and myself. I have them to thank for passing on their wisdom, kindness and understanding of craft to my father, and for showing my father and I that a writer's life is a life well lived.

This book would never exist without the enduring and tireless support of the Macansantos and Supnet clans. I stand on the shoulders of men and women whose courage, fortitude and joy have made me the person I am today. I am deeply grateful to have a cousin like Andrew Viloria who has been a constant source of encouragement and support, as well as humor. I would be remiss in my gratitude if I forgot to mention Binky Puno, Nancy Puno, Florita Wilhelm, Larry Abando, Christine Yra-Garcia, Charles Viloria and Kate Puno-Daquinag for their encouragement and thoughtful responses to my work. Huge thanks to Geraldine Puno-delos Santos, Teresita Supnet-Viloria, Elizabeth Supnet-Yra, Carol Lucero and Joy Ebuen-Yra for opening their homes to me during my wanderings around America. I would not be the writer

I am today without my lola Peregrina, who passed down to me her love of literature, dance and laughter.

To my college best friend, Katrina Lallana, thank you for reading and supporting my work long after we graduated. Friends from the Philippines, including Agnes Paculdar, Fiona Paredes, Romylyn Boñaga, Mary Cita Hufana, Dennis Gupa, Cesario Minor Jr, Niccolo Vitug and Razilee Ramos, thank you for sticking around. Sir Allan Elegado, my dream was to hand you a copy of this book, and I was heartbroken to learn of your untimely passing. I would not be here without you.

To Grace Talusan for being an early and constant supporter of my work from faraway Boston, we may not have met in person, but your faith in my work means the world to me. Ellen Darion, I knew we were kindred spirits when you said that my work has a "hauntedness" about it. Thank you for seeing these qualities in my work that would have otherwise remained invisible to me.

To Paul Beatty, when we met at the Auckland Writers Festival in 2017, you listened when I told you about my own self-doubts after this story collection failed to find a publisher during an initial round of submissions. Your insistence in pushing back against these doubts has helped me remain resolute throughout the years it has taken me to find a home for this book. I still have my copy of *The Sellout* in which you wrote, "Monica, 'I don't know?' Don't stop! Keep the faith!"

To the person who is holding this book in their hands – thank you for reading.

GSP STAFF ACKNOWLEDGMENTS

We first encountered Monica Macansantos's wonderful short story collection late in 2020 when our managing editor, Katherine Day, noticed it in the unsolicited manuscripts channel.

Astutely, she saw that it would suit GSP's list very well. I felt the same when I read it, and in turn, the student publishers at GSP responded with great enthusiasm.

The authenticity of Monica's voice, the energy of her writing and the varied settings – in Monica's home country, the Philippines, and among the Filipino diaspora in the US and New Zealand – gave the collection distinctive appeal. Despite the contemporary settings and her own youth, Monica's stories exhibit an old-fashioned sense of character and its consequences, which adds unusual complexity to an already rich brew.

There is also something deeper operating in Monica's stories, which all center around relationships – relationships consolidating or fracturing, reaching a natural end, or quietly working their way towards, if not always mutual understanding, then at least acceptance. Monica astutely weighs the balance of love and how it shifts – quickly or slowly – not only in the great romances, conflicts and friendships of the young, but also (and perhaps most interestingly) in their families of origin.

Producing *Love and Other Rituals: Selected Stories* has been a great experience for GSP's editorial team. Monica embraced the collaboration with GSP's student editors, designers and proofreaders, but also stood her ground on editorial decisions that mattered to her, including the question of how to style words from Filipino languages. She persuaded us to standardize such words in the text (i.e. not to use italics), and in return graciously agreed to a Notes on the Text which contains translations of key terms (these notes were chiefly produced by Tegan Lyon, Olivia Camilleri and Luzelle Sotelo). We hope readers enjoy the results!

This project was unusual for GSP in that two student cohorts worked on the book. In semester 1, a strong editorial team, led by Fiona Wallace and including Laura Franks, Rowan Heath, Natalie Keenan, Olivia Camilleri and Tegan Lyon, carried out a round of structural editing and then copyediting. Designer and typesetter Natalie Forsyth worked tirelessly to produce the collection's stylish and readable setting, while production editor Taylor Doyle developed a striking cover concept featuring a human heart, which helped inspire the wonderful Australian and US covers designed and executed by Nathan Mifsud in semester 2. Tegan Lyon led the proofreading team in semester 1, which left a set of second page proofs for the semester 2 editorial team to work with. In semester 2, production editor on the Australian edition, Zoë Hoffman, did a great job with Natalie Mulligan, Chloe Hogan-Weihmann and Jack Firns in getting the book to final proofs, ably assisted by Alex Zelembabic's typesetting. Natalie, production editor of the US edition, and Chloe also worked on the preparation of the text for the US edition, with Zoë in charge of proofreading and Jack taking in the changes. The editorial and marketing teams from both semesters, but most notably Natalie Keenan and Zoë, contributed to the creation of the book's blurbs. The social media and sales & marketing teams worked extra hard to promote and sell the book in three markets: Australia, New Zealand and the US.

Thanks to Alex Dane, for stepping in at short notice as the publisher in charge of sales & marketing in semester 2, Tim Fluence, for his valued feedback to Natalie regarding the text design, the School of Culture and Communication for its funding of the first printing, Kerin Forstmanis for her assistance with the author contract, and Ingram Spark for printing and distribution, both here in Australia and in the US.

We wish Monica every success with this, her first book.

Sybil Nolan
Publisher at Grattan Street Press

GSP PERSONNEL

Semester 1, 2022

Editing & Proofreading

Lead Copyeditor
Fiona Wallace

Chief Proofreader & Copyeditor
Tegan Lyon

Copyeditor & Proofreader
Natalie Keenan

Copyeditor & Proofreader
Rowan Heath

Copyeditor
Laura Franks

In-house Translator
Luzelle Sotelo

Design & Production

Production Editor
Taylor Doyle

Designer & Typesetter
Natalie Forsyth

Ebook Production Editor, Copyeditor & Proofreader
Olivia Camilleri

Submissions Officers

Commissioning Editor
Sarah Hooper

Commissioning Editor
Eleanor Jordan-Gahan

Sales

Sales Manager
Claire Crawford

Sales Analyst
Luzelle Sotelo

Sales & Marketing Officer
Hui Chen

Marketing & Publicity

Marketing Manager
Isabelle Kulick

Publicity Manager
Alexandra Pearce

Events Manager & Proofreader
Sophie Goodin

Content Creator
Jessica Tan

Events Officer & Content Officer
Jialu Cheng

Content Writer
Reann Linn

Content Writer
Sarah Hooper

Website & Blogs

MZ Blog Co-editor
Aislinge Samuel

MZ Blog Co-editor
Andrea Septien Uribe

Website Producer & Website Proofreader
Jenny Varghese

Publishing Blog & Website Editor
Georgia Jennings

Book Review Editor & Proofreader
Marlo Kennedy

Book Review Editor, Reviewer & Proofreader
Lachlan Kempson

Social Media

Social Media Manager & Commissioner
Naomi Harrison

Social Media Content Producer
Georgie Hindle

Semester 2, 2022

Design & Production

Production Editor (AU Edition)
& Chief Proofreader (US Edition)
Zoë Hoffman

Production Editor (US Edition)
& Proofreader (AU Edition)
Natalie Mulligan

Copyeditor (US Edition)
& Proofreader (AU Edition)
Chloe Hogan-Weihmann

Lead Designer & Typesetter
Nathan Mifsud

Typesetter, Designer & Copyeditor
Jack Firns

Typesetter, Designer & Copyeditor
Alexandra Zelembabic

Marketing & Sales

Sales & Marketing Officer
Siobhan Lake

Marketing Officer
Amy Kayman

Marketing Officer
Amy Thompson

Commissioning Team

Commissioning Editor
Lee Parker

Submittable Manager
& Proofreader (US Edition)
Jasmine Hewitt

Website, Blogs & Social Media

Publishing Blog Editor
& Proofreader (US Edition)
Lachlan Blain

MZ Blog Co-editor
& Website Producer
Lochlainn Heley

MZ Blog Co-editor
& Content Creator
Joanna Lean

Website Editor
& Book Review Co-editor
Carla Di Maggio

Social Media Manager
Heidi Instone

Digital Content Creator
Felicity Smith

Academic Staff
(Semesters 1 & 2)

Publisher
Sybil Nolan

Managing Editor
Katherine Day

Digital Publisher
Alex Dane

Industry Associate, Sales
& Marketing
Susannah Bowen

ABOUT GRATTAN STREET PRESS

Grattan Street Press is a trade publisher based in Melbourne, Australia. A start-up press, we aim to publish a range of work, including contemporary literature and trade nonfiction, and re-publish culturally valuable works that are out of print. The press is an initiative of the Publishing and Communications program in the School of Culture and Communication at the University of Melbourne and is staffed by graduate students, who receive hands-on experience in every aspect of the publication process.

The press is a not-for-profit organization that seeks to build long-term relationships with the Australian literary and publishing community. We also partner with community organizations in Melbourne and beyond to co-publish books that contribute to public knowledge and discussion.

Organizations interested in partnering with us can contact us at coordinator@grattanstreetpress.com. Writers interested in submitting a manuscript to Grattan Street Press can contact us at editorial@grattanstreetpress.com.